6-27-08

To: SUSANNB — NIECE —
MY N[ew]
WELCOM[E]

Uncle Verne [signature]

The Saga of Robert E

By

Verne Foster

1663 Liberty Drive, Suite 200
Bloomington, Indiana 47403
(800) 839-8640
www.AuthorHouse.com

© *2005 Verne Foster. All Rights Reserved.*

No part of this book may be reproduced, stored in a retrieval system, or transmitted by any means without the written permission of the author.

First published by AuthorHouse 05/13/05

ISBN: 1-4208-3324-3 (sc)
ISBN: 1-4208-3325-1 (dj)

Library of Congress Control Number: 2005901300

Printed in the United States of America
Bloomington, Indiana

This book is printed on acid-free paper.

Dedication

To my wife Liz for all her help editing and proofreading this book for me.

Prologue

It is mid March, 1865, and the last few weeks of the Civil War. A fierce battle is raging between a Union cavalry unit and a combination of Confederate infantry and cavalry. The screams of pain of the dying and wounded are only drowned out by the murderous gunfire. The stench of fresh blood and death is overcome by the smell of gun smoke. The sound of cannon fire is no longer heard since the overwhelming attack of the Union cavalry has been so drastic and compelling that the big guns are abandoned. It is man against man. A vivid nightmare in reality. In this onslaught, the Union forces have again outnumbered the Rebel forces at least three to one and the tide of battle has turned into an imminent defeat. As the Rebels begin falling back, four of their officers make a break down a road through the forest.

In the heat of the onslaught, the relentless Union Captain is far ahead of his men and is a witness to this retreat. He has just reloaded his Colt revolver and without hesitation, gun in hand, and being the true leader in battle, yells, "We've got'em on the run! Let's get'em!"

With that, he heads full stride after them knocking over a Rebel soldier as he heads toward the road they are taking. His horse is a magnificent beast and readily closes the gap between them. He is a battle savvy veteran and knows all the tricks of the trade. He has learned well from the enemy. He watches carefully the men on horseback ahead of him for he knows well the lengthy procedure for reloading his ball and cap Colt and doesn't wish to waste one precious shot. The man in the rear merely reaches over his shoulder and fires blindly at the Union Captain hoping for a lucky hit or to un-nerve him.

The Captain rides smoothly and steadily with no bounce in his saddle as he aims his revolver. One shot and the Rebel is knocked out of his saddle when the .45 caliber ball crashes into his back. The Yankee never slows down as he passes the now riderless horse.

Again, he is carefully watching for any offensive motion. He is drawing closer as the next man, now in the rear, turns in his saddle to fire. The Yankee's aim is again perfect. Blood spurts from the Rebel's neck as he is literally knocked out of his saddle. This time, the Captain is slowed down by the man falling from his horse. One of the other two men grabs the opportunity to take a shot. He fires at the Yankee officer. The Yankee has already pulled the hammer back and immediately fires back. A little too hasty. A miss! He takes another quick shot at the Rebel. Another miss, but it causes the Rebel to retreat.

Once free from the confused and riderless horse, the chase is on again. The men have gained some ground from him and are rounding a curve out of the Union officer's sight for a second or two. He has to slow his gait to a walk as he advances to the curve, gun cocked and held in position to take a shot. Sure enough, as he approaches the curve, the third man has dismounted and fires at him. He answers with a quickly, but, this time, a deadly aimed shot and the man lurches backward. Now, he wonders, "Where is that fourth man?"

A shot rings out as a horseman suddenly bounds from the brush! The Union officer then feels something hit him on the right side of his head near his eye. In a smooth reflex motion, he fires at the man on horseback. The Rebel jerks the reins and causes his horse to fall with him. Since the falling Rebel is to the Captain's right, he quickly dismounts putting his horse between them. The Rebel's horse staggers up and off leaving its rider lying on the ground. The dying Rebel officer looks as if he is trying to say something. The Captain walks over to him and sees he is still trying to fire his weapon. His hand goes limp and he slumps back.

The Captain looks down at him as he holsters his now empty revolver. Everything is suddenly blurring. He wipes the side of his head with the back of his hand and sees the blood covering it. He staggers back to his horse and, with great effort, pulls himself up into the saddle. He slowly and aimlessly rides off, but in the same direction they had been traveling.

And so begins, "THE SAGA OF ROBERT E".

Chapter One

He sat tall in the saddle. It was easy to tell this man and his horse were worn and tired. He had been riding for a long time and had no idea where he was. Yesterday was forever and today even worse. He wished he had a canteen, but could not reason as to why. Every time he would try to think, his memory had no response. How long he had been in the saddle was anybody's guess. He suddenly found himself riding through an old cotton field now overgrown with grass. He stopped while his horse fed on the tasty fronds. There was a stream up ahead, so he spurred his horse to move on.

He dismounted at the water's edge and habitually moved upstream from his horse. He cupped his hands in the cool liquid and drank the fresh clear water. Then, he removed his hat and splashed the water on his head and marveled at it's calming affect as it ran down his hot face. It was only then that he realized it was a very warm day. As he looked at his coat, it was dirty and bloody and in much need of washing, as was he. As he rubbed his face with the clean, cool water, he noticed blood mixing with it and staining his hands. He felt his head and his hair was clotted with blood. He tried to remember what had happened, but as he called upon his memory, it just wouldn't respond.

His solitude was suddenly interrupted by a woman's voice shouting, "Get yore hands up, Yankee!"

1

He looked up and wading into the shallow stream were three young women, one with auburn hair, a sandy haired girl, and a dark complected brunette. All were armed, but the most threatening was the red head in the lead with a shotgun. He stared at them for a moment as they came closer. They seemed oblivious of the water they were wading in soaking their skirts. He could see the big "rabbit ears" on the shotgun were pulled back and cocked for firing. This girl meant business.

The brunette hollered, "Get your hands up, you dirty Yankee dog, 'fore I put a rifle ball twixt yore eyes!"

The redhead admonished her and said, "Now Mercy, remember yore name!"

As he squatted there looking at the three, a similar scene flashed in his mind with the noise of battle and a bunch of men with guns yelling. His mind went blank at this and he fell face first into the water. The running stream had opened up his wound and the water was turning red around his head. He was face down in the stream and motionless. He would have drowned had it not been for the redhead's quick action. She moved quickly and, seeing that he was obviously unconscious with blood coming out of his submerged head, she clicked the rabbit ears shut and handed the gun to the smallest girl. She pulled his head up out of the water and yelled to Mercy, "Get in here and help me!"

The two women dragged the limp figure of a man up onto the dry land. They saw that he was breathing. He coughed a couple of times, but there was no attempt to respond to their questions. Time stood still for him until he finally awoke. He was now on the porch of the big house. His coat had been removed and he was in his shirt sleeves. His head was clean and bandaged. Now it was time for introductions all around. He asked, "Why did you call me a Yankee?"

"Well, now, that's an easy one", Mercy retorted. "Yore wearin' a Union Captain's uniform!"

She held up the blue military coat with its gold shoulder insignia and his blue hat with its gold insignia. This puzzled him and he shook his head to clear it, but that caused his head to spin and hurt and he almost fell over.

The redhead spoke, "I'm Hettie Lee. Some people think my husband is kin to the "General", but that's up for grabs. What's yore name?"

He thought for a moment and then replied, "For the life of me, I don't know."

Mercy was quick to say, "Yer derned right, mister! It could be yore life here!"

Hettie again calmed the girl. The women looked at each other trying to fathom whether to believe him or not. Then Hettie spoke again, "Well, surely you got a name!"

The young man shook his head and replied, "I guess I have, but I just don't know what it is. As a matter of fact, I can't remember anything before I rode into your field. It is as if I just woke up!"

"Well," Mercy said, "We searched yore coat and hat band and there ain't no papers there. By the way, yore gun is slap dab empty. No balls and no caps. For that matter, no powder!" She paused then continued, "Look in yore pockets and see if you got something that might tell us who you are."

He did so, but his pockets were empty except for a couple of gold coins and a pocket knife. "Well, two twenty dollar gold pieces. At least I'm not broke."

Mercy was the next to speak and said, "Hmmph, depends on how ya look at it. Thanks to you Yankees, there ain't nothing to spend it on round here. Y'all sacked everything and took it with ya!"

"I'm really sorry about that, but I don't remember being from around here...I mean, everything's strange to me."

Hettie spoke, "Well, I'm inclined to believe him. After all, his horse was worn and wet and that blood is a good day or two old."

"Now, Hettie, don't go getting soft on us." Mercy chided.

"It's not that I'm getting soft; it's just that this is sort of a mystery and it interests me. I mean, now what if this were Jeff and with that wound, he could be havin' lapse of memory or something."

Both girls nodded and agreed he was probably telling the truth as Mercy questioned, "Well, if that's so, then we done got us a Yankee pris'ner, but then, he ain't really a Yankee, huh?"

Rose, the third girl, finally spoke, "Yeh! That puts a sorta different light on it now, don't it? We've always wanted to have a Yankee pris'ner instead of bein' one and now that we got one, he ain't."

Looking confused, she added, "Well, sorta."

"Rose, stop! Yore talkin' in riddles again!" Hettie then paused and said, "But that is true. It ain't quite the same!"

Mercy now chimed in almost disgustedly, "Yeh! That sure messes it all up!"

The young man asked, "Just how are you girls related? I've heard your names and, uh, let me see. You're Hettie and you have a husband, but Mercy and Rose here are, well, as I said, how are you related?"

"Well, I'll be polite and tell you even though it ain't none of yore business," Hettie replied, "Rose and me are sisters and Mercy's mom was a bonded slave...well, sort of. Of course, that never did make no difference or sense to any of us. We always have considered ourselves sisters. Even when our parents were alive and had a whole bunch of slaves, they were all more like family and we all worked as if this was our place."

"Yeh!" Mercy chimed in, "That is until our men went off in the Army and you, or them Yankees, killed everybody off 'round here that stood up to them."

Hettie put her hand up for Mercy to calm down and continued, "Well, I'm married and Mercy's sort of engaged... that is, we think we still are, uh, me married and her engaged. We don't know what has happened to our men. Jeremiah is

The Saga of Robert E

her man and Jefferson Lee is mine. Now Jeff's family was a small clan and were not land owners. They were what people called 'sharecroppers', so they didn't have no slaves. Well, slaves didn't normally have any last names, but our daddy gave all ours the Summerall name.

Mercy picked up the explanation, "We don't know what happened to our men. Rose over there ain't never been married neither, but she was bein' courted by a fine boy who also went off to war and we ain't heard from them since. It's been over two years."

The Captain queried, "You say Mercy was a slave?" He turned to Mercy and said, "May I say you certainly have a beautiful complexion and your hair is quite beautiful. You don't look, er, colored to me...well, I mean..."

He could see he was burying himself deeper here when Hettie cut in on his stammering, "Nobody said she was colored and nobody said she was a slave neither!"

The Captain quickly apologized realizing he had obviously made a social blunder here, to say the least. Hettie spoke up immediately, "Well, actually, it's been said that Mercy's mom was half colored and half Cherokee. To tell the truth, I think we all have the same daddy."

Rose gasped, "Hettie! We don't know that! And besides, we're not even sure Mercy's mama was half colored either. Mom or daddy never did talk about it and we never saw her. You're older than us, but you were just a little baby yourself. You can't remember. All we know is daddy telling us about how he traded a wagonload of corn for Mercy's mama and since she was just about to have Mercy, he said he got a 'two for one deal'. Daddy always gave special care to her and when she died at childbirth, he buried her with the family."

Hettie challenged, "Yeh...well now don't that tell you something, girl? And just look at her! She sure looks a lot like us and besides that, she's surely got daddy's temper! So, let's face it. She's our sister! We've known it in our hearts all our lives and that's that! I don't wanna hear no more about it!"

Verne Foster

The Captain pondered this and said to himself, "Yep, there is no doubt about it. These girls are definitely sisters

Chapter Two

In an effort to change the subject, Rose asked, "And just what shall we call you?"

The man shrugged and said, "Whatever comes to mind, I guess."

Mercy's eyes lit up as she said quite mischievously, "Let's call him Robert E. I sure like the sound of that." She could not keep the grin from her face.

The girls giggled as they readily agreed. Him being a Yankee and all, no better name but Robert E after their great general.

"I must say that this seems like a joke or something...what am I missing?" the young man asked curiously.

"Why whatever do you mean, suh?" replied Hettie in her most southern accent.

"Well, the way you all talk about this 'Robert E'...you referred to him as 'General', then, you want to call me by his name...why?"

Hettie looked at the other girls and then spoke, "You mean you really don't know who General Robert E. Lee is?"

"Nope."

She continued, "Well, how about General Grant...or General Sherman?"

The soldier replied, "I have no idea who you are talking about. Are they your heroes or something?"

"How dare you, suh! To even compare them as such!" screeched Mercy, also letting her southern drawl give her away.

"Whoa there...compare them together...uh...I mean, which ones?" he stammered.

Hettie took over saying, "Now calm down, Mercy. Can't you see he's totally confused?" With this, she turned back to him and explained softly, "Captain, we are in a war. The North against the South. We're the South and General Robert E. Lee is our commanding general. The other two despicable monsters are yo're dirty dogs that loot and kill!" Her voice getting crisp and her accent getting deeper as she spoke. "They sack ever' farm and town in sight and after they rob and kill the folks, they burn down tha'r homes and move on!" Her anger becoming very apparent.

The Captain could see this was quite a touchy subject here and looked down as he moved his head back and forth. There was a moment of silence, then he spoke, "I am so sorry. I just do not know anything about that, but I can certainly agree it is terrible."

After a few second of silence, Hettie, the obvious leader here, clears her throat and takes control of the conversation quickly as she says, "Well, enough about that! At least for now."

Still silence, and then the Captain speaks, "Well, uh, why don't you tell me about your family? You said your parents had a lot of slaves and ran this farm. I mean, it's not burned down and they're not around...or are they?"

Rose spoke ahead of the other two as tears swelled in her eyes, "The slaves are all gone and our parents are dead."

Mercy spoke sharply, "I guess they figgered they'd done enough to us when they killed 'em, so they let us and the house alone." There was more silence as the girls spirits changed from anger to pain.

The Captain said in a soft voice, "Tell me about it...that is, if you can, or, uh, will."

The Saga of Robert E

The girls spirits darkened and you could tell it was a painful memory. Hettie started, "The Yankees came up and wanted our two cows and our horses. That was all we had left by then. Pa had greeted them with this here shotgun in his hands. When he argued, they just shot him down where he stood without warning."

Almost crying now, she continued, "Mom ran to him and as she reached for the shotgun lying across his stomach to move it out of the way, they shot her too. We'll never actually know what she was goin' to do. We do know that she didn't even know how to use it. It looked like she was just goin' to move it off him." Her southern accent became even more obvious as she remembered the horrible incident and continued, "But them soldiers just opened fire and there the two of them died! Right out thar'! Right in front of us!" She slowly pointed toward the front yard at what was left of the gate.

Robert E, almost in tears himself, shaking his head in pity, almost whispering, said, "I am so sorry! So very sorry! If I am a Yankee, it makes me very ashamed!"

"Well, one thing we do know...you've obviously been in a gunfight." Hettie continued, "That wound on yo're head's deep. Took some skin with it. Had a time pullin' the skin together so I could sew it up with my needle and thread or it would never heal! Yo're lucky it grazed off'n yo're thick skull instead of goin' on in. It should do good now. I could'a sewed up a seam on a dress with the number of stiches it took. Then I doused it down good with coal oil and bandaged it all up."

Mercy was the first one to speak of it and said, "Well, it's startin' to get dark now. It's time to fix something for supper. Ya'll hungry?"

Hettie and Rose said, "Oh, yeh...and how about you, Robert E?"

He seemed to be lost in thought...just staring. Their question brought him back and he replied, "Uh...yes...I guess so."

As they walked toward the back to where the kitchen set off from the back porch, Hettie asked, "What was you thinking about, Robert E? Somethin' coming back to you?"

"Sort of, I guess. I was thinking about the shooting. Those men shouldn't have done that."

Mercy exclaims, "Dern right they shouldn't have! They was renegades! Probably from that General Sherman's outfit...used to doin' what they want...just plain mean! We've had a lot of that lately...which reminds me, girls, what are we goin' to do with him tonight?"

"We'll discuss that over something to eat. For now, let's just fix some food." Hettie advised.

The table was on the back porch between the main house and the kitchen. It had six chairs around it. The porch served well in the summer for a dining room. They had had warm weather for a couple of weeks now. Warm days and chilly nights. Spring was in the air.

Rose spoke, "It's nice to eat out here in the cool of the evening. It does get hot in the house. Right now is best... real cool most of the time."

Mercy chortled, "You think it's hot in the house, try that kitchen on fer size. That wood stove really puts out the heat." She turned to Robert E and added, "We got a table in there too for the cold times."

Hettie went into the kitchen with Mercy. Rose motioned for Robert E to sit down at the table. He sat down in one of the chairs facing Rose as he did so. He put his elbow on the table and leaned back with the chair turned sideways to face her. She asked him, "Don't you remember anything? Anything at all?"

The Captain thought for a moment and replied, "Well, back when you were talking about the soldiers shooting your parents, there seemed to be something, but I'm not sure...well, I mean...a thought popped into my head about some gunfire, like I was in it...well, sort of." Robert E spoke thoughtfully like he was trying to remember. Then, he said,

The Saga of Robert E

"That's when you asked me about being hungry and I lost it. It seems like I was being shot at. There was a lot of noise."

"Can you remember it now?"

"Uh...nope...it's gone."

About that time, Hettie called out from in the kitchen, "Hey out there...we need some help in here to hurry things along. Robert E...you can come pump us up some water. Rose...get the table set."

Mercy was boiling something on the big cook stove. Water was kept hot in the big kettle and it didn't take long for her to make the tea.

Rose queried, "Hey, I thought the Yankees stole all our tea and sugar."

Mercy answered coyly, "They didn't look hard enough for that last bag of sugar. I had it hid. As for the tea, it's sassafras. I'm boilin' it now. We got plenty of them little trees."

The Captain was pumping water into a pitcher at the sink and replied, "Hey, sassafras tea. I know what that is. Tastes almost like root beer...sorta...doesn't it?"

Hettie asked slyly, "Now just how do you know that?"

Robert E stopped pumping and, with a puzzled look on his face, he said, "I don't know...I just don't know, but I know what sassafras tea is for some reason."

Hettie dismissed it and said, "Well, think about it, but meantime, put that cool water from the well into those glasses that Mercy's put the boiled tea in and fill 'em up."

Robert E replied, smiling, "Yes maam."

The girls had warmed up some left over lima beans and Hettie had made some fresh pan fried cornbread. As she brought the plate full of pone to the table, she said, "Lucky for us the Yankees don't like cornmeal...and they missed our meat cooler out back, so we still got some white side pork. It's cooked into the beans, so you won't have to salt 'em."

Rose came in from somewhere with a couple of nice sized tomatoes and started slicing them. As she brought them to the table, she said, "I'm sure glad they didn't stomp down

Verne Foster

our vines. These were too little to be picked and have turned out to be real nice."

Hettie replied, "Yeh. Like Reverend James' down the road. They trampled his garden after they took the vegetables."

Robert E shuddered at that remark. How coarse could one be?

Chapter Three

After supper, the girls agreed that Robert E should sleep in the barn. It was a cool night and, after all, it just wouldn't look right for an unattached man to be sleeping in the same house with three ladies. This was fine with Robert E. Mercy was the one to bring him a blanket and see to it that he was comfortable. As she started to leave, she turned, smiling, and said, "Now, you remember...you're our pris'ner and we don't want you runnin' off."

"I am a gentleman, maam. I wouldn't think of it."

He was in the middle of a nightmare with men yelling and screaming, gunfire, explosions, fire, and all the things he imagined hell to be when he was suddenly awakened. In all that, something was different. Why he awoke was unexplainable to him, but a noise nearby made him smell danger. He got up and went to look outside when he heard it again. Up by the house, he heard the snort of a horse. He eased his way up there and saw two men getting off their horses. They were at the open porch between the kitchen and the house. By instinct, he had verified his sense of danger. He darted back into the barn looking for his gun the girls had put there with his things. When he returned, the men were already inside the house. The girls had left the back door unlocked! He slipped into the house and as he got to the stairs in the foyer, he heard one of the girls scream and a man's voice laugh. It was obvious they had caught the girls by surprise or he would have heard a shotgun blast instead.

Slipping up the stairs, he got to the first floor where the commotion was coming from. Apparently, all three girls slept in the same bedroom for companionship and safety. It hadn't worked out that way for them tonight.

One of the men was standing just inside the door with a gun on them while the other had picked Mercy to start trouble with. She was certainly a pretty thing with her long black hair and dark complexion. He had her by her neck and was just starting to pull her nightgown off when Robert E stepped silently through the door. Knowing his gun was empty, he could only hope a bluff would work. It was worth a try, so he jammed the barrel of that six gun against the man's head, pulled back the hammer on that single action revolver with a loud click that only a Colt can make and growled, "Change of plans!"

The man with the gun automatically raised his hands in reaction. It worked! Robert E quickly grabbed the loaded gun from the man's upraised hand, but just as he did, the other man pushed Mercy away and went for his gun. Robert E fired purely out of reflex that even he did not recognize. The man's head bolted back as the ball smashed into his skull. He was dead when he hit the floor.

Mercy quickly showed her bravado and took his gun from his body. All this was in the dim light of the lowered house lamp on the washstand. Hettie turned up the lamp and only then could they see who they were dealing with. They were wearing the same kind of blue uniform Robert E was wearing. It just so happened that their six shooters were the same issued Colts as Robert E's, so now, Robert E had some ammunition.

Hettie walked over to the man next to Robert E and slapped him so hard that it made a popping noise as it turned his head. He winced and went into a cower saying, "Please! Please don't hurt me! Mercy! Mercy!"

The Saga of Robert E

    This roused Mercy as if he'd called her name. She immediately got right in his face and snarled, "Please don't hurt me? Please don't hurt me? Why you no good renegade! What you had planned for me...did you hear me whimper like that? Well, you called for mercy! Ya got me! That's my name...Mercy!" Then, she kicked him where it hurts the most. He silently sank to his knees. He probably would have groaned, but he could not muster a sound of any kind. Robert E stopped her and helped him to a chair.

    Robert E gave him a few minutes to recover and asked him where he was from. The man was slowly getting over the shock of the kick, but was able to answer, "We left our company. We were in a battle with Johnny Reb and everybody was getting killed...hundreds...thousands! We just left and kept going. We've been on our own for weeks now."

    Rose was the next to speak, "Well, what are we goin' to do with him?"

    Mercy quipped, "Let's just take him to the hog pit and string him up!"

    Hettie surprised Robert E with she said, "Well, maybe we should just skin 'im like a deer or something."

    Robert E and the girls had moved away from the man in the chair by that time and were standing to one side of him when, all of a sudden, he bolted for the window and jumped right through it. They ran to the window and looked down. Though it was not a full moon, there was light enough to see the still body below lying amid broken glass. Mercy said sarcastically and coldly, "Well, I guess he forgot how high up he was."

    Robert E bounded down the stairs and out to the limp form on the ground. Sure enough, he wasn't breathing. It looked as though he had broken his neck. Hettie was the first to follow asking, "Is he dead?"

    Robert E answered, "Yep. Most assuredly."

    By this time, the others had gotten there and Mercy said, "Well, if this ain't a fine kettle of fish...what next?" Then she turned to Robert E with a loving expression on her face and said That was a very brave thing you did back there! You could have been killed! We knew your gun was empty."

Robert E replied, "Ah yes, but they didn't and I was counting on that...and it worked. Besides, everyone who's ever used one of these guns knows just what that loud click means without looking."

Mercy asked suspiciously, "And you know that because...?"

He paused thoughtfully, then replied, "I really don't know. Some things just seem to come to me." Then he looked around and asked, "So...what are we going to do with this mess?"

Hettie replied, "Well, we're goin' to have to clean up that mess upstairs and scrub the floor to get rid of all that blood before it soaks into the wood." She turned to Robert E, "Robert E...you think you can wear any of their clothes?"

"Not really. Their pants are too big and I don't need another coat. However, we do need their valuables and guns and all."

Mercy chirped, "Yep...and we got to bury 'em to get 'em outa the way."

Rose asked, "What about their horses? They're branded, aren't they? And the saddles? Well, anyway, let's check and see."

After they looked, Rose said, "Sure enough. Telltale brands and insignias on the saddle blankets and all."

Hettie spoke up, "Well, that ain't a big problem. Sometimes, we get stray horses from up north way where the battles are apparently bein' fought."

"Yeah," Mercy retorted, "they just wander up!"

"Sounds plausible," Robert E obliged, "Isn't there a way we can alter the brands?"

The girls nodded the possibility was there. By daylight, the horses were in the barn and the two new graves could hardly be noticed out back. Robert E was walking back from the family burial ground when Hettie called to him, "Breakfast... hot coffee, flapjacks, molasses and fried fatback."

The Saga of Robert E

Somehow, that sounded really good to him. The smell of bacon frying and a girl calling out to him that breakfast was ready. Yep, mighty good! He wasn't sure just what fatback was, but he definitely was ready to find out.

Chapter Four

The days went by and the girls taught Robert E about farming and the peculiarities of the area and its people. They also made an agreement with him. For room and board, he could stay and help them repair the place and, literally, get on with life. These were very wise women, especially Hettie. She had made the statement that though life may be a little tougher right now, you don't just stop living. You move on. Robert E understood that and he was slowly getting used to his condition. He would have things pop up from his subconscious like "flashbacks", but he was also learning to sort them out and try and put them into focus in hopes that someday it would all come together.

Within a couple of weeks, things were looking a lot better with a man's help on the old plantation. It was becoming quite obvious to them, under Hettie's leadership, that since slavery was coming to an end, conditions of working would be quite different. Of course, slavery was never quite accepted by the Summeralls. At least, in the last two generations. Hettie was a Summerall. A family who had come from Scotland. The name had changed through the last couple of hundred years somehow from Summervail to Summerall. Their slaves were bought, yes, but they were not only given room and board, but when marketing time came, they were paid a portion of the crops, etc. It had been more like a large extended family.

Verne Foster

Hettie had once explained it saying, "Jeff and Jeremiah went off to fight the Yankees together. They did everything together like brothers. Jeff and Jeremiah were a lot alike. They support the cause of the Confederacy because neither one of them liked somebody telling you how you can live."

Robert E was curious about the war and Hettie and the girls would educate him on occasion while they sat on the old porch in the cool of the evening sipping their sassafras tea. In their opinion, the war was not about just freeing slaves, especially since plenty of Yankees had them. Rather, it was more about "States Rights". The sin of being told how you can live and can't live. Irrelevant of memory, or lack of it, Robert E was getting quite an education at the hands of these girls. It was not just a political attitude, but from the grass roots level of those who were living it. He was fast becoming "Robert E" instead of "The Captain". His memory was starting to come back gradually, but only in little vignettes. Only pleasant things, though, like when he was a teenager or even younger. When he would push himself to try and nail down those little episodes more vividly, they would disappear leaving him blank and even sometimes forgetting what his thoughts were. It troubled him, but the girls were a big help to him and would encourage him to just keep trying. He noticed that every time he would try and remember something about his military past, it was almost like his subconscious mind was fighting him and he'd just go blank.

The time came when everyone agreed that he was ready to meet some of the locals. The first one would be the old preacher. He lived about a half mile down the road towards town. The one that they had told about the Yankees stomping down his vegetable garden. His name was Normal James. Reverend Normal James to most folks around. He was up in years and had been the local preacher for as long as the girls could remember. He would be the first one they would introduce Robert E to. First thought, they had to figure out just who Robert E would be.

The Saga of Robert E

Rose said, "Let's just say he's Mercy's cousin from Carolina."

Mercy was the first to jump on that. She chided, "Girl, who do you think we're goin' to fool with that? I'm dark skinned with black hair. People have remarked that I look like an Indian. He's light skinned with hair almost the same color as Hettie."

Both Rose and Hettie looked at each other for a minute as the reality of it sank in. He even looked a little like Hettie. They solved the problem, though. He was their cousin from Florida. One of the Summeralls from down near Alligator Town in Florida.

Hettie said, "Daddy talked about his cousins down there all the time."

Robert E chimed in, "Okay. Now we're getting somewhere. I am now Robert E Summerall. So, let's go try it out on this Reverend Mister James. By the way, how do these trousers look on me?"

The girls had gathered him up some of Jeff's clothes to wear and they were just about the same size. To this, Hettie replied, "Well, you're a little lean in the waist for 'em, but not too bad. They're a lot better than those Yankee blue trousers people would recognize a mile away. Oh, and you'd better not wear no Yankee hat neither."

"Yeh! Mercy chirped, "I was kinda thinkin' about that all along. Good thing we ain't had no company around."

Rose added, "Yeh! And that's sorta unusual. Not even any Yankee dogs awantin' to take our stuff."

"Dunno," Mercy thought out loud, "We've been so busy 'round here gettin' things goin' again that I ain't really thought about it."

"Well, the lull has been real good. We've got a lot done." Rose added.

Mercy went on with, "Say, Robert E...You might not be able to remember anything about our past much (her accent getting more and more southern as she would emphasize a point...a feature of their speech that he had noticed changed

Verne Foster

back and to from deep southern lingo to a more moderate English) but you sure got a good head on yore shoulders when it comes to fixin' things and havin' ideas about what we could do with our land to make a go of it. Maybe the Lord allowed all this to happen to you just so you could help us." She smiled as she said it.

The girls chuckled at this as Robert E shrugged his shoulders and grinned with them. It caused him to wonder just what did happen to him and why he had ended up here. They talked about the war going on "up there" and all. What part did he play in it all?

Chapter Five

They had three horses now, but there were four people. Working with the horses came easy to Robert E for some reason. He had taken the alternative and had been training them to work together. Now, he hitched them to the girls' wagon and pulled it around to the front of the house. The fence had been mended and the gate was fixed. There was a whippletree at the gate and he pulled up to it and threw the reins around it. He dismounted from the wagon and yelled, "Ladies, your carriage awaits you."

And so it was that the four of them started out toward Reverend James' place. Mercy had come up with an idea for another bench seat in the old work wagon and Robert E and her added it in place just behind the regular bench where the driver sat. They all agreed that it was a good idea and looked fine. Robert E, not only enjoyed doing that kind of work, but he seemed to have a natural talent for it. Even though his memory wasn't working, his imagination certainly was. He had found some old green barn paint in one of the sheds and some whitewash and had painted up the old wagon. It was now a two seater and looked really good with its green seats and wheels and white body. Now, as they started off down the road, a song came to him. From where, he had no idea. The tune just seemed to come out. He started whistling the tune to "John Brown's Body Lies A Moldin' In The Grave." Well, Mercy certainly recognized it and immediately started singing loudly "Dixie" as if a duel were on. Hettie caught the spirit of the thing and looked at Robert E, who was driving, and asked him where he got that song.

"Dunno," he replied, "just popped into my head. I guess it has words to it, but I don't know them. What was that song Mercy was singing? It sure is pretty."

"Yeh, it is," Hettie said, "But we don't know it all. Just a couple of lines."

Mercy chimed in, "Well, Johnny Reb sure likes it. They sing it all the time."

Robert E was puzzled now and asked who this Johnny Reb was. The girls laughed and Rose was the first one to explain, "That's what you Yankees call our boys in gray."

Robert E was even more puzzled now and asked, "You mean your men?"

Mercy answered, "Not just our men, but the whole Confederacy. Jeff Davis and all. We're considered rebels and so they refer to any Confederate as Johnny Reb."

Rose came back saying, "Actually, we kinda like it and we're rather proud of it."

Mercy added, "Yeh! And real proud of it. The men in gray! Johnny Reb!"

Rose and Mercy were really getting into it when Hettie chided, "O.k., now! That's enough from the back seat!"

They both looked at her, but saw a little smile on her face, so they knew it was in jest.

"Well, looka here, now. We're almost to Reverend James' place."

Hettie informed Robert E.

The house sat way back off the road amid some small trees. What was left of the fence was standing with sections missing. Hettie told Robert E to just take a short cut through the field anywhere and head for the house. He did so and headed the horses in that direction. As they pulled up to the front porch, they could hear men's voices coming from around on the side porch. They sounded irritated as one was

The Saga of Robert E

saying, "Listen here, you poor excuse for a human being! We know what you've been up to and if we can just catch you at it, we'll shoot you dead!"

As Robert E reined up the horses to a stop, they were in plain sight of the men. and they turned to look at the four in their painted up wagon. The one who had been ranting was a Union Lieutenant and he had a Sergeant with him. They faced the visitors and questioned in a commanding tone, "And just who might you be?"

Hettie was quick to reply, "We're parishioners come to see the Reverend. How you doin' today, Reverend James?"

Reverend James tipped his hat and smiled as he said, "Mighty fine, Miss Hettie. The soldiers here were just leaving. We can talk in just a minute." He then came over to the wagon and extended his hand to help the ladies down.

The Sergeant, who had been almost ogling the girls, amazingly enough came with him. The Lieutenant stood back and did not interfere as the three men helped the girls off the wagon. The Sergeant remarked politely as he tipped his hat, "That sure is a nice looking wagon you have there."

Hettie replied, "Yeh. We're tryin' to brush off all that dirt your comrades tried to bury us under."

Grasping the moment to save the conversation, Robert E surprised himself at his political aptitude as he explained, "Yes. We had some old barn paint and whitewash and are trying to spruce it up. We were just coming over to show it to Reverend James here."

As he spoke, he walked over to Reverend James trying to get the soldiers' attention off the horses. They certainly didn't need to take too much notice in them where they might discover the U.S. brand. Reverend James quickly took advantage of the interruption in an attempt to prevent any further questioning by the soldiers and said in a very pastoral style, "Now, Lieutenant, you're welcome out here anytime and you will find I have nothing to hide. As a pastor, I am trying to keep a neutral and non-political stand here." His speech style got to the point that it sounded as if he was starting to preach as he said, "An-n-n--n-d wha-a-a-a-at ever-r-r-r the good Lord wants....sooo be it."

The two soldiers suddenly found themselves in an uncomfortable position with the sudden appearance of these people. They took this change of events as a chance to take leave and maintain their control of the matter. Besides, they did not want to hear another one of his sermons, so they mounted their horses, tipped their hats as they nodded politely to the girls and said, "Ladies." Then they rode off.

The preacher said in relief, "Whooooeeeee!"

This was all strange to the girls. This was a side to Reverend James they had never seen. Why was the Yankee Lieutenant talking to him like that and threatening to kill him?

Chapter Six

Reverend James was an old man, but he was quite agile for those years as a result of a lifetime of hard work. Though his farm seemed run down, he still had a garden growing. There were still several sources to get flour, meal, and other cooking staples. Also, most of the fruit trees were full of young fruit. The Yankees had taken much of his crops and attempted to destroy most everything else. So, with the fruit just now popping out, who knew what tomorrow would bring.

Everyone in Georgia had heard of Sherman by now. While those in Florida might have referred to him by his nickname, "Cump Sherman", the people of Georgia all referred to him as something else. He had burnt his way from Atlanta to the Atlantic. Those of a civilian nature cursed him while those of a military nature understood what he meant when he said, "War is cruelty and you cannot refine it." Some would later interpret this as actually being, "War is hell!" In any case, he was a true soldier without political instinct and was bent on winning a war. No politics involved. His theory was if you destroy the enemy's strongholds and supply sources, you minimize his power and you will be successful. He was. Only the future could know just how successful or unsuccessful his campaign would be.

Neighbors to the North had been on the searing edge of Sherman's sweep. There were stories about the "scorched

Verne Foster

earth". Some had headed south to stay with friends and relatives to get out of the battle zone and told of the carnage that was prevalent. Even in the worst times, people survive and find a way to eke out a livable existence. That was what was happening here. Not having had any raiders in a couple of weeks, the girls and Robert E had made out fine. Things were actually beginning to level out. There had been plenty of rain and the soil was excellent for any crop. Their little garden had been left intact and it sure helped. Plus the scrounged and hidden stuff they had stashed away had made life pretty good for them.

Reverend James had brought out a pitcher of cool water and some glasses. He poured the liquid into the glasses only filling them up about a couple of inches. Robert E noticed this, but dismissed it until he downed a big gulp. He tried to say "Wow", but it had taken his breath. It literally exploded in his head. The girls frowned as they looked at Robert E curiously and then realized what had happened. Reverend James was serving his "concoction"! Some folks called it "White Lightening".

Robert E was still gasping when Rose chided, "Now Reverend! You should have warned us about what yore servin' us to drink here."

It was noticeable that the girls' speech would go heavily southern when they were getting emotional. "Just you look at him! He can't even breathe!"

The old man laughed and said, "Well, I guess you're right. So what brings you here and who is this young man?"

Hettie was first to reply, "Now just a minute, Reverend. First, you tell us what's goin' on with you! Just what're you doin' that warrants them threaten'n to shoot you dead?"

Robert E had caught his breath by now and interrupted, "Hey! Now why don't we just start from the very beginning. You are Reverend James. I am Robert E. Summerall, the girls' cousin from down Florida way. I've been helping them fix up their place. You know the girls already. Now, that seemed to be a real serious conversation you were having

The Saga of Robert E

with the soldiers." He suddenly shook his head and leaned against the table as he hesitantly said, "Er, uh, oh boy! What in the devil is that stuff I just drank? My head's starting to spin!"

All four of them were watching him now as Hettie spoke up knowingly, "He calls it his concoction. Actually, he has a still somewhere and likes to spring his strong drink on poor unsuspecting victims." Turning to the old man, she shook her head and said, "Shame on you! A man of the cloth!"

Reverend James replied sheepishly, "Shucks, ya'll. I gotta git my fun where I can find it at my age."

Mercy made no attempt to hide her sudden anger. She shot back, "Ain't nothing wrong with yore age, you ole coot! Yore just mean to the bone!"

There was a sudden protective nature in this girl when it came to Robert E. Both the other girls and the old Reverend James noticed it. She was clearly and highly upset because Robert E was the victim and she was letting them all know she didn't like it. Hettie put this in the back of her mind to ponder. After all, Robert E was a fine cut of a man and obviously a gentleman.; and the prolonged absence of their men without any word for so long had not made their hearts grow any fonder...especially with what they had to go through. As she mulled it over in her mind, she realized she had taken a shine to Robert E herself. Now, Mercy was showing concern for him. The only one who didn't seem to care one way or the other was Rose. She thought to herself, "Oh, well, Rose was still quite young."

Robert E was continuing to react to his drink. He suddenly had to sit down to steady himself. He had taken a big swig and swallowed it all before he realized what it was. He might not know who he was, but it was becoming quite obvious to the girls that he definitely was not a drinker. Of course, though, what he had drunk wasn't fit for even a drinker!

Mercy asked him in a very concerned tone, "Robert E, are you all right?"

He just shook his head and put it down on his arm on the table. She moved to his side and turned to the Reverend and asked, "Just how strong did you make this stuff this time?"

He shrugged his shoulders and replied, "Well, I, uh, well, usually I run it through twice, but I had to cut it short this time and it, well, it could be a little stronger." The guilt was showing strongly as he almost stuttered.

Mercy's anger and the Indian in her was clearly showing now as her eyes had an Asiatic slit to them. She literally hissed as she spoke, "We come all the way over here for a social visit and you try to poison us. Let me tell you, ole man! If you've ever prayed, you'd sure better pray he's O.K!" She even startled her sisters as she added, "You ain't never seen me mad!"

Reverend James' voice quivered as he tried to be humorous and replied, "Oh no! Yes I have! You've got the temper of a wildcat!"

Mercy shot back at him, "Oh no! You don't git what I just said! I said you ain't never seen me mad! As mad as I'll be if you've hurt Robert E!"

The Reverend thought to himself that this little spitfire had special feelings toward this man. Hettie stopped the mayhem by interrupting and said, "Well, Mister Reverend James, we'll just have to come back to finish this visit. Right now, it looks like we'd better get our cousin back home."

The Reverend apologizing helped them get him into the back of the wagon. Robert E had passed out by then and Mercy chose to sit in the back with him. Rose got up on one side of the front bench as Hettie mounted the other side. She looked down at Reverend James and said, "We've got some talkin' to do. We'll be back later. I want to know more about them soldiers." With that, she let off the brake and slapped the reins on the horses as she yelled, "Giddap there!" The horses responded immediately and effortlessly obeying her driving pulls on the reins and the wagon rolled away.

The Saga of Robert E

Reverend James stood and watched them drive away as he removed his hat and rubbed his balding head with a kerchief to wipe away the sweat. He pondered Hettie's curiosity and wondered just what or how much she knew. He knew she was no fool and how dangerous these girls could be. He thought about how they had assumed the man's job of running the farm and surviving as well as they had. He realized he probably had some tall explaining to do later if he was smart. Those three made much better friends than enemies.

There was very little conversation on the way home. Robert E was asleep with his head in Mercy's lap. As Hettie pulled up the reins, she posed the question, "Wonder why ole Reverend James didn't ask us more about Robert E. He didn't even ask about that fresh scar on his head?" She dismissed it realizing a lot had happened all of a sudden.

The next morning, the sun was coming up driving away the mist from the open fields leaving only the shady areas with the evidence of the overnight's heavy dew. Mercy was the first one up and was in the kitchen making the morning coffee when the other two girls came down.

Hettie asked, "You been out to check on Robert E?"

Mercy answered she hadn't had time yet. She said she figured to wait until breakfast was ready. Suddenly, Mercy looked out toward the barn and said matter of factly, "Oh my God! Somethin's wrong!" Watch the coffee while I go check on him!" Hettie had seen this before with Mercy. It was like she could tell without seeing.

Mercy came off the back porch running. She went straight into the barn where Robert E slept and to her shock, he wasn't there. He was gone! She called to him and went running back to the house screaming, "Oh, Hettie! Rose! Oh, he's gone!. He's gone!"

Hettie and Rose met Mercy on the back porch steps. They could see the tears flowing from Mercy's eyes. Hettie tried to reason as she said, "Well, maybe he's just down at the river."

Verne Foster

Mercy, visibly shaken and now crying, sobbed out, "No! You don't understand! He took his horse! He's gone! I mean, he's really gone!"

Chapter Seven

It was after breakfast and the girls had discussed all the possibilities they could think of as to the whereabouts of Robert E. So, after the morning chores, Hettie decided to ride over to Reverend James' place to check and see if Robert E might have gone there for some reason.. She saddled up the roan and was on her way. There was a nice breeze blowing against her face as she rode east. She thought about the comfort this horse gave her with his smooth gait and strong legs. Her long auburn hair was down and as she rode into the wind, it blew it back of her as if she were riding at a faster rate then she actually was. The military horse was well trained and had a soft gait that kept her from bouncing in the saddle. Actually, she was enjoying the ride as she reined up at Reverend James' place. There was no sign of life anywhere except for a couple of cows in the side pasture. There was a well barn in the immediate back yard and an older and larger one way off in the distance at the end of his clearing. Beyond that was just woods. Reverend James liked to call it his own hunting ground.

Hettie dismounted and wrapped the reins around the whippletree a couple of turns. She went up on the side porch to the door. The house had a front door, but no one ever used it. Usually, by this time of day, you could see old Reverend James sitting in his favorite chair on the side porch as if he was waiting for you to call. No one anywhere

Verne Foster

about today, though. It all seemed so strange. Robert E and his horse gone. No one at Reverend James' house. She double checked by opening the side door and hollered in. No answer. She then walked back down the steps and out toward the first barn. As she neared the neat little building near the house, she could tell no one was about there either. She looked back at the big barn. She hadn't been there since she was a little girl and her daddy used to bring her and her sisters over on Sunday afternoons for a sort of family get together. Several of the people from the church would always congregate there for dinner and some singing.

The old barn was surrounded by a three rail fence that formed a corral. As she approached it, she could see some saddled horses toward the back of it. She lifted the single rail that formed a gate and replaced it. As she neared the barn, she could hear voices. One was definitely Reverend James. None was Robert E's though. She then quietly slipped closer and listened. She thought she recognized a couple of the voices. Now that she was closer to the horses, she saw that two of them were definitely army horses. Where had she seen them before? And, the voices were so familiar. Then, she remembered the Lieutenant and the Sergeant. "Yes! These were two of the voices!" she thought. There were a couple of more voices she did not recognize, though.

This was certainly not the time to make an error. She had to try and see who and what these men were doing in there. She approached the window cover that could be raised for light and air when supported by a stick. She tried to lift it out a little bit. It worked. She could see inside the barn. There were several men there standing by the wagon loaded with something covered by a tarp and all tied down. The big back doors of the barn were open. There was an old road heading off into the woods from there. It looked as though they were getting ready to take a load of something off through the woods or somewhere.

About that time, the Lieutenant said, "Well, get that out of here as soon as you can. It looks like the war will be

The Saga of Robert E

ending any time now. Grant is pushing hard and you Rebs are caving in. This might just be the last load."

With that, he turned to the Sergeant and said, "Let's get mounted. We have to be back in town by mid morning." Turning then to Reverend James, he asked, "By the way, Reverend. Did you find out anything about that man that was with your neighbor women? I don't cotton much to somebody just showing up out of nowhere like he did!"

Reverend James said, "Aw, he ain't nobody. Just the girls' cousin like they said. I've know'd them all their life and they do have relatives down in Florida."

With that, the Lieutenant began walking toward the open doors and said over his shoulder, "We can't take any chances this late in the game!"

Hettie ran back to the other barn and circled around the house from the other direction. She had left her horse at the front. She peeked around from the side porch. Fortunately, the men all came out talking about something and it slowed them getting on their horses. She slipped her horse out to the road and rode quietly back toward home. She slowed down as she thought about what was in that wagon. It was just dark enough in the barn looking against the light to where she could not make out any of the faces or the possible shape of the load in the wagon. She suddenly reined up and headed back down the road toward Reverend James' place. As she neared his property, she saw the other men leaving and heading toward town in the opposite direction from her. She was just too far away to see who they were, but one rode an Appaloosa. The spotted buttocks was clear to be seen. "Hmmm," she thought, "No one around here rode those. That is a western horse."

She had led her horse off the road and into the trees at the edge of the Reverend's clearing. She heard a horse snort and stayed where she was. In a minute, Reverend James came out and rode off toward town in the same direction the other men had ridden.

"Well," she decided, "Now is the perfect time to see what's going on back there."

She left her horse tied in the trees off from the road so no passerby would notice it. She circled around the shady side of the house away from the morning sun and on back to the big barn. No one seemed to be around now. As she came to the big barn where the wagon was, she circled it quietly. The big doors on the back were closed now. She tried the window cover she had moved earlier. It was loose and she crawled through it. As she dropped to the floor, she could see the wagon in the darkness of the barn. Only little beams of sunlight filtered through the cracks in the walls. There was still the aroma of cigar smoke in the air.

She hurried over to the wagon. It looked like boxes were under the canvas. Their square corners formed little pyramids in it. She had to be careful and not disturb anything that might be noticed by the men. The canvas was tied down pretty good and she could not lift any of its edges enough to tell what was there, but it was definitely wooden boxes. She then decided she would untie one of the knots at the back of the wagon. She carefully picked at the rope until she could untie the knot. Threading the rope from its cinch, she was able to lift the canvas just enough to see one of the box ends. It had "U.S. ARMY" stenciled on it. She pulled at the tarp until she could see more in the little ray of light that was shining on it now. There it was. "Volcanic Arms Company, New Haven, Conn.".

Could this be the new "Henry" repeaters? She was almost wild now as she pulled at the rope to loosen its bind on the tarp. Finally, she exposed the lid to the box. It was soft yellow wood nailed at the ends. She hunted desperately for something to pry with. She found a piece of wagon rim metal and forced open one of the boards enough to see inside. Sure enough! Under a cover wrapping of burlap, she found rifles. New ones. She pulled three of them from the box. What to do now? She became weak in the knees as she suddenly realized what this was. A shipment of "Henry" rifles.

The Saga of Robert E

Her whole body trembled as she felt the adrenalin rush. She had heard about the new and better rifles that were being used by the Union now. These were apparently some of them. But what were they doing here? On closer inspection, she saw the inscription in the metal, "NEW HAVEN CONN. PATENT FEB 14, 1854". This gun took bullets. No ball and cap stuff here. She had heard talk of a Benjamin Tyler Henry teaming up with a couple of men of handgun fame named Horace Smith and Daniel Wesson. She hurriedly put the greasy cloth back down and found a rock and pounded the nails back into their holes sealing the crate again. She then pulled the tarp back down and retied the rope as best she could. She knew it would not be as tight as it was, but maybe they wouldn't notice. She stepped back with the new rifles in her hands and inspected the load. It looked untouched. She then headed for the window she had come through and just as she was about to open it, she heard horses coming up outside!

Chapter Eight

The sound of the horses outside continued around to the big back doors of the barn. Hettie was almost in a panic. What to do? Well, as she steeled herself against her panic, she began to reason again. "Hide, fool!" was her first thought. There were several places in the barn she could hide, so she ran over behind a stack of bags of feed. She crouched behind them and waited. She heard the clanking lock and chain being pulled through the holes in the doors. The big doors swung open and there were two men there with a one-horse drawn dray. They loosed it from the horse and both men grabbed the tongue and pushed it back into the barn. It had a bunch of smaller boxes on it, but no cover. As they pushed it along side the larger wagon, she could hear them talking.

"Where's that Reverend James? He was supposed to be here to help us. This thing's heavy," complained the first man.

The other man answered, "Oh well, it don't matter none. We've brought the ammo for them rifles like we had to do, so let's git outta here."

It was then that Hettie noticed they were Yankee soldiers. The one that had driven the wagon took a saddle from it and put it on the horse he'd used to pull it with. As he tightened the cinch, he said, "Well, that's it. Our job's done. Now all I want to see is some good old gold pieces."

Verne Foster

As they shut the big doors, she heard one of them say, "Yeah...it's his worry now. Let's move out!"

The big doors once again were closed and locked. It was dark again except for the myriad of little strips of sunlight dimly lighting the interior. Hettie waited until she heard them ride off. She went to the window cover and cracked it a little to see out. She watched them ride toward town.

"Ammo for the rifles, huh?" She hurried over to the smaller wagon and looked at the smaller wooden boxes. Sure enough. They were marked ".38 Cal. Cartridges". Using her trusty wagon rim strip again, she opened one of the boxes. What she saw was a strange sight to her. Bullets! Brass jacketed bullets. The boxes were clearly marked "US ARMY". This caused her to inspect the rifles more closely. She had never seen a rifle like this one before. She picked up some shells and began to load the rifle. Nope. There was no open breech. Instead, this rifle had a lever action and loaded in a tube under the barrel from the side. A repeating rifle that could be fired as fast as you could work the lever. "What will they think of next?" she thought.

She decided to open a couple more of the ammo boxes to be sure they were all the same. While she had them open, she found a burlap feed bag and took handfuls of cartridges from each box she had opened and loaded them into it. She decided she had enough when the bag became almost too heavy for her to carry. About sixty or more rounds were a load for her. When she added the three rifles to this, it all was quite a load for her little frame. She tied a big granny knot in the end of the bag and laid it beside the rifles. Then, she resealed the boxes and relocated them behind a couple of the others so the difference in weight would not be noticed quite so quickly. Now, to just get out of here while the getting was good. She found an old piece of rope and tied the rifles together so they would be easier to carry. She eased the board window cover open a little and saw no one around. She dropped the rifles and bag of shells outside on the ground and climbed out. Looking around, she

The Saga of Robert E

saw there was apparently no one there. She circled around the west side of the little barn and the house anyway just to make sure, keeping close to the heavy trees and overgrowth. She reached her horse and used the knot in the burlap bag as a fastener on her saddle horn. This allowed her to have a free hand for the reins. She eased her horse out of the trees and brush and when she got to the road, she spurred the great beast into a run. You'd think she was racing against someone the way she rode, crouched down and spurring the horse for more speed. Well, actually, she was, for it wasn't long after her dust settled that Reverend James came riding back home.

As she approached her house, she started calling out to Mercy and Rose. She rode directly to the barn before she stopped. Her horse was almost snorting for breath after that run. Rose came from around the front of the house and Mercy had been in the kitchen and came running out from there. Hettie dismounted and unloaded the guns and bag of shells. The horse went straight for the water trough. Hettie told the girls to come into the barn with her. They were doing their best to try and fathom what was going on, but the only clue was that Hettie rode in fast and she had some rifles like they'd never seen before. Once in the barn, Hettie showed them the rifles and began to untie the croaker bag. Mercy was the one who was the most interested in the weapons. Rose was still asking, "What in the world is happening? Where have you been? And what in the world is all that?"

Now Mercy had an innate attraction to weapons. She took one of the rifles and inspected it. She said, "Ya load this thing from the side. Hey, this is one of them new "Henry" repeaters!" She held her hand out and said, "Let me see some of them bullets!"

Though the rifle was oily, it made no difference to Mercy who appreciated its newness and artistry. She quickly loaded it and held it up as if she were going to fire it. She looked down the long barrel and then brought it back down working

Verne Foster

the lever and unloading the shells. She then said, "This is one heavy gun!" She looked at the sight and marveled at its simplicity, then said, "Well, we're listening. This is some kind of miracle rifle. Now where in the world did it come from and how did you get ahold of it?"

Hettie started, "Well, you're not going to believe me, but I'll tell you anyway." She paused, took a breath, and said, "Reverend James."

Mercy and Rose looked at each other and in almost perfect unison, hollered, "Reverend James?"

Mercy then chided, "Aw-w-w, come on-n-n-n!"

Hettie was calmer now and related the story to them. The two girls just sat there looking at each other, stunned in disbelief. Then, Mercy asked, "Hettie, do you know what this means?" Then, she suddenly paled and asked, "Ugh! Do you think they've done something with Robert E?"

Hettie told her what she had heard and Mercy let out a heavy sigh of relief. Hettie looked at Rose and then asked Mercy, "Mercy, just how do you feel about Robert E? I mean... what with Jeremiah and all?"

Mercy said, "Aw, I don't believe me and Jeremiah ever really loved each other. You know, sorta like family and all."

Hettie broke in and said, "Mercy, you're in love with Robert E, aren't you?" Mercy started to say something and Hettie cut her off with "Now don't try and fib out of it. We've both noticed how you acted around him and all, especially when you saw how Reverend James' white lightning knocked him crazy. And, how upset you were when you found him gone and all."

Mercy looked down and tears came down her cheeks as she replied, "I've never felt the way I do about anyone like I do for Robert E. I just dunno. I don't know what to think...I mean...oh, it's so confusing!" Almost crying, she continued, "He knows I'm part Cherokee and part something unknown, so I don't think he would ever consider me...."

The Saga of Robert E

Hettie and Rose chimed in at the same time, "Now Mercy, you really don't know just what your heritage is. Your grandpa could have been anything. We just don't know. What we do know is that we've got the same papa!"

Mercy suddenly straightened her face, took a deep breath, and said coolly, "Well, none of that matters now anyway, does it. He's gone to who knows where. Maybe even dead of all we know. Anyway, we have much more serious problems to handle now!"

Both Hettie and Rose pondered how strong a young woman Mercy was. There was one thing they knew for sure. She was definitely their sister.

Chapter Nine

Reverend James rode his horse around to the back of the big barn to the double doors. He dismounted and fiddled with his keys as he walked over to the lock and chain. He would have used the smaller side door, but it was secured with a board and braces on the inside. You had to come through the big doors to get into the barn and then open the others from the inside. He pulled one of the doors open. As he looked inside, he saw the second wagon. "Hmmm. Well, I see they've brought the ammo." he said to himself.

He had led his horse inside the barn where he could unsaddle it more easily. He plopped the saddle on a bin wall and removed the bit and reins. Then, he slapped the horse on its rear and it trotted outside to munch on some grass. He then walked over to the second wagon and looked at the boxes. "Now this is a brazen thing for them to do! An open wagon full of boxes of ammo and them clearly marked US ARMY. Them soldiers certainly have a lot of gall, but then, maybe that's a good way to get by unnoticed."

As he thought about it, knowing the two soldiers that had brought the ammo, he could picture them in his mind. He also knew them well enough to know that all they were interested in was their money.. The Lieutenant and Sergeant, though...they were different. They had been doing this for a long time and had made a fortune. Rifles were in huge demand both locally and out west. That wasn't his area, but

Verne Foster

he knew the Indians paid for them in gold, or at least, their representatives did."

"These were a different type of gun from any he had seen. These were the new breed of weaponry. The newest! Ever since the Lieutenant had ran across him helping runaway slaves get out of the territory, he was forced to help in the illicit business the Lieutenant and Sergeant were conducting. As he thought about the Lieutenant, he wondered why he was so persistent in finding out about that cousin of the girls. Back in town, awhile ago, he thought he might have seen him before. When he said he thought he might be a Yankee soldier, I told him it was impossible. But now, that I think about it....naaaa...I was right. He's just like the girls said. Their cousin up from Florida to help them out. Besides, if he did come up from down there in Florida, he'd be a Reb anyway."

He continued to talk to himself out loud, "Aw, who cares anyway. From what we've been hearing, the war is just about over. No telling what our business will turn into or just what we will be trading or moving. We've moved all kinds of supplies that had been scrounged and sent to wherever or whomever paid the best price."

Of course, he had made a lot of money with them, so now, he was just as much a thief as they were. He actually considered it his patriotic duty to help in the underground railroad and was quite content with the money he was making with his "mountain mixture". Sometimes, it turned out almost 200 proof. That meant you could water it down better'n a hundred per cent and still have good booze. The stuff he had given Robert E was almost 200 proof. Lord knows what would have happened if the girls had drank any of it. "I sure am glad they didn't take a sip. I forgot that I had that pitcher full of the full strength stuff to water down and fill up a couple of jugs with."

As the reverend thought about his dealings, he had some second thoughts, but what could he do now? And anyway, all the Reverend was expected to do was to provide the shelter

The Saga of Robert E

for the goods until they could be picked up and shipped away. He never asked where and really didn't want to know. He was a Southerner and he kind of figured that this was a way to keep those new guns from killing more of the Rebs. What a mixture of loyalties. Just when his poor conscious thinks it has him in a bind, he comes up with something that knocks it out. The Reverend had been known to say, "Oh, I have a conscious all right, but I just make sure I never listen to it".

He finished his inspection and said to himself, "Well, everything looks like it's ready to go. I'll just go in and forget it's here. The boys will be by soon enough to move it and I'll be through with it."

Now, back at the girls place, Mercy had gotten some coal oil and some rags. Rose was fixing some lunch while Hettie and Mercy worked on the weapons. They carefully cleaned the grease off the rifles and took little soaked patches of cotton and ran them down the barrels with the cleaning rods they already had there for their own guns. By the time lunch was ready, the girls had three beautiful rifles all cleaned and polished. Gun oil was something every farm had and the girls had done a great job lubricating them with it. Hettie practiced with the lever while Mercy was more interested in getting used to the new sights. They were simple enough, but apparently effective. They wanted to practice firing them, but decided it might just draw some unwanted attention, especially if they fired too rapidly. Besides, it is easy to tell the difference in a shotgun blast and a rifle even from a distance. Furthermore, they didn't know what might be going on at Reverend James' place.

There was quite a contrast in the two camps. Reverend James was sitting on his porch sipping a little of his concoction and had no interest where those guns were going. At the girls' place, that was all they could think about. Hettie was thinking to herself, "We know where these guns came from, but where are they going? And just what can we do about it?

Where in the world do we start? And, since Robert E is gone, could he be in on this?"

Her thoughts were interrupted when Mercy spoke, "Look here girls. I want to test these guns out. Let's take the wagon on out to the ravine and see what they'll do. That's over an hour's ride from here and no one ever goes within miles of there."

The girls agreed because they too were anxious to see what these rifles would do. So, they wrapped them and the ammo back up in some burlap bags, put them in the wagon, loaded up some snacks and a bucket and dipper for water. They would drink fresh sweet water from the river that ran through there. It was always cold and satisfying. All three girls were small enough to all sit on the front bench and as Hettie flapped the reins and kicked off the brake, the horses started with a jerk that almost made Mercy and Rose lose the shotguns they were holding. So away they went on a very special quest, not realizing what lay ahead for them before the day would be over.

Chapter Ten

The Union patrol was moving warily through the woods. The sun was high in the sky as they slowly rode easterly. Early that morning, they had left camp and were covering the area for possible signs of any Rebel activity. They had been in the saddle for several hours spreading out over a wide rank and had circled from camp starting from the West and were now slightly easterly to the camp. These were seasoned soldiers, all having survived many battles. As a matter of fact, their leader was a man that had been given a battlefield commission. He had been the top Sergeant serving next to his company commander until that officer was lost in a recent battle. He was of Irish descent. He had been called "Sergeant Pug" for so long, he still had a habit of answering to that. Technically, he was actually acting Lieutenant until his papers were finalized and, being on the front, paperwork came slowly. In those days, the Union Army actually was sort of two armies in one. If you were of enlisted rank and were given a commission, they would discharge you at your enlisted rank and re-enlist you as a commissioned officer. So, "Sergeant Pug", who was actually Sergeant Patrick MacHenry, as of about three weeks ago, was now Lieutenant Patrick MacHenry.

It was about time for the patrol to stop for a mess break and were looking for a good spot to eat and relax. The silence was suddenly broken by a shrill whistle and one of the men calling out, "Sergeant Pug...er... uh...I mean, Lieutenant MacHenry...over here! Over here!"

The Lieutenant quickly drew his revolver and headed toward the shout. The rest of the patrol drew their rifles and cocked them as they cautiously followed their Lieutenant. Since they were ball and cap type weapons, they wanted them ready to fire. As Lieutenant MacHenry rode up to the scene, there was a man lying face down on the ground. His horse was standing beside him. The horse's reins hung loosely to the ground showing a definite relationship between horse and rider.

Drawing up to the scene, he holstered his revolver and dismounted. What he saw was confusing. Here is a man with Union Army trousers and boots with a civilian coat. His horse was definitely U.S. Army complete with the US brand. So, on size up, this was definitely not a Rebel. He appeared to be asleep or unconscious. The Corporal that found him had been transferred in from Company K, 37th Illinois, as one of several replacements since this company had taken so many losses in the recent battles. Lieutenant MacHenry reached down and took the man by his coat and turned him over while the Corporal stood guard with his rifle. What he saw was something he could not believe. It was his commander, Captain George Fitzhugh Custis himself. Pug was so stunned that all he could say was, "Oh my God! Oh my God!"

A couple of the other soldiers had dismounted and came over to look. One of them turned to the others still in the saddle and yelled, "It's Captain Custis!"

A yell went up from the men as they quickly dismounted and came running over to the group. As they surrounded the man on the ground, they saw he was dazed. Something was very wrong with him. He was conscious, but not quite alert as he ought to be. Lieutenant Pug told the Corporal to lower his rifle and relax. Having been in Company K, his rifle was a very special weapon. Companies A and K of the 37th Illinois Regiment were the two companies that had been issued the rare repeating rifle for testing. It had been designed after

The Saga of Robert E

the highly respected Colt revolver. It had the advantage of rapid fire from the ball and cap cartridges held in the cylinder. There were two models of this rifle. One was a five shot .56 caliber and a six shot .44 caliber. The Corporal's was the .44 caliber six shot model. Big problem was that bits of lead could fly into the face of the shooter sometimes since the cylinder was held so close to the shooter's face plus the loud noise. Even worse, there was the possibility of all chambers in the cylinder misfiring at once. This would put the shooter in risk of mutilation as the bullets struck his hand holding the barrel in front of the cylinder. Yet, many of the men using them liked them. The Corporal's had never given him any trouble but the deafening noise. He didn't mind that because of the fire power it gave him.

Lieutenant Pug reached down and gently took the man by the chin and, facing him up close, said, "Captain Custis...do you recognize me?"

The man looked at him wearily and finally said, "I think so. You look familiar."

"Captain Custis...I'm Pug...do you remember?"

At that, the man smiled and said, "Yeah...I believe I do... uh, yes! Sergeant Pug!"

Lieutenant MacHenry smiled as he replied, "Thanks to you, sir, I'm a Lieutenant now." The man's eyes suddenly dulled and he just stared at the Lieutenant. Pug exclaimed, "Captain! Captain Custis! Are you alright?"

The man asked, "Who did you say that I am?"

"Sir, you are Captain George Fitzhugh Custis. You were the commander of our company. Company B of the..."

At that, the man frowned in confusion and, shaking his head as if he was saying "no", he replied, "Then who is Robert E?"

Lieutenant Pug said almost laughing, "The only officer I know of named Robert E is General Robert E. Lee and he is the head general of Johnny Reb."

"Are you sure I am George Custis?"

Verne Foster

"Sir, I am very sure. You and I have fought together too long for me to think otherwise." The Lieutenant then noticed the big scar on the Captain's forehead. He continued, "Captain, you seem confused. Could it be from that wound you got on your forehead?"

The Captain felt his forehead. The left side first, then, finding no scar, moved his hand over to the right side. There it was. It was still sensitive to the touch. He asked again, "Then you're sure I'm not Robert E?"

Lieutenant MacHenry assured him he wasn't. He further said, "Not only are you Captain Custis, you are one of the fightingest men I have ever served with. Why, the last time I saw you, you were charging a whole pack of Rebs with just your revolver, screaming and yelling, 'Let's get 'em men!'" Pug paused a minute giving it time to sink in. The other men were looking at each other in the realization of what was wrong...Amnesia!

The Lieutenant continued, "Why there was so much confusion and noise goin' on that we didn't know which way to shoot first. When the smoke cleared and Johnny Reb had cleared out, you were no where to be found."

The Captain was just moving his head back and forth in confusion.

Pug continued, "Sir, we looked high and low for you, but we couldn't find hide nor hair of you. We saw a trail of dead Reb officers in the direction you had last been seen heading, but you were no where around." Pug had been squatting all this time. He stood up and told the men to stand the Captain up. They reacted immediately in a very protective and respectful manner, reaching down and taking him by the arms and slowly helping him up to a standing position. The Lieutenant cocked his head slightly, and looking at the Captain as he asked, "You O.K. sir? Not dizzy or anything?"

The Captain nodded. The Pug asked, "Sir, can you remember what happened?"

The Captain thought for a minute and then shook his head. He spoke softly, "I am so tired." With that, he suddenly went limp. The Lieutenant barked out an order, "Get the Captain on the wagon. I want to take him back to camp right now. Maybe the regimental doctor can make some kind of sense out of this. A man who is one great Union Captain one minute and then thinks he is General Robert E. Lee the next! I surely don't know what to do."

Chapter Eleven

It was mid afternoon now on the same day as the girls' wagon followed the old clay road out toward the ravine. It was a road that veered off the main road and wound its way up into the foothills. The ravine was a slit through one of the foothills that looked sort of like the Lord just took His big finger and drug it through a mound. This area of Georgia wasn't far enough north to be in the high mountains, but rather, it was fairly flat land for the most part, with some hills to it. The mountains were near enough, but basically, the foothills were the only mountains visible. Mercy always liked to ride out there and stand atop the foothill and look all around at the wild country. She claimed it was so high, she could see clear into Alabama. She would imagine what the wide Chattahoochee River looked like and would someday like to cross it. The girls would humor her about it, but they found themselves doubting she could see that far, even from that high up. It was well over a hundred miles to the river.

It was rather wild country, though, that had all kinds of land in an admixture of types. There were the flatlands that looked more like prairie. There were the beginning foothills that would slowly get higher and as you traveled further north, became mountains. Then, there were the deep forests where the mainly traveled roads disappeared into a mass of trees. The ravine was located in the first

Verne Foster

foothill area that stretched out about three to four miles wide and slowly rose in height as it meandered north. The ravine was ground level where possibly, at one time long ago, a huge river flowed through cutting a slice out of it. It was a flat, rocky area about a half mile wide with a river deep enough for a horse to have to swim to cross it. It was crystal clear with a million small stones for its bottom. There were a couple of places you could cross, but if you did not know where they were, you'd be over your head. Mercy knew every inch of it. She had played there even as a child. That knowledge would certainly come in handy now. It was Mercy that suddenly told Hettie to stop. Hettie pulled back on the reins, put her foot against the brake lever, and hollered, "Whoa team!"

Rose and Hettie wondered what was going on in Mercy's mind, but was respectful of her innate cunning and instincts. Just like this morning when she suddenly said, "Something's wrong!". Here, she was saying it again. She stood up in the wagon and was looking down the road curiously. She said, "Hold on. Let me check this out!"

With this, she jumped down from the wagon and walked forward ahead of them a few yards looking at the road as if she were listening for something. Hettie and Rose heard nothing. They were still quite a way off from the entrance to the ravine and still riding the flatlands. The forest was fairly close to them to their right. About a five minute ride through wild grass from the road they were following. Mercy squatted down on the road and ran her fingers across the ruts in the old dried out clay. It hadn't rained in several weeks. There'd been a dry spell and it had warmed up a bit. Cool nights and warm to cool days, but no rain.

Mercy hollered for the girls to come there. Now, she was about fifty feet down the road from them. They climbed down off the wagon using the front wheels as steps. They knew enough not to make any unnecessary footprints here, so they walked up the sides of the road to Mercy. As they looked at her with the foothills behind her and that shotgun

The Saga of Robert E

under her arm, she looked pure Indian. Her long black hair was tied in the back out of her way. She told them to look as she pointed to the tracks in the clay. Tracks that could barely be seen, yet, Mercy had sensed or seen them from the wagon. Mercy exclaimed, "Listen! There it goes again!"

Hettie and Rose looked at each other, then at Mercy and chimed, "There goes what again?"

"Sounded like shots in the distance," Mercy said as she stood up, letting some of the loose dry clay sift through her fingers as she watched it flow through the air. Hettie had seen her do this before. She was testing the direction of the wind. Sure enough, the sand drifted toward the wagon. Mercy continued, "Girls, we got something wrong here. Them's wagon and horse's tracks. Yep...horse's tracks...and you know something else?" She looked off in the direction of the ravine and said, "Them shots sound alike. They're rapid fire!"

She turned to Hettie and asked, "How many men did you say you saw down at Reverend James' place?"

"Oh, five or six. I'm not sure. Why?"

"Well, I just don't think we're goin' to be alone in the ravine...if we go there."

Rose asked, "Well, what do we do now? What if that's the men Hettie saw this morning?"

"Well, more'n likely, that's them! We're gonna hafta' find out."

"And just how are we supposed to do that?" Rose snorted sarcastically.

Hettie told Rose to hush and let Mercy think. She knew this countryside better than anybody around.

Well sure enough, as if answering, Mercy spoke in authority, "We'll go the old Indian trail. Up the back way to the top. Hardly no one knows it's even there. It'll take us to the top and we can look down from the trees up there into the ravine and never be seen."

Rose asked, "Well, what if they're up there too?"

Verne Foster

"Well, we'll just have to take care of that when we come to it."

Hettie almost chided, "Now Rose, don't be a stick in the mud! We have the element of surprise. No one even knows we're here."

"And they don't need to find out, neither!" Rose retorted.

Mercy became the leader now. Following her was like following a scout. Well, actually, they were. Hettie drove the wagon very slowly behind Mercy as she walked along the side of the road ahead of them, looking for something. Just what? No one knew but Mercy.

Hettie thought to herself, "Yep, this sure reminds me of some of those tales the men would bring back from the West about following their Indian guide."

Now, they headed through the grass toward the tree line. They were moving slowly now and when she looked back, she saw Mercy sweeping the trail and obliterating their tracks with a small bush. She did that for a ways and then came and hopped up on the wagon with the other two and said, "Now. Let's continue our journey along the trees."

They were traveling over near the trees now and a good distance from the road. The swift breeze caused the grass to soon stand back up. No one should notice their trail now. Mercy suddenly instructed, "As soon as you get to that big rock on the right up there, just on the far side of it is where the tundra begins, circle around the rock and head into the trees. You'll see an old trail there."

Sure enough, just as Mercy had said, just past the big rock (that was as high as their heads) was the tundra. They turned into the trees and there was the old trail. Here Mercy stopped them again and jumped down, running ahead for a ways, checking the trail. Apparently, she was satisfied with what she saw. She motioned for Hettie to come on and she got back up on the wagon. They drove on up the slope between thick bushes and trees. Finally, the trail ended with only a foot path continuing on up the slope. The trees were

The Saga of Robert E

so thick now that it was almost dark as night. It felt cool and damp. The smell of rotting leaves combined with the smell of pines gave an almost mystic atmosphere to the place. Mercy had been watching all along for anything unusual. She was out walking ahead of them now. It was apparent that she had inherited a whole bunch of her grandma. The Indian was showing all over her now. The trail suddenly narrowed again at another boulder even larger than the first. Mercy came and took the reins of the horses from Hettie and tied them to a tree limb. Then, she said in a hushed tone, "Nobody's been this way for a long time."

This was the best news the other two girls had heard in a while. Here, they would have to leave the wagon and horses. They continued on up on foot with their weapons. Mercy carried the three loaded repeaters. Hettie carried two shotguns and had put their ammunition in one of the burlap bags. Rose had a loaded revolver stuck in her belt and was happy to carry the bag of ammo. They were like a little army. A real little army. Loaded to the gills with ammo and weapons, their hearts beat like trip hammers as they neared the top, wondering what they would find there. As they reached the top, the trees did not thin out. They were old and big and some of them even grew out over the edge of the ravine. Sure enough, they had the whole place to themselves.

Suddenly, before they could even set their load down, Mercy held up her hand and whispered hoarsely, "Hush! Listen!"

They could hear the voices of several men below. They seemed to be aggravated about something. It was apparently not a party going on down there. The girls inched forward toward the edge of the ridge ever so quietly following Mercy's every movement and instruction. As they peeked over the edge from behind a bush, they saw an unbelievable sight. Rose almost screamed as Hettie grabbed her mouth with her hand. Lo and behold! Hettie recognized the appaloosa!

Chapter Twelve

The girls were well hidden in the mass of trees and bushes at the top of the ravine. Mercy had crawled out on a limb for a perfect view. Hettie had eased to the edge behind some tall bushes with Rose beside her. There, hardly two hundred feet below them, was a sight they certainly did not expect to see. There was a camp there. A complete campsite with three tents, several wagons, some loaded with tarps covering them and some still empty. There was what looked like a chuck wagon next to the water's edge. There were several horses tied to a line that had been stretched from a couple of posts that had been set in the ground. Among them was a second appaloosa like the one Hettie had seen earlier. However, the man she had seen riding off from Reverend James' has his appaloosa with him and was holding its reins like he'd just dismounted.

This was a strange admixture of men. The two soldiers Hettie had witnessed putting the wagon in the barn were there with their horses. The raised voices of the men made it clear for the girls to understand what was said as the sound bounced off the ravine wall and up within earshot. It seems they were wanting to get paid right away so they could leave, but apparently, that was not the deal that had been made. There were several men dressed in apparently western gear. Three of them wore wide leather leg covering. The girls could plainly tell they weren't from around here.

Verne Foster

Besides, the strangers were wearing side arms in open holsters, not like the military. Their large brimmed hats also told them they were possibly from the West and not local people. There were also four Indians with them. They all wore buckskin trousers and boots. A couple of them with no shirts and the other two wore cloth shirts with no sleeves. The two that had no shirts wore vests. They were much darker skinned than Mercy, but their cold black hair was long and down to each shoulder. The two with the vests wore headbands around their head and their hair hung loose. The two with the shirts on wore their hair in long braids. Who were these men? It was quite obvious they were from the West somewhere. Their attire. The obvious Indians. The appaloosa horses. The girls could think of no one having an appaloosa around this neck of the woods. Apparently, the man on the appaloosa had just ridden in and he was talking to one of the westerners. He was possibly the straw boss of this outfit. They were the ones having the argument with the two Union soldiers.

The girls could hear one of the men say, "Hey! We're here to get our gold and get out of here!" The two men were apart from the rest of the group. The two soldiers were standing in front of their horses facing the two other men.

The one with the appaloosa looked at his cohort and said, "You reckon we ought to go ahead and pay 'em off now?" The westerner nodded to his boss. The appaloosa man was now turned facing his partner. This made the two soldiers at a right angle to him. Suddenly, as fast as lightening, he drew his revolver and shot both of them down. All three of the horses shied with a loud whinny. The two army horses backed off a few paces, but the man's Appaloosa settled quickly as if he was more used to it. Apparently, he had had this experience before and so long as his rider was right there, he was alright. He raised the gun to his lips and blew the smoke out of the barrel. He grinned at his partner, then hollered to the others who had stopped what they were doing and stood watching as he held his gun up ready to level it

The Saga of Robert E

quickly. "Anybody else got any ideas about getting greedy?" They all shook their heads and went about their business of what looked like breaking camp.

The girls backed off from the edge of the ravine. Rose was the first to speak, "I still can't believe what I just saw and heard!"

Hettie then pondered, "Hey! I wonder if the load of guns and ammo is still at Reverend James' barn?"

Mercy remarked, "And, I wonder if he knows just what kind of men he's dealing with?"

Hettie answered, "Well, we sure do."

Mercy climbed back up the tree over the ledge and looked down. The man with the appaloosa hollered, "Hey! Let's get ready to go!"

"Sam! You're the official Indian agent from Oklahoma, so, where's the gold we're going to pay for all this with when the other wagons come?" the westerner asked.

Now it all made sense to Mercy. This well dressed man was an Indian Agent doing the dealing for the guns. About that time, one of the Indians, who had been inspecting his newly acquired repeater rifle, gave out a yell, started jumping around, and quickly fired several rounds into the air. The other three Indians gave the same yell, but did not fire their rifles. They just raised theirs in the air over their heads in a sign of acceptance.

The Indian Agent hollered, "Hey! I said let's get ready to go!"

His western partner, hollering above the noise, and, in more of a challenging tone yelled, "Hey Sam! I'm beginning to think there ain't no gold. Maybe those soldiers were right." Putting his hand on his holstered weapon, he added, "And if there ain't, then that would mean I won't be getting my share either."

With this, Sam stopped and turned to face his partner who had apparently set this whole deal up for him. Sam's face had drawn cold and hard as he said, "Now you ain't by any chance saying you don't trust old Sam, are ya?

Verne Foster

The westerner said, as he tightened his grip on his gun, "Just show me the gold, Sam. I want to see the gold!" The westerner knew by Sam's face it was a showdown. He drew his revolver, but Sam had his gun out too fast. Mercy didn't even see him draw it out of its holster. Sam fired, hitting his partner square in the middle of his chest. The shot knocked him backwards and he dropped to the ground with his hand still gripping his gun that had never left its holster. Sam walked over to him and looking down at him mockingly said, "The streets of heaven are paved with gold! Go look there!" With that, he shot him again. The man had taken his last breath.

The other two girls had come to the edge by now and watched the sequence of events below. Hettie and Rose scampered back into the trees. Mercy watched as Sam snarled loudly, "Get rid of this mess before that Lieutenant and his sidekick get here with the rest of the stuff!"

Mercy eased catlike back down the tree and came over to Hettie and Rose who were in shock. Mercy announced to them, "There is nothing we can do but try and stay alive. If we leave now, we'll probably run into the other wagons from Reverend James' place."

Fortunately, their horses and wagon were well hidden on the far side of the foothill. No one should hear them if they make a noise. Then Hettie said, "Why don't we go back to the edge of the woods and watch for the others and when they pass, we can hightail it outta here?

Mercy retorted, "Well, that's a good idea providing they ain't already passed and we don't know it."

Rose added, "Well, we gotta get outa here somehow! What're we gonna do?"

Mercy looked at them and back at the edge of the rim and replied, "Whatever it is, we need to do it soon!" Thinking for a minute, she continued, "Apparently, they plan to move out late in the day and drive at night."

The Saga of Robert E

Hettie said, "Well the way that Sam guy's killin' everybody off that mentions gold, I want to be as far away from him as I can get!"

Mercy eased back out on her tree and looked below. Everyone was busy and occupied burying bodies and breaking camp. She eased back down again and walked over to her waiting sisters and said, "Let's give Hettie's idea try!"

Chapter Thirteen

It took a little time for the girls to retreat down to their hidden wagon. The horses were content in the quiet forest and all was peaceful there. Hettie climbed up into the driver's seat of the wagon while Rose gathered the reins and handed them up to her. There was easily enough room to turn the rig around if you just knew how to handle the horses...and Hettie did. It would take having them back up and go forward until the rig was in the position of choice. This was easy for Hettie for she had long mastered the art of team driving. They had had a team of oxen that they used mainly for land clearing and farming, but it was long past since their own Confederate army had conscripted them into military service. Things had long gotten desperate for the South and with the lack of horses and mules, some units had to substitute even oxen to pull the cannons and caissons.

As she was maneuvering the rig into position, the thought came to her just how much circumstances had made her change. The petite little lady of the plantation in her long dress that her husband had left was not the same girl she was then. She was now a very self sufficient woman quite capable of taking care of herself no matter what. Also, she now wore denim trousers and boots instead of the long dresses she once had. Only on Sundays did the girls wear their dresses. As she thought of these changes, she remembered they were wearing their dresses when they found Robert E.

Yes, things had certainly changed with the war and all. Now, she was truly a proven survivor. This war had made her and her sisters a tough bunch to tangle with. The locals had long acknowledged their prowess and held a high regard for them.

Once the wagon and team were turned around, the girls headed back to the edge of the woods. As soon as they could see the clearing up ahead, Mercy motioned for them to stop. She then jumped down from her perch on the wagon and trotted to the edge of the forest. She disappeared for awhile. Just as the two girls were getting concerned and contemplating doing something foolish, Mercy returned.

"Well, they've obviously already gone by."

Rose quizzed her, "How in the world can you tell?"

"Simple deduction. Two heavy wagons have gone by since we were on the road and an extra pair of horses too."

Now Roses' curiosity mounted and she continued, "And just what told you that?"

"Just as I said, Rose. Simple deduction. First, horses tracks. Then, heavy wagon tracks over 'em. Then, horses tracks again. Apparently, two loaded wagons with two horses tied to the rear one."

Rose shook her head and said smiling, "You know, Mercy, I'm glad I'm on your side."

"Well, that tells me it should be safe for us to make a run for it. Let's move on out...slow and easy."

There was no argument from the girls and Mercy climbed up on the back seat with her shotgun. Rose had the other one. Hettie started the team up and they moved at a walk. Once at the clearing, she moved cautiously around the big boulder and stayed close to the trees. They were traveling parallel to the road that was several hundred yards away over to their right now. Hettie was looking for a sign of their tracks in the grass where they had come over from the road on their way out, but the heavy breeze had blown the tall grass to and fro so much, there was no sign of any tracks they might have made.

The Saga of Robert E

As Hettie started to steer the team over toward the road, Mercy quickly warned, "No, no!" Stay over close to the trees. We want to stay away from the road for awhile and not leave any noticeable tracks in case they might be coming back this way and see them. Besides, we don't want to disturb any of those fresh tracks out there on the road. Let them think they're the only ones that have been along here."

By now, Hettie had the team on a trot. Soon, they came to the point where the road turned back toward the main road. Also, the trees were thinning out to just flatland fields. Now, Mercy said it was alright to move on over to the ravine road and head on back down the main road toward their place.

"What'er we goin to do now?" Rose asked.

"Well for now," Hettie and Mercy agreed, "we're headed home."

It didn't take the girls near as long to get back to their place as it did going out to the ravine. You would have thought Hettie was driving a chariot in an arena race instead of an old farm wagon. Fortunately, the girls did not meet anyone on the road. Now their house sat a ways back from the main road surrounded by big oaks and maple trees. As Hettie started to turn into their lane back to the house, Mercy warned, "No! Don't turn here. Go on down to the bridge at the river and pull off where you can turn around. Then, come back and turn in from that way. If anybody notices our tracks, they won't be coming from the direction of the ravine."

Hettie just nodded in understanding a good plan while the more younger and impulsive Rose seemed amazed at all the forethought. So, Hettie drove the team down to the stream and pulled off the road. She could feel the horses wanting to go on down to the water, but she steered them back onto the road and made her turn-around. She let them trot on back to their lane and on into the yard, but drove them straight around to the barn. They did first things first. They unhitched the horses from the wagon and tended them as they drank from their trough. They had really had a

Verne Foster

workout. But, some cool water and brushing was just what the doctor ordered.

Once those chores were done, the girls headed into the house with the rifles and shotguns. The shotguns stayed out for immediate use and the rifles and their ammo were securely tucked away for safe keeping; but not too much so just in case they were needed. Mercy was very quiet. She seemed to be in deep thought.

Hettie asked, "Anybody hungry? I'll fix something."

Neither of the other two girls were the slightest bit hungry and just shook their heads. Hettie fetched a pitcher of cool water out of the pump and the girls sat around the table in deep thought sipping their water. Rose was the first to speak, "I just can't help but wonder what's goin on out there now."

"Well," Hettie said in a devilish tone, "I'll just bet if anybody asks about gold, that Sam guy will probably shoot 'em dead!"

This brought a grin to the girls' faces. The seriousness of it all settled in for they knew that this was probably the final time and all of them and the guns would be gone to who knows where. More than likely, from what they saw, out west somewhere. Apparently, the Lieutenant and Sergeant were bringing the final load to them and would get paid for the whole deal.

Hettie raised a question, "I wonder just how much all that stuff is worth in gold?"

"A whole lot." chimed Mercy, "A whole lot. The way the war is gong now, they're probably much more valuable out west in that war." She was silent for a moment, then asked, "I can't help wondering what's goin on at old Reverend James' place? Judging from what we saw and what we heard that Lieutenant tell him yesterday, he might be dead too."

Hettie thoughtfully asked, "Well, you think we ought to go over there and see for ourselves?"

The Saga of Robert E

Rose almost hollered, "Hey! I'm for letting sleeping dogs lie!"

Mercy had other ideas though. She had been in deep thought every since they had gotten back. She said, "Tell ya what. Let's get cleaned up and in our dresses and go pay him a visit."

Hettie averred, "I'd give a purty penny to know just what's in that old back barn now."

Rose had made a good point though and pushed for it. It was getting late in the day and by the time they could do all that, they would be returning in the dark. Besides, the horses needed a rest. With that thought, Hettie backed off and said, "Oh well, we probably couldn't find out what was out there anyway, and what the devil, it can wait until tomorrow."

Mercy thought about it and agreed saying, "Oh, I guess yore right...and besides, we have had enough for one day!" Now Rose was quite happy with that decision. "We do need a plan, though," Mercy continued, "You know, a way to go just in case we do get linked to all this and have to protect ourselves."

Rose added, "Yeah, and just what would we do if we did get involved and somebody came after us?"

Hettie reasoned, "You know, we don't even have anyone to go and report this kind of thing to. I don't see anything we can do but stay out of it and count our blessings."

So, as the dusk of the day approached, it found the three little adventuresses trying to figure out just what the best choice for them was. They were starting to come out of the shock of their experiences today and realize just how serious this problem was that they had suddenly been caught up in. There were so many questions that needed answering before they could even try and decide what to do. What approach to take to the circumstances. So, they all agreed it would be best to just stop and stay put until they could figure it all out. A sign of the pressures of the day setting in became evident when Hettie said, "You know, if I had some of that ole reprobate Reverend James' concoction right now, I would probably turn to drinkin!"

That was quite a statement for a teetotaler. The remark had an impact on Mercy though. The very mention of Reverend James' concoction caused memories of Robert E to come flooding back to her. Her eyes clouded up as she thought of the ride back home with his head in her lap and how concerned she was for him. Then, there were a thousand questions as to just what might have happened to him. Was he alive? Dead? Questions as to his whereabouts were flooding her mind. Little did she know what had happened to him in such a short length of time. Yesterday, he was here and all was well. Today, it was as though he never existed. So very much had happened.

Hettie was the first to notice Mercy's face and asked, "Oh, Mercy! What's wrong?"

That brought it to Rose's attention too and she tenderly asked, "Oh Mercy, what is so bad that it's making you weep?"

Then Hettie, being the wise person she was, realized what just might be wrong here. With the remark about old Reverend James' hooch, memories of Robert E had emerged. She turned to Rose silently mouthing, "Robert E."

With that, both girls moved over to Mercy and hugged her in a gesture of silent understand. A loving gesture of concern and that they knew without saying what was wrong. Their thoughts were all the same now. They all were wondering just what had happened to their Robert E. Not knowing what to think, they all wept together. The common mystery of what happened to him filled their thoughts. Was he alive, dead, or did his memory come back causing him to suddenly flee back to the North in the middle of the night? And the things all around them now were so desperate. All these thoughts came thundering down on them now like a heavy blanket. They hugged each other trying to fight off the fear that was so vehemently trying to overcome them.

The Saga of Robert E

But these were strong and self sufficient women now. The events of the war and today would only serve to make them stronger. They all three now knew they were truly survivors.

Chapter Fourteen

The wagon carrying Captain Custis soon arrived at brigade headquarters. The Union had cleared the area of any enemy threat. The commander was General Absolom Davis and his brigade was comprised of 2000 cavalry and 7000 infantry, not counting artillery. He was awaiting orders from General Sherman to join forces with him for an assault on the Confederate stronghold at Richmond. The patrol, led by Lieutenant Pug MacHenry, had made the trip in double time. As they came into camp, they reined up at the infirmary. The guard watches had long recognized them and made no effort to slow them down. This was a tent city complete with a hospital set up. The General was standing in front of a large tent that served as headquarters for him and his staff. The hurry of the wagon and patrol caught his immediate attention. Lieutenant Pug rode straight to him and dismounted, saluting and reporting, "Sir, we've made a fine discovery! We have found Captain Custis and he's alive! Confused, but alive!"

The General knew about the missing Custis because he was the one who had approved Lieutenant Pug's field commission. He was naturally interested in this latest turn of events.

In the meantime, the patrol had taken the Captain into the infirmary tent. The chief physician looked up from his table and asked, "What's this?"

Verne Foster

The Corporal announced, "Sir, this is Captain Custis...he was missing and we found him. He seems confused and needs your help, so we've brought him to you."

The doctor told them to have him sit down. The Corporal gave the doctor a full report on what had happened. The doctor looked at the wound that was healing quite nicely now and said, "Hmmm...looks like a bullet wound. Took some hide with it. Whoever took care of that did a dern fine job!" Then he asked the Captain how he felt.

By now, the Captain was lucid and alert. He answered the doctor, "I feel fine now. I was a little whoozy out there, but I am alright now."

The doctor looked up over his spectacles and replied, "Well, let's just see for ourselves now."

After hearing the report about his state of mind, the doctor started with some questions, "Son, just who are you?"

"I am Captain George Fitzhugh Custis."

"So, tell me what happened to you."

Custis began, "Well, we were in the battle of Washingtonville and we had split the Reb forces in half. They were hightailing it south and we were in pursuit. They reached a grove of trees and turned on us to make a stand. We kept right on charging and broke their line. Then, they started retreating in all directions into the woods." The Captain suddenly stopped and frowned. By this time, the General and Lieutenant Pug had entered the area. The doctor asked the Captain to continue. With a confused look, he replied, "That's all I remember!"

Lieutenant Pug spoke up, "Doc, let me tell you what happened out there then. We were all shooting and dodging bullets. We had split the line and the Rebs were all over the place running and shooting. We were moving up on them when their main line in front of us started to retreat. Shooting at us and running. They would stop just long enough to take aim and fire, then move on. The Captain didn't even slow down. I know he alone must have killed more than a dozen Rebs. He never slowed down. He was on his horse charging and yelling something. We couldn't make out what he was saying because of the noise. The last I saw of him, he had reloaded and was riding right into them hollering at the top of his voice. I stopped to reload and when I looked up, he had ridden well into the trees. That's the last we saw of him! Ridin and Shootin!"

Custis had been listening to Pug and his face lit up and he almost yelled, "Wait a minute! I remember now! I had shot a couple of Rebs and was firing at some ahead of me. Yes...there were four of them. I got the first three and was after the fourth. He had gotten a little ahead of me and I was looking for him. He suddenly came charging out of the trees and we both got off a shot at each other. I felt something hit me in the head, but I didn't stop. I remember getting off my horse to check him because he had fallen off his horse and it looked like he was trying to say something. I remember walking over to him. He was trying to fire his weapon, but he never made it. My weapon was empty now. I had gotten him with my last shot." His voice tapered off and a frown came upon his face as he said softly, "That's all I remember...until I woke up in that barn."

The General broke in asking, 'Captain, were you held prisoner? I need to know if there are any Rebel forces near here. It's important."

The General repeated himself, "Tell me Captain! Were you held prisoner by a group of Rebs?"

Custis answered slowly, "No sir. I don't remember much of anything. All I know is I woke up in a barn. I wasn't guarded or anything. I must have been there for awhile because there was a pair of civilian trousers laying in the hay beside me and my uniform trousers were hanging on the stable wall near me. My boots were under some straw and my horse was there with me. My saddle was laying over in the corner of the stall. I didn't waste any time and dressed as quickly as I could and saddled my horse. I couldn't find

Verne Foster

my jacket, but I grabbed this coat that was hanging on a nail by my trousers. I grabbed it up and took off."

He thought for a minute in silence, then continued, "Now there was this big farm house there. I lit out toward the North and, well, it all seems to run together after that.

The General quizzed, "How'd you know which way was north?"

"Well, sir, the moon was bright and I knew it was well into the morning, so I figured if I kept the moon on my left, I would be headed north."

The General then asked Pug, "Was he armed when you found him, Lieutenant?"

Pug replied, "No sir."

The General then turned back to Custis and asked, "Do you know why you weren't guarded?"

"Not exactly, sir. However, as I think back, I can vaguely remember a lady helping me." His eyes suddenly brightened and he added, "Yes! Yes sir! I remember these ladies helping me now. One of them was the one that dressed my wound!"

The doctor interrupted, "General, judging from his wound and what we have heard, it is quite apparent to me he has had a lapse of memory and was probably taken in by a family who took care of him. It would be consistent with his symptoms and, if he suddenly regained his memory, he would probably, in shock, have reacted from his military training and escaped at all costs."

Lieutenant Pug spoke, "Sir, if I may, he was totally confused when we found him. It was chilly and he was laying on the ground without his coat on, and, he, well, he kept thinking he was General Lee."

"No, Pug," Custis interrupted, "I remember now. That is the name they gave me. Those ladies. The ones that took care of me."

Pug asked the doctor and the General to step over by the door. They moved away from Custis and Pug began, "Just for your information, Sirs, I've ridden with the Captain for years and I know a lot about him. Actually, he is kin to General

The Saga of Robert E

Robert E. Lee. Distant as it may be, but kin. Maybe that's why he thought his name was Robert E."

"Good point, Lieutenant." the doctor agreed. He than asked Pug, "Did he actually call himself General Lee?"

Pug replied, "Well, er, no sir. When me and my men recognized him, we called him by name and he just kept asking me if I was sure he wasn't Robert E. He never said Lee. We just assumed he meant the General."

"Well," the General quipped, "you know what we say about assuming anything."

Pug almost bowed up as he continued, "Sir, now that's a man we all would ride directly into hell with, if you want to know how we feel about him. As a matter of fact, we have done just that!"

General Davis nodded, "I certainly understand and I agree with that. I am wiring General Sherman about all this and, oh, by the way, your promotion papers went through. You are no longer an acting Lieutenant. As a matter of fact, my recommendation was also accepted and you are a full fledge First Lieutenant now."

Pug queried, "Uh, don't you mean Second Lieutenant, sir?"

General Davis turned and looked him in the eye with a look of mischief as he sort of cocked his head and said, "Never correct a General, son! I just promoted you and I am also promoting Captain Custis to Major."

Pug was awe struck and speechless.

Then, the General said, "Congratulations, First Lieutenant MacHenry." As he continued, he took a more serious tone, "And furthermore, when all this checks out, and I am sure it will, I am going to recommend him for that new medal that the President approved for honor above the call of duty when facing the enemy of the Union in battle. The Navy already has it and now, the Army has finally accepted it as well. The medals are different in looks, but they are awarded for the same reasons." Then, the General grinned and said determinedly

Verne Foster

"So far, there has not been a commissioned officer to get one,. I want to see if we can make him the first!"

Chapter Fifteen

As Pug re-entered the tent, the doctor was saying, "Well, Captain, you look fine to me. You seem to have your memory back and are stable; but, if you have the slightest problem... something you can't explain, and I mean anything, then I want to see you immediately!"

Custis asked, "Well, like what? A lot of strange things have happened to me already."

The doctor replied, "Periods of absence, forgetfulness, dizziness, or especially passing out, blurred vision, any of those kind of things."

"But as long as I'm o.k., then I'm all right?"

"By all means. Carry on as usual. You should be remembering more and more as time goes on."

Pug went to Custis' side and took him by the arm as they started toward the door. As they walked, he said, "Sir, you ain't going to believe this, but you are no longer a captain."

Custis pulled away and replied, "Oh, no! What now?"

"Well, sir, you and I both have been promoted and you are now a major and I'm a first lieutenant." Custis frowned as he tried to absorb this news. Pug continued, "I know things are happening fast for you, but they are for me too. Well, anyways, the General wants to see you as soon as possible. He'll explain it all to you."

Verne Foster

Pug guided him out and toward the headquarters tent. Custis was trying to make sense of what Pug had just said, but Pug just kept telling him to wait until he saw the General. As they approached the HQ tent, a lieutenant colonel was at the door. He seemed to be expecting them. He stepped into the opening and, with a loud voice, announced, "General Davis, Major Custis and Lieutenant MacHenry have arrived, sir!"

The General replied in a happy sound, "Send them in. Send them in."

The two entered and stood at attention before the General as they saluted and reported.

General Davis gave the command, "At ease, gentlemen. Sit down."

They sat on two benches made from fresh hewn lumber. The General was reading something that looked like a wire. It was. He looked up over his Ben Franklin style glasses and said, "Gentlemen, there are a lot of things happening right now and it seems that you two are a big part of them. First, I will deal with what I told the Lieutenant. Custis, I have promoted you to Major and your associate here to First Lieutenant. Also, I wish to have the 'Medal of Honor' given you."

Custis started to say something, but the General put his hand up for silence and said, "Major, you must follow my orders. You seem to be good at that so far, so don't stop now!"

"But sir, I was only going to ask what it was."

"Well," said the General, "That's not surprising. You're not the only one who is not familiar with it. You just go on busting your butt being a good soldier and you never think of the consequences. Well, I do. Seems this medal was refused at first by the Army, but the Navy thought it a good idea and put it into action. Then, the Army thought better of it and decided they could use it too. Well, it was originally made for everybody but commissioned officers, so, until now, no

The Saga of Robert E

one has challenged that and no officer has been awarded it."

A look of determination was on his face now as he continued, "By God, it's a pretty medal. Prettier than the Navy's. Ours is a bronze star with a silver eagle holding it and the ribbon is the old stars and bars. All red, white, and blue. The Navy's is different. It's silver with a dull looking ribbon...well, that's enough of that! Everybody up the line is in full agreement with my move, but the wire I just got from Sheridan deals more with our original wire we sent earlier about your being found alive. Seems he knows more about you than you think. He knows about your family ties to General Lee and contacted General Grant." A look of excitement came on the General's face as he frowned and said, "Looks like we're in the last days of the war. I am sure you have heard of General Custer?"

The new major nodded. General Davis went on, "Well, he is with Sheridan and is making his usual brilliant self known to the enemy. We all know of his feats at Cedar Creek and how he held off General Jubal Early's infantry long enough for General Sheridan to re-form and thus made it possible for General Sheridan to make his famous ride and ultimate victory."

"Oh, yes sir. Everybody's heard about that by now. That was back in October." the Major replied.

The General continued, "Well, he has remained with General Sheridan for the whole shebang. They're calling it 'The Appomattox Campaign'. Custer made great strides at Dinwiddie Courthouse and Five Forks at the start of all this. They have Lee cut off from all his supplies. However, General Custer and his brother, Captain Tim Custer, have both been re-assigned to ride with General Grant as we speak, and we are moving out tonight to join General Sheridan for an assault that might just be the last one of the war! I've already given the order to move out. It's what we've been waiting for."

Custis looked at Pug and then back at the General as the General warned them, "This is highly confidential. The only reason I am telling you all this is that when General Grant found out about you, Custis, my boy, he said he wants you to report to him as soon as we can get you there!"

Custis was in awe. He could only stutter trying to find the right words. The General saw this and calmly said, "Look here, Major. Our battle plans have changed so much in the last hour that we don't even know how we can get you to him unless you just ride with us, so I am appointing you two as my aides and I am appointing our Lieutenant Colonel Jean Conant, my present aide-de-camp, as commander of the 6th Regiment. That way, you can not only be of great service to me, I can keep my eye on you until we can move you on to report to General Grant. And...by the way...go to supply before they are completely loaded up and get you a fresh uniform and those maple leaves. We want you to look good when we join General Sheridan."

"Does General Grant want us both?" Custis asked.

"I am not sure about that. The wire wasn't detailed. It just said Grant wanted you sent to him immediately. Now 'you' could mean both of you. I haven't been able to get more word from General Sheridan. He is in the field apparently starting his move and expecting us to move with speed to catch him. It seems General Lee is making a stand at Richmond; however, General Grant got around him and is taking Petersburg as we speak. We have a long, long way to go in a short, short time!"

"Wow!" was all the two could muster.

General Davis ordered, "Well, there you have it men. Get your things ready 'cause we're moving out!"

The two officers left the General in the tent. As they got to the door, the Colonel that had greeted them was gone. Pug said, "Well, it won't take me long to move my things."

Custis laughingly said, "Me neither. I'm already packed."

The Saga of Robert E

They laughed as they parted. Pug for his tent and Custis for the quartermaster. As he neared it, they were already loading the wagons. He had to hurry, but had no trouble getting a new uniform. He also got a set of shoulder bars for Pug. He had to wash up at the mess tent because everyone else had packed up and was moving out. It was the only place that still had a vat of water. As he changed and was checking his horse, it seemed like people were running in every direction all over the place. Tents were all down now and soon, the camp would be history. Major Custis was wondering just how far they had to move when, suddenly, he heard the blast of a train whistle. He thought, "It will take a mighty long train to move this many soldiers."

It was a brigade of two different regiments. One was cavalry and one was infantry. They had sixteen big guns and many wagons. It was a complete unit in itself. Self reliant. However, with 1600 to 1800 cavalry and 4500 infantry, this was still going to be a long, long train. Well, sure enough, it was. The infantry worked with the artillery loading the big guns and when that was done, suddenly, here came another engine up to the one that was pulling an endless stream of cars. Flatbeds, coaches, every kind of combination he had ever seen. Then, something he had never seen before. The late arriving engine had backed its way up to the camp and they were loading firewood in the tenders of both of them. They attached the two engines together somehow and within less than an hour, they were ready to go. He was seeing things happen that he had never imagined before. The train would not take everyone. Some of the cavalry units had already ridden out. They would make the trek on horseback, but these units were used to hard and long rides to move from one battle front to another.

The General called for his staff which now included Custis and Pug. They boarded the train which would be the fastest mode of transport. The cavalry mounted and started out ahead of them. Half the cavalry had already left and was far ahead of the rest of the units. As was said, they would ride

Verne Foster

hard and long. The General had a car for his top officers and his staff. It was quite comfortable, but not the most plush of quarters. In time of war, you will find that quite often you have to sacrifice comfort for practicability. This was the scene here. General Davis wasn't one for luxury anyway. He was a man of quick thinking and daring and it was often said of him that he seldom took time for leisure, but was always about a mile ahead of it.

The loud blasts of the two engines echoed through the late of the day as each car of the train took its turn at the beginning jerk as it started moving. The train was crowded and uncomfortable with so many men aboard, but each had his own breathing room and that would suffice for the moment. As the train slowly picked up speed, Custis thought, "Well, I thought we would never do it, but here we are not only moving, but picking up speed. We're on our way, but to where? What lies ahead for me now?"

The one good thing about this most unusual train was that it had a "mess" car they were rigging up from a dining coach. The rations might not be the best of menus, but they would certainly suffice. Other than the periodic toilet stops and taking on water and more wood, the trip would be fast and furious. As he looked around the General's car, he thought how fortunate he was. This was undoubtedly the most comfortable spot on the whole train.

Chapter Sixteen

Night had fallen back in the foothills of northern Georgia where the girls were. That afternoon, Hettie had ridden over to Reverend James' place, but found no one there. She boldly rode back to the big barn and lifted up the window cover. The wagons were gone just as she had thought. Now the question was, "Where was Reverend James?"

She looked around for the horses she had seen earlier, but none were there. Maybe he had ridden into town. Town was just a little group of buildings. A couple of stores and a big barn where they used to have auctions for livestock, cotton, and all kinds of things. Since the war, no one really had anything to sell anymore. The Yankees had taken most all of the animals and even some of the wagons. As for law, there was nothing available because martial law had been the order of the day. If you had a problem, you had to report to the commanding officer who used the combination store and post office for his headquarters. It worked out pretty good because you could get your odds and ends in shopping done, mail your letters, and also handle any legal problems you might have all at the same time. Only thing was that there wasn't much of anything in stock in the store except a few bolts of cloth and sewing stuff. The Army had taken all the other stuff for their use.

As Hettie thought about this, she wondered what she could do about what had happened that day. Who would she report it to? The commander was a captain and that lieutenant and sergeant were probably his assistants and therefore he was probably in on the plot with them. Maybe not, but who's to know? She could just see it now. She goes to the so-called commander and reports all this that had happened and would probably not make it home alive. "Nope," she thought, "that ain't such a good idea." What to do? She rode back home and the other two girls came out to greet her asking her what she had found out.

"Nothing!" she replied as she unsaddled her horse. Mercy took the saddle and swung it up on the rail of the stall. "Reverend James ain't there!" she announced.

"What?" they chimed together. "Well, where is he?"

"I have no idea! Those wagons I saw were gone and the place was empty. His horses weren't even there."

Mercy reasoned, "Heck no! That makes sense. They're the ones that went past us out there at the ravine!"

"You're probably right!"

"I know I'm right!" Mercy was bristling now. "Reckon he went with the troops out to the ravine?"

"Maybe, but then, maybe not. Maybe his body is lying around somewhere out there by now!"

Rose squeaked, "You don't reckon they killed him, do ya?"

Hettie retorted, "Well, you saw how easy it was to get killed out there today, didn't you?"

"Well, now! Ain't we in a fine mess! We need help from the law but the law not bein around here is exactly what we need the law for now!" Rose sputtered rapidly.

Both Hettie and Mercy quipped, "Rose! Yo're doin it again!"

"What?"

"Yo're talkin in circles, that's what! When you get like that, we can't even understand what yo're sayin!"

"What I was sayin was..."

Hettie and Mercy stopped her saying, "Forget it, Rose!"

The Saga of Robert E

As the girls walked back up on the side porch of the house, they heard a man's voice moaning, "Help! Help me! Mercy... Hettie! Anybody...help me!" They ran around to the front porch and lo and behold, there was a man lying there on the steps. His horse was standing at his feet. He had apparently gotten off and tried to get up the steps, but that was as far as he could get. Rose had a hand lamp with her and held it down close to him. His face was all bloody, but she was able to recognize him. It was Reverend James. They turned him over and asked him if he'd been shot.

"No, but they beat me and left me for dead."

Hettie asked, "Who beat you?"

He coughed as he spoke, "It's a long story. I think I have some busted ribs. Can ya'll help me, please?"

"Sure," Hettie said, "what're we thinking of. Let's get him into the house." They helped him walk into the house. Rose ran and got a blanket and spread it out on the settee. As they helped him sit down, they took off his coat and shirt. By this time, Rose returned with a pan and a pitcher of water.

Hettie continued, "Get us some cloth for some bandages and tear off some long strips for his ribs." He didn't need any prompting to hold his ribs and not breath deep. They bathed his face and head and cleaned the blood off so they could see just where the wounds were. After a lot of work and time, they had him all bandaged up. Those long strips of muslin were just the thing to hold his ribs in place.

Hettie told Rose to fix him some hot sassafras tea. Mercy took the bloody water and threw it out after she rinsed the cloths out. She could wash them later. Now, it was time for some answers. Hettie and Mercy pulled up a chair and straddled them leaning on the chair backs. They just watched him for a few minutes with no one saying anything. Rose came in with the hot tea. Mercy had tied his ribs nice and tight with the bandages, so he wasn't in as much pain as he was earlier. They shoved the parlor table over in front of him and Rose sat the tea down on it. As he took a sip, he looked up at three curious faces staring at him. He could tell it was time for confession and these girls weren't going to take no for an answer.

Reverend James finally spoke, "Boy, I shore wish I had some of my concoction right about now." He flinched as he caught the look in Mercy's eyes. He reflected on the last time he'd seen Robert E and what she'd said. His guilt gave him away as he looked at each of them... not saying a word...just looking at him. He thought, "That Mercy's ready to scalp me. I just know it."

Hettie's voice finally broke the silence, "I'll just bet you'd like to have some of that devil's brew, but you ain't gettin any! We ain't got any and therefore, yo're goin to be doin without any!" She leaned toward him, her arms still folded on the back of the chair, and very methodically, stated, "Now. It's time for some straight answers, Mr. Reverend James. Did you get this out at the ravine?"

Reverend James almost dropped his cup. His mouth sagged as he stuttered, "Wha...wha...what do you mean?" Hettie continued her stoic stare at him as the other two girls moved in closer. He was truly nervous and intimidated by these girls' judging attitude. He slowly set his cup down on the table for fear of dropping it. He looked around into each of those determined faces. Hettie was poker faced. Mercy had pure contempt in her cold eyes and he felt a cold chill as he looked at her. There was no love lost there. Even Rose showed an unusual lack of pity. All was quiet. Waiting like an animal for its prey. He remembered back in the barn when the question was asked about them and he denied they knew anything. Even then, he had a feeling that there was something awry. Now, he realized the truth and finally spoke, "Well, er, you see, uh...why are you asking about the ravine?"

Mercy cut in abruptly, "Listen here, you old coot! Quit playin games with us or I guarantee you'll be worse off than when we found you!" He could see the real anger in this girl's

The Saga of Robert E

eyes as she continued, "There ain't no love lost between me and you! I ain't forgot what you did to Robert E!"

Reverend James wanted to ask about Robert E, but decided he had better go ahead and tell what had happened. "Well, girls, as I said awhile ago, it's a long story, but it came to an end today! I was a pick-up point for contraband from the U.S. Army and some other misdeeds. That Lieutenant and his Sergeant had me by the butt. It all started out simple enough with a little job here and there. I considered it politicking at first. Then, as it got bigger, I kept having to rationalize what I was doing."

"We had that figgered out already." Hettie said, "Now answer my question. Were you out at the ravine today?"

Reverend James admitted, "Yes! Yes, but I had a reason."

Mercy chortled, "I'll just bet you did."

He looked up at her then back to Hettie realizing his best bet was to deal with Hettie. "I was supposed to get paid off in gold for my part in this last shipment of guns." He lowered his head as he continued, "Things were getting too hot for us because of them."

Hettie interrupted, "Them? Them who?"

"The guns. We have done this a lot, but the Lieutenant was getting spooked and said this would be the last time for us to deal with them, uh, the stolen guns, that is."

Hettie asked, "How'd you get them late model repeaters, anyway?"

Now this completely put the Reverend into a state of shock. His swollen eyes opened as wide as they could in surprise as he exclaimed, "How'd you ever know about that?"

She answered slyly, "We know a lot more than you can imagine, so you'd better start leveling with us. Were you a part of what went on out in the ravine today?"

The Reverend shook his head in amazed question as to how they could possibly know all this as he said, "Wasn't supposed to work out that way. The Lieutenant was supposed to bring me my gold and take the wagons out there, but something happened and the plans were all changed. Instead of me just watching them empty the barn, they said I would have to go with them and I had to help get the teams ready. When I asked where the Sergeant was, he said it was none of my business. Just do what he said. So I did!"

Hettie asked, "Did he pay you in gold?"

"No! That's just it! He said he didn't have it, that I'd have to go with him so we could collect it on delivery."

"So you drove one of the wagons."

"Yes, I drove the one with the ammo. We hitched my two work horses to the wagons and we tied our ridin horses to the back of the wagon he was drivin."

Hettie and Rose gave Mercy a knowing glance. Hettie continued, "Well, tell us what happened when you got out to the ravine. Was there a man riding an appaloosa still there?"

Now, the Reverend almost lost his breath. All he could do was shake his head in disbelief and asked, "How do you know all this stuff?"

Mercy barked, "Just answer our questions for now!"

He obeyed, saying, "No, but I know who you're talkin about. He was gone and only a couple of the Indians and a guy from out west was there. When I saw what they were doin, I guess I panicked."

Hettie asked, "What were they doin?"

"They were burying bodies! That's what they were doin!" He stopped for a minute and gulped, then, continued, "I asked what had happened and the westerner hollered, 'The same thing happens to anybody who asks a lot of questions!'. By this time, me and the Lieutenant were afoot and standing by my wagon. The Lieutenant was as quick as lightening when he drew down on that westerner. He must have read the guy's eyes and beat him to the punch cause there he was standing there with his gun pointed at the guy when he asked in a deathly slow voice, 'The man asked you a reasonable question. It don't look good to me and I can't help wondering

The Saga of Robert E

if their fatal question was something about where the gold was.' I just froze in my tracks. I could hardly breathe. It was deathly quiet. By this time, the two Indians had walked over to where we were and just stood watching."

Here, the Reverend, who was now sweating profusely, reached his cup and sipped the last of the tea from it. As he put it back, he continued, "That's when the westerner turned nervous and stammered, 'Well, you see, uh, it ain't up to us. The boss rode out a ways on business with the rest of the wagons. We were waiting for you to come with this load. He'll be back anytime now.' By now, my mouth was as dry as dust. I felt death all around me."

By this time, Reverend James was truly shaken and was showing his fear. It was then that Rose seemed to have pity on him and poured him some more tea. His hand shook as he tried to lift it to his swollen mouth. His wounds were getting more painful now and he was spilling the tea. Rose quickly retrieved the cup from him. He closed his eyes for a moment, then opened them again quickly and said, "Oh! Every time I close my eyes, I see it all over again!"

"Well, tell us the rest...see what?"

"I suddenly didn't care about no gold. All I wanted to do was get outa there! I had seen enough. They could have it all. The gold, the guns, all of it! I had had enough! I told 'em they could have my share. All I wanted was to go home. I started for my horse behind the wagons and I can remember some shooting. That's all I remember until I woke up at dark. There was a horse nearby. I pulled myself up to where I could get on it. Man, I just know I was dead and came back. It was awful. I ain't never been in so much pain. I sure wish I had some of my concoction!"

Chapter Seventeen

The girls decided it would be best to get the Reverend back to his home where he could rest easier. They concluded that for him to try and ride his horse was just impossible. Every time he took a breath, he groaned with pain. Maybe it would be best for him to be home where he could get his concoction to help him get by the night. Since there was no way he would be able to ride a horse, they elected to take him in their wagon. They made a pallet in it so he could lie down and headed for his place. It was a very painful ride for him. Every bump caused him to yell. Every turn of the wheels brought groans and moans of agony from him. He kept saying he was going to die. The ride was killing him, but he made it alive to his house. It took all three of the girls to get him inside where he could lie down. They lit the oil lamp and adjusted it low just so he could see. He continually had asked for his jug, so that was one of the first things they brought him.

Hettie said, "We left yore horse at home on purpose. Two reasons for that. One is that we don't want you goin nowhere. You ain't goin to feel like it anyway. Two is that we need to borrow her because we got business to do and we only got two horses. Rose will need one and besides, you ain't fit to take care of no horse anyway."

He took a big swallow of his concoction and put the cork back in the jug. He waited for it to go down so he could get his breath. Then he answered, "Anything you girls say. If ya need anything, I'll be right here. I might not be able to walk straight or talk plain, but I'll be right here." The girls grinned at each other as he took another swig. Now that was a given.

The ride back was dark and late, but was far less taxing not having to constantly hear his moans and complaints. Once back at the house, they realized how tired they were. They agreed there was no use going out to the ravine at night, so they decided to get a good night's sleep and rise extra early so they could get out there as close to daybreak as they could.

The next morning, they were up well before daylight as was their routine anyway. In those days, you got up early and got your chores done. When everything is done by hand, it takes longer. They had fed their horses and were now sitting around the table with their morning cup of coffee. The coffee pot was always on the back burner where the heat was the least. Hettie had warmed over some biscuits cut in half in the iron skillet on top of the stove and had put them out on the table with some molasses. The girls just dabbled at a biscuit half, though. No one was really hungry. The adrenalin was flowing too fast. Hettie was the first to speak, "Well, let's take those new rifles with us and head out to the ravine. I can't stand another minute of this not knowing."

Rose said, "If it's all the same to you, I'll take my shotgun. I know how to use it and might need to without wastin any time."

Hettie had rubbed down Reverend James' horse the night before and fed her. Her soothing talk and calm tone had impressed the mare. Hettie's natural expertise with animals made it easy to make friends with her. The mare had made no attempt to shy the night before and seemed to enjoy Hettie's gentleness. So, Hettie cautiously approached her and, after giving her a turnip and talking to her, she was able to put the saddle and harness on her without incident. Now

The Saga of Robert E

came the test. Hettie put her foot in the stirrup and hoisted her slim body up into the saddle. No problem. The mare had reacted well to the lighter weight of the girl and her gentle approach. The other two girls were on their horses already. Rose liked to carry her shotgun across her saddle ready for use. Mercy and Hettie carried two of the new rifles with them. All three headed out toward the ravine without further ado. As they rode away, Rose told Hettie, "You sure have a way with horses, don't you?"

"Learned it from Pa." she smiled back.

It took them the better part of an hour to get to the ravine. The sun was up now and burning off the haze that had been defying it. You take the old road to the ravine from the main road and as you approach the ravine, at first, you see to your right the foothill starting to rise. It is at the end of a flat area of land. The trees on it sort of form an edge for it. The forest cuts a straight line toward the ravine and as you make the bend to head into it, the hills on both sides are red clay. You are actually riding on the floor of the ravine. The river is fairly wide and gets deeper in places, but there is plenty of flat ground for you to ride through the gap. You can tell by the ridges cut into the sides of the foothills that the river must have been that wide and much deeper at one time eons ago. However, the bottom was sandy like the river bottom, so you found yourself riding on sort of a beach. Mercy and Rose were on army horses and their saddles had rifle carriers on them. Hettie preferred to keep her rifle in one hand across her saddle in front of her. Mercy was in the lead and held up her hand. The three reined up. They were at the "gate" as it was called. The girls took the rifles up and cocked them. Rose now had the rabbit ears pulled back on her shotgun and all positioned the weapons with the butts on their thighs. They were now ready for anything that might move. Nothing did.

They rode on into the ravine. About a hundred yards into the ravine, they could see ahead the area they had been looking down on the day before. Mercy told them to

Verne Foster

hold up and cover her as she rode on in. There was a horse standing by the river and something lying over toward the ravine wall to her right. In fact, there were several things on the ground that she could not quite make out from where she was. Hettie and Rose showed true ingenuity when they eased apart from each other so they would not make a single target.

As Mercy approached the horse, she could plainly see what was lying several feet away. It was a Union soldier. Since they seemed to be alone now, the other two girls rode on in. Mercy looked up at them with a look on her face of a mixture of disgust and unbelief. She said, "This is the Lieutenant from town and that's his horse over there. Must have gotten thirsty and moved over to the water."

There was what apparently were to be three graves over near the wall of the ravine. One was just a small bit of a mound, but the other two were unfinished and had the body of a man in each one. Apparently, something had stopped them from finishing the job. Possibly the Lieutenant had something to do with it. A little farther, down the river, were some boxes. All three girls were dismounted now and walked over to the boxes about a hundred feet away. Hettie spoke, "Why these are some of the rifles and ammunition I saw in the wagons."

As they inspected them, Mercy just shook her head and said, "This just doesn't make good sense."

They counted five boxes of rifles and seven boxes of ammunition. What did this mean? By now, the girls were getting used to seeing dead bodies, but this was utterly amazing. What happened here? The three girls looked at each other trying to find an answer to all this puzzle. Rose was the first to speak, "I can tell you what happened just from what we saw yesterday. The poor old Lieutenant mentioned the 'G' word and got killed for it."

Hettie chastised, "Now Rose, this is no time to be funny."

The Saga of Robert E

Rose came back, "Who's tryin to be funny? I'm dead serious...oops, that didn't come out right."

Hettie and Mercy suddenly looked at each other. They walked back to the dead Lieutenant. He was lying face down in the dirt and dried blood was all over the back of his head and had run into the ground. Mercy spoke first, "Hey, remember what that ole coot said? He heard some shooting and then couldn't remember anything else?"

"Yeh." said Hettie.

Mercy continued, "You thinking what I'm thinking? Remember the Lieutenant had asked about the gold? He had drawn his gun out of sudden distrust. Then, the Indians had come up by them, right?"

Rose proudly chimed in, "See! I told you what happened! One of those Indians got around that Lieutenant and shot him in the back of the head."

Mercy shook her head and said, "That ain't no gunshot hole in his head. It's too big. More like a hatchet or something."

Hettie posed a question, "That caused them to leave in a hurry alright, but why did they leave all those guns and ammunition?"

Mercy perked up and said, "To lighten the load!" She faced Hettie and asked, "How full were those wagons in the barn?"

"Oh, they were packed all the way up past the sideboards. Must have been at least two dozen cases of rifles and fifteen or so cases of bullets."

Mercy surmised, ""That's exactly what they did. They never intended to pay the Lieutenant or anybody else for the guns and bullets. There wasn't any gold. Only a bloody mess. That westerner must have made a play and it caused the Lieutenant to shoot him. That's when the two Indians got into it and one got the Lieutenant and the other went after Reverend James."

Rose questioned, "That's all well and good, but if the Lieutenant shot one of them, where is the body?

Hettie added, "Well, he must not have killed him. Seems like they must have hurriedly threw off some of the stuff to lighten the load so they could travel faster and catch up with the others."

"Sure makes sense to me," Mercy said, "I guess yore right. It sure makes sense from what we can see here. They were caught off guard while they were burying those three guys and didn't finish the job. Probably just too time consuming to have to bury two more people."

"Apparently so." the others agreed.

"Well, question is, what do we do now?" asked Rose.

Hettie explained, "Well, we shouldn't leave all the guns and ammunition out here. We can go back and get the wagon and come back and load it up and take it to our barn."

Rose moaned, "And then what? If that Sergeant comes looking for the Lieutenant and we got those guns and stuff, he might think we did it."

"Well, now that you mention it, sister dear, just where is that Sergeant?" asked Hettie.

They all looked at each other in wonderment. Hettie spoke, "Well, let's take the Lieutenant's horse back anyway I can't bear the thought of leaving him out here." Then, mischievously added, "Besides, he'll be some good company for the others."

Rose queried, "Well, how about the bodies and all? Should we give them a decent burial?"

Mercy spoke, "Well, actually, I feel just like those other guys did. Let's just get outa here. We can decide about comin back with the wagon for the stuff when we get home."

Chapter Eighteen

By the time the girls got back to the farm, they had pretty well decided to return and get the guns and the ammunition. They would hitch up their wagon and bring the load back and store it in the back of their barn with the other stuff that was stored back there. Then, they would check on Reverend James. Next, they would check all around to see where that Sergeant was. No one must know that they had the guns or knew anything about all this that was going on. The one key to all of it was still Reverend James. However, the bad guys must think he is dead, so they figured they should warn him to keep out of sight.

Hettie took the saddle off of the Lieutenant's horse and rolled the very noticeable military blanket up in a roll. By the time she had led the horse into a stall and hung his bridal up, Rose had a hole dug and they buried it. They threw the saddle into the back stall and piled hay over it. The saddles were nothing special to notice from any other kind since many of the officers used their own saddles. They would have to come up with a plan to take care of the U.S. brand on the horses though. By this time, Mercy had hitched up two of the horses to the wagon. After watering them, the girls agreed they were still not hungry after all they'd been through. Knowing the boxes would be heavy, all three girls would be needed to load them.

Verne Foster

After the horses had a suitable rest, all three of the girls boarded the wagon and headed back out toward the ravine. It had been over two hours since they had left the ravine and the sun was up and hotter than before. They let the horses move at a slow gait because of the heat and realized it would take longer, but why should they hurry? No one ever went to the ravine and certainly, the dead men weren't going anywhere. So, just as they had planned, they would do all this and then check on Reverend James when they got back. Up ahead was the turn off toward the ravine. Their tracks onto the side road were still there undisturbed. This gave them a feeling of comfort. On they went until they approached the bend in the road toward the "gate". they checked their weapons. They had un-cocked them previously, but now, they cocked them just in case, even though they knew the only thing they would probably need them for was if the buzzards had found the bodies. They rounded the bend and continued on down beside the river. Even though they strained their eyes, there was nothing to see now. They looked at each other in disbelief. Hettie slapped the reins on the horses and they bolted forward. As they came to the site where they had left all the carnage and guns, they didn't find anything. They dismounted and each took a different direction looking carefully around them. There were no bodies! Also, there were no boxes! Nothing was there but some disturbed dirt where the shallow graves had been leveled out. They could tell the dirt had been disturbed, but even the dead Lieutenant's blood had been removed. Somebody must have cleaned up the mess and took the guns and ammunition. No tracks were there. They had swept the sand and covered most of the site up. Mercy picked up a stick and went over to where the three gravesites were. She poked around in the sand, but found nothing. The girls were speechless. Hettie finally spoke, "Well, we didn't see any tracks coming in, so what do yall think?"

The Saga of Robert E

Rose quivered out, "Oh, my god! You don't think there's ghosts out here, do you? I've heard all kinds of weird tales about this place!"

Mercy chided, "Oh, Rose! Don't be silly! Yall stay here and let me do some tracking."

Rose and Hettie stayed by the wagon while Mercy went trotting off down by the river toward the westerly end. Soon, she was almost out of sight when she turned and waved her arm for them to come to her. They climbed aboard the wagon and, staying close to the water, moved down to where Mercy was. Mercy said, "Yall get down and come here. I've found something."

It was about a couple of hundred yards west of where they had been. Sure enough, there were horses and wagon tracks. "Now what," the girls thought. Mercy spoke, "Well, all this had to have happened in the last three hours!" Hettie nodded in agreement.

Rose asked, "Ya don't suppose they were here and waited for us to leave this morning, do you?"

Hettie shook her head, "Nope, or we'd be buzzard bait too. I figure this was a big coincidence. I think that those guys must have caught up with the others and told them what had happened and they figured to cover their trail and came back to clean up the mess. This would give them more time to get on outa here with no one the wiser."

Rose asked, "Well, what do you think they did with all those bodies?"

"They probably plan to dump 'em way out there somewhere."

Mercy they surmised, "Yep. That's just what they did and I figure something else too. They saw Reverend James and the Lieutenant's horses were gone and with all those tracks we made while we were here, they probably know now that someone else was here."

Rose looked at Hettie and cried, "Oh no! You don't reckon they'll come after Reverend James, do you?"

Mercy thought for a moment and replied thoughtfully, "I really don't think so. For two good reasons. One is that they don't want to take the time and if they're headed out of here, it won't matter. Two is that with all these tracks, they might just think it ain't worth the trouble to go up against a crowd. Just skeedaddle and leave no clues for anyone to speculate on."

"Sure makes good sense to me." Hettie commented.

"Well, it does seem quite reasonable, the way you put it." Rose agreed.

"Well, either way, we'll be checking on the Reverend soon enough." Hettie said thoughtfully.

Mercy was gazing north in thought. She had her hand up to her chin and was looking up the trail,. It went north for quite a way and then it makes a turn to the west and on up the foothill. It meanders through heavy trees and there is a steep slope on your right as you head west where the road sort of dips and as it continues on up northwest. If you bear west there, you start on up into higher ground.

Hettie asked, "What's on yore mind, Mercy?"

Mercy took her hand away from her chin and replied, "Well, I sure would like to know just what happened here and the answer has to be up that way." She was pointing up the trail.

Both Hettie and Rose cried out almost in unison, "Well, we don't! We already know too much as it is! Let's just head back to the farm. We need to check on Reverend James anyway!"

Mercy still had that curious tone as she answered, "I'll bet they've dumped those bodies down that west slope where it will take days for the smell to tell anybody they're there. By that time, the critters will have all probably had a good feast. All that will be left of them will be a bunch of bones and some torn clothes. They'll chalk it up to just some war casualties."

Rose almost shouted, "I don't care what they chalk it up to or whether they're ever found! I don't care whether they

The Saga of Robert E

ever chalk it up! The guns are gone! The bodies are gone, and we're still here! I just want to clear outa here!"

Hettie offered, "Well, she's right. There's nothing we could do if we found them. The only thing we came back for was the guns and the bullets."

Mercy acquiesced and said, "Well, I guess yore right. Let's get outta here."

So, the girls turned the wagon around and headed back the way they came. It took the better part of an hour to get back to the farm. Hettie immediately went over to the Reverend's horse and put its harness on it while she caressed her nose and let her drink some water. She then put the saddle back on her. She told the other two, "Yall go ahead and take care of the team and wagon. I'm goin to check on Reverend James."

They both replied, "Ain't you goin to need some company there?"

"Nope. I'm goin to take one of our six guns with me. If I get into trouble and six shots won't get me out of it, it won't matter anyway."

With that, she spurred the horse and rode off toward the road and on down to Reverend James' place. When she got there, she dismounted and walked up onto the porch. She banged on the door as she entered calling out, "Reverend James, it's Hettie." She heard a muffled reply and headed for the couch where they had left him. He was laying on the couch facing the back of it on the side with the broken ribs.

He slowly turned over and looked at her. He was a mess. His face bore all the marks of a beating. He looked at her through swollen eyes and with a silly grin, he said, "Hello there, darlin. Ju come to take me away to heaven?"

That silly grin and his swollen face certainly didn't go together, but they were together, and really made for a comical combination. She looked at him with mixed emotions. He was snockered! She answered, "No. I've just come to check on you. How are you feelin?"

"I ain't, hee, hee, hee."

105

She said, "Yore drunk as a skunk, but I'm goin to tell you something that might just sober you up."

He just smiled his silly grin and replied, "O.K. What?"

"They know you ain't dead and we don't know but what they're comin for you right now."

Sure enough. The grin left his face and he thought for a minute, then spoke, "Leave me my shotgun where I can get to it. I'll just have to wait for 'em."

Hettie asked, "I need to know where that Sergeant is or stays. Do you know where I can find him?"

"Not really. The times I have ever met with them in town, well, we usually met outside the general store and talked while we were on horseback. I believe they have a camp on the other side of town. Why do you ask?"

"You just stay put. I'll be back to see you when you sober up. Meanwhile, don't dare answer yore door!"

As she left, she saw him take another slug from the jug. With the information she had just given him, he would probably drink himself into a coma. She thought as she closed the door behind her, "Well, that's not a bad idea given the circumstances. If they do come for him, he won't answer the door and if they do kill him, he won't even know he's dead."

She smiled and almost chuckled at her own wit as she rode off toward town.

Chapter Nineteen

"Town," she thought as she rode. "Now that is a joke if there ever was one. It ain't even a settlement."

It was about a twenty minute ride from Reverend James' place. As she neared the settlement, it was almost vacant. Hardly anyone was on the street. She rode past the big auction barn and on to the general store. As she reined up there, she dismounted and wrapped the reins around the whipple tree. She stepped up onto the boardwalk. There was a single door that was open and a screened door to keep the flies out. When you enter, the little post office area was straight back. On your left was a desk and chairs and a wooden filing cabinet. On the desk was a nameplate, "Ronald J. Beck, Captain, USA". The couple that owned the place were the "Bowdens". Mrs. Bowden was behind the cage of the post office. Mr. Bowden was behind the counter on the right wall as you enter. He smiled as he nodded politely, "Good day, Mrs. Lee. Hope all is well out at your place."

Hettie smiled and walked over to the counter. She had known the Bowdens all her life. She replied, "And a special good day to you, Mr. Bowden."

How may I help you today, Mrs. Lee?"

Hettie looked around and replied, "Well, I was just wonderin if any of us had some mail."

Verne Foster

Mrs. Bowden had come out from behind the cage now and answered, "No. I wish I could say yes, but, you know these days and times."

Hettie nodded, "Oh yes. Oh yes."

Mrs. Bowden remarked, "Dear, I was so hurt to hear about your mom and dad. Haven't seen any of you three in a long time."

"Well, we've been quite busy out there. Mendin things and paintin up and all."

She could tell Mrs. Bowden was about to burst with curiosity. Finally, Mrs. Bowden subtly said, "I understand you all have a guest, a young man, staying with you."

Hettie could almost see the cat fur growing on the old lady's neck. It was apparent that some rumors were flying around about Robert E. Hettie kept her temper and explained, "Oh, you must mean Robert E. He's our cousin come up from Florida way. He helped us a lot in some fixin up, but he had to go back."

"Oh," Mrs. Bowden said almost sadly, "Well, I guess he was a blessing to you three girls."

"Oh yes. He was a great help. Fixed up our wagon and painted it all up. Right purty like now. We sure were sad when he had to go back home." Hettie then asked Mrs. Bowden where the Captain was.

"He hasn't been here today as yet, but he's usually here for awhile most days."

"Hmmm, well how about his Lieutenant or his Sergeant?"

Mr. Bowden looked at his wife and back to Hettie before saying, "Well, I guess he does have a Lieutenant and maybe even a Sergeant, but they've never came into the store. Now we've seen such a couple of times out there at the edge of town just sitting on their horses and talking to the Reverend James, though."

Hettie's eyebrows raised with curiosity as she asked, "Well, did the Captain ever notice 'em?"

The Saga of Robert E

The couple exchanged glances again and just shrugged their shoulders as he replied, "Don't think so. Come to think of it, both times we saw them, the Captain was gone off to who knows where. There are days we don't see him at all."

As Hettie pondered this, Mrs. Bowden said coyly, "By the way, dear, we have noticed you girls never wear your dresses much. You seem to always be in pants. Why is that?"

Hettie kept from taking offense and replied, "If you'll remember, Mrs. Bowden, we all dressed quite ladylike before this here war ruined everything and changed our lives. So, we decided that if we had to live and work like men, we were goin to dress like 'em'. Besides, we only got one dress apiece to our names and we just about ruined them in the river a couple of weeks ago!" As soon as she had said it, she wished she had not, but her anger had taken its toll with this little gossip hound.

Mrs. Bowden's eyebrows lifted as she replied, "Oh? How did that happen, deary?"

Mr. Bowden, who was looking ashamed by now, said, "Mama, it's none of your business."

Just to quell any more rumors, Hettie quickly responded, "No, Mr. Bowden, it's alright. We all know how Mrs. Bowden is." Hettie continued calmly with a lie, "We had an ole hog that came up just as we was dressed to come to town and were chasin it around and it ran right into the water with us right after it." She stopped for a minute trying to decide what else to say.

Mr. Bowden very interested now, asked, "Well, what happened?"

Having enough time to think, she said, "Well, it got away from us and hightailed it on off and left us there in the mud and all in our one and only dresses. I ain't got all the stains out of mine yet." Hettie was quite pleased with her story when she saw both of them shaking their heads in a kind of pity.

Verne Foster

Mr. Bowden spoke, "Well, that's too bad. Messed up your dresses and no bacon either."

"Looky here...Where does the Captain stay? Does he have soldiers and all?"

"Oh yes." Mrs. Bowden answered. "There are several of them coming in to see him all the time. They're nice looking young men, too."

Mr. Bowden spoke, "Their camp is just up the road. Must be about two dozen of them. If you're planning to go up there, they're about a ten minute ride on your left. Just follow the road north."

Hettie started to thank them when Mrs. Bowden offered, "Now, I've got some nice ready made dresses that could be made to fit you girls by just taking them up a little here and there. That is, if you ever want to wear a dress again, deary."

Hettie dug her nails into her palms, but managed a smile and said, "Well, that's a very nice and proper offer, Mrs. Bowden. I'll tell Mercy and Rose what you said." She almost stomped out of the store. Once outside, she mounted her horse and just as she started to pull on the reins, Mrs. Bowden had come out onto the boardwalk and queried, "Oh Mrs. Lee. Isn't that Reverend James' horse?"

Hettie nodded as she replied, "Yep. The Reverend is sick and he's our neighbor. We're having to tend to him a little."

Mr. Bowden came out about that time and said, "But I thought no one could ride him except Reverend James. We used to kid him that you had to be a praying man to do it."

Hettie looked down at them and replied, "That's true, but I'm not a man and I'm great with horses. Learned it from my dad." With that, she spurred the animal and hollered, "Gidyap!" Away they went like the wind.

Watching her ride off, Mrs. Bowden remarked disgustedly, "Hmph...she's no lady! Just a show off! Wonder what it's going to be like out there if and when her man Jefferson comes back?"

The Saga of Robert E

Once away from the settlement, Hettie slowed her animal down to a comfortable trot. Sure enough, in a few minutes, she could see some smoke trails heading up to the sky. As she came nearer, she could see the little group of tents. As she rode up to the camp, she saw a soldier sitting on a rock with his rifle across his lap. The camp was about fifty yards on back off the road. As soon as she neared the soldier, he stood up holding his rifle across his chest and said, "Maam, you can't go in there unless you have official business."

Hettie had been looking at the camp and several of the soldiers had stopped what they were doing and were looking over at her. From the way old Mrs. Bowden had talked, her, with her half coat and trousers, and wearing her hat, she wondered if they could even tell from that distance if she were a man or woman. Apparently, from the way they were looking at her, they could tell she was a woman. She had stopped her horse and was now looking down at the soldier. She leaned forward and inquired, "Is the Captain here?"

"No maam."

"Well, how about his Lieutenant?"

The soldier looked puzzled and said, "Maam, we don't have a Lieutenant here."

Reality was beginning to set in on Hettie. She had to collect her thoughts for a minute. Shaking her head, she said, "No Lieutenant? Well, how about your Sergeant?"

"Yes maam. Matter of fact, he's the one in charge today. Here he comes now."

Hettie let the Sergeant walk up to her as she scrutinized him. This was not the man she had seen with the Lieutenant. She asked, "Is there more than one Sergeant here? One that wears a lot of stripes on his sleeves?"

The Sergeant looked almost hurt, but remained in a polite attitude as he replied, "No maam. I'm the only one, but my three lonely stripes seem to be enough to get the job done."

Hettie sensed his hurt pride and apologized as she explained she didn't mean to demean his rank at all. She said, "It's just that I heard you had a Lieutenant and a Sergeant with some things under his stripes out here. I guess I was misinformed."

The Sergeant asked, "Well, maam, is there something we can do for you? The Captain is gone for a couple of days, but I am in charge until he gets back. Is there a problem?"

Hettie shook her head and replied, "Uh, no. Not really. I've just never been out here before and was just curious. Well, good day, gentlemen."

The Sergeant doffed his hat and said, "Maam, come back anytime. It's been a pleasure just seeing you."

She smiled as she rode off. As she rode back to the farm, she just couldn't understand what was happening. She wondered where the Captain was and if, too, he was involved. She was so deep in thought that she almost rode right past Reverend James' place. She pulled the right rein and the horse readily obeyed and they headed up to the house. She again wrapped the reins around the post and walked across the porch. She knocked on the door twice as she opened it. The house was so quiet. It almost alarmed her. Her tension was eased as she came across the room. Reverend James had moved over to the table and was sitting with his back to the wall and the shotgun laying in front of him. He had a bowl of vegetable soup and had torn off a piece of fresh biscuit and was dunking it in it.

Hettie looked puzzled, so he said, "Mercy and Rose came to see how I was and brought me some food. I sure appreciate you girls." He looked at her for a minute and then said, "Hey...you look as worn as I look bad. Where've you been to make you look so frustrated and tired?"

Hettie pulled out a chair and sat down across from him. Looking him straight in the eye, she said, "Now I'm through playin around! Just who was that Lieutenant and Sergeant?"

He calmly finished his bit of biscuit and he thought for a minute, then said, "On my own soul, I don't know. I've done business with them for quite a while, but it was always on their terms. I never asked. I talked to them in town a couple of times, but I told you before, we never even got off our horses and it was always at the edge of town."

"How about the Captain that's in charge out there at the camp?"

"Ain't never done any business with him. Fact is, I ain't never seen him. I've tried to steer clear of him all I could."

Hettie knuckled down and said, "I'm too tired to play anymore games. Too much bad stuff has happened and I don't want you beatin around the bush! Do you know for a fact that the two men you dealt with were actually attached to the soldiers there in town?"

Reverend James dipped another piece of biscuit in his soup and carefully put it in his swollen mouth while he was in thought. Hettie waited. Then, he looked at her in an almost surprised look (it was hard to tell with his swollen face) and thoughtfully said, "You know, come to think about it, I never saw them actually go into town. Just the edge of it. Old Mrs. Bowden was always peerin out her store window and I know she saw us, so I always figured they were. I never did see them head out toward the camp. Maybe Mrs. Bowden knows somethin."

"Well, I've got news for you, old man! They ain't! Nobody has ever heard of them and there ain't no such people out there!"

Surprised, Reverend James asked, "How do you know that?"

"Because I just came back from out there and there ain't no such people. And now, I got my doubts about that Captain, him bein gone all day so much."

Reverend James tried to smile through his swelling and said, "Well, that is probably because he loves to hunt and him and a couple of his men go out huntin for meat rations all the time. Venison is on their menu out there all the time."

Verne Foster

    This made sense to Hettie. Her anxiety was somewhat relieved and she got up from the table and said, "Well, that might just explain his absences...and the real Sergeant on duty out there seems to be on the level too."

    As she walked toward the door, she looked back and said, "You still have to be careful. We still don't know what has happened to this Sergeant with so many stripes on his sleeve. We'll be back and don't worry about your horse. She's in good hands.

Chapter Twenty

Another morning broke and Custis awoke with it. He had not moved a muscle all night and as he tried to stand, it was as if he had to activate each body part individually. Finally, he was standing. It was not until now that he realized just how exhausted he'd been. It must have been a jerking of the train that brought him out of his deep sleep.

As he stood, the train was slowing down for a stop. He almost lost his balance going forward for a second. He sat back down and looked out the window. They were coming into a town and would take on water here. It would also be a short breakfast break as well. As the train came to a stop, the men were all disembarking and many headed for the trees. As he stood up again, the General was toward the rear of the car from him preparing to disembark. He looked back at Custis and motioned for him to come on with him. Pug was awake now and Custis told him the General wanted them. Pug jumped up and followed Custis immediately, rubbing his face with his hands and moving his head around in a circle trying to get some of the stiffness out.

As Custis stepped off the train, the General was waiting. He said, "Walk with me, Major." Custis obeyed. As they walked together, the General told Custis his latest news. "Look here, son. We're headed north as fast as we can move. We're almost to where we're to join with General Sheridan. Seems we're near the final battle of the war."

Custis and Pug looked at each other. The General continued, "We received a wire while you were asleep telling us General Sheridan's troops have just intercepted a big Rebel train from Lynchburg that was headed for Appomattox. It was full of food apparently intended for Lee's troops. According to the wire, we have the Rebel army boxed up in that area. Our troops have taken the Appomattox Station. It's about two miles west of town. All routes are being cut off and we think there's not much left of what they refer to officially as 'Lee's Army of North Virginia'. We're still about a day's ride from there now, but even so, after the men have all been fed, we will be under full battle alert status, so get ready."

After a rest break and some rations, Custis and Pug started back to the car. As they got to the entrance, a major handed Custis a paper and said, "These are your orders. Be on that train when it leaves here. The General has wired ahead that you are with him and we will be joining forces late in the afternoon."

They climbed aboard. With that, the train powered up and gave a "choo..choo..choo..choo" as the big wheels of the engines slipped on the rails. Finally, the train jerked and started moving toward the northeast. The train seemed to be a mile long or more. The longest they'd ever seen. As Custis stood there, he suddenly realized he could remember everything. The girls came immediately to his mind. He immediately thought of how outwardly tough, but yet, inside, so caring they were. As he was retracing all that had happened with them, his mind kept going back to Mercy. After awhile, she was the center of his every thought as he hopped aboard the slow moving coach.

It had been a long and tiring day without incident and was starting to get dark when they neared Appomattox Station. There was no sound of battle anywhere. As they approached the station, they could see the campfires ahead. Pug chortled, "I sure hope those are our troops."

Custis replied, "You're right there! I expected all hell to be breaking loose. With all I've heard about General Gordon

The Saga of Robert E

and those guys, I figured a full fight to the finish to be going on."

The train started slowing down for a quick stop before they were at the station. As it came to a halt still southwest of the station, a Colonel boarded their coach with a message in his hand. It was from General Meade. The General read it and announced to his officers, "Gentlemen, we are under a temporary truce with the Rebs." He then gave the order for all to dismount and prepare camp along with the other troops.

General Absolom Davis dismounted the rail car amid salutes from the troops. He loudly announced, "Men, the reason it has been so quiet today is that we are in temporary truce with General Lee and his army.

I want you to be alert, but it's been a long and burdensome ride, so make yourselves as comfortable as you can. Get some food, then pitch your tents. I believe that is in a good order of sequence." With that, the troops gave him a big "hoorah". Smiling, he turned to Custis and Pug.

Looking tired, he said, "Well, gentlemen, it has been a long day for us all, but we know not what will await us at any time. It's Saturday night. Tomorrow's Palm Sunday. Maybe all this will be over by Easter."

Over by Easter. "Wow", Custis said, "You hear that, Pug?" That's only a week away."

Pug grinned and nodded in agreement. About that time, General Davis came back to them and said, "Major Custis, I want you and your Lieutenant here to meet with me as soon as the headquarters tent is pitched. I gave you written orders this morning because I did not know if we all would make it or not. We have, so, we'll talk about your futures."

They replied, "Yessir" and saluted the General. He returned it and went toward the camp's headquarters area. Custis and Pug walked over to the area where they were pitching the mess tent. The cooks said,

"It'll take us a little while to get ready, but we'll hurry. May we suggest to the Major and Lieutenant to get your sleeping bags set up and by that time, we ought to have you something to eat."

The Major replied, "Sounds good, Sergeant. We'll be back later."

Actually, Custis was not really that hungry, so the time element wasn't that important. Thoughts of the girls kept coming back to him. It puzzled him why he kept thinking of Mercy. Her neat way of dress. Her sweet smell of vanilla. The cute way she would wrinkle her nose when she laughed. The other girls were nice in their own way, but for some strange reason, he kept going back to Mercy. He liked her spirit. What you saw was what you got. That little body of hers contained not only fire, but a lightning bolt ready to hit.

As they approached the officer's area, a sergeant handed them a blanket roll. Most of them were just putting the rolls on the ground and staking out their own area. The tents were being used for other things. No big ones had been brought along on this trip. The main objective was to move as many men at one time as possible.

Everything was going well, it seemed. A report that the Rebels were established just east of the town was not so troubling since the truce was struck, but the more experienced minds were quite wary of all the possibilities of battle action those Rebs were capable of. Even though ease was the order of the day, full battle alert was the condition of their camp. This meant you would eat, sleep, and keep your weapon and ammunition with you at all times. No matter where you were or what you were doing. Word was that the Rebs were only a mile east of Appomattox. Only a little over three miles away. General Gordon's troops were close and they were capable of anything, as were General Pendleton's, even in their weakened condition.

Major Custis and Lieutenant MacHenry had eaten their rations when word was delivered to them that General Davis and General Sheridan himself had been in conference in the now general headquarters tent. It was now located between

The Saga of Robert E

the new troops bivouac and the rest of the force at Appomattox. They were to report to General Davis immediately. They did so and there, they were introduced to General Sheridan (who had just secured Appomattox Station). The cavalry that had set out ahead of them had turned easterly and joined forces with the rest of General Sheridan's horsemen to the south. General Grant's forces now stretched out from General Sheridan's all the way around to Danville on the east. General Sheridan said to them, "Gentlemen, as I understand it, we have approximately 140,000 Union troops surrounding General Lee's army of roughly 30,000."

The information was so awesome to Custis and Pug as well as the other officers there, that it was hard to comprehend. General Grant himself was less than five miles away to the east. The union was now tightening a noose around the Rebs. At that time, a messenger came from the intelligence tent with a wire from General Grant. He gave it directly to General Sheridan who read it aloud, "Have sent under flag of truce to officially discuss with General Lee terms of surrender. Hold your posts until further notice, but take any such action as necessary to defend against any attack from the enemy."

Things were sure starting to get stickier and stickier. Now, it seemed that the end of the war could come as soon as Palm Sunday!

Major Custis addressed General Davis, "Sir, can you give me any idea of just what my duties are to be here?"

General Sheridan looked at General Davis and said, "Let me answer that for you." He then turned to Custis and asked, "You are the one related, at least by marriage, to General Lee, are you not?"

Custis replied, "Yessir. My grandfather and General Lee's wife's father are first cousins."

General Sheridan continued, "Well, that is what seems to be your assignment here. Not only are you the first commissioned officer to be put in for the Army's 'Congressional Medal of Honor', but, well.." He hesitated here, then, as

Verne Foster

if making a tactical decision, he said, "You see, when it came to General Grant's attention that he had an officer in his command that was directly related to General Lee, he decided he wanted him to be at the signing of the surrender. He's known it was an imminent thing for over a week."

"But Sir, why would he want me to be present at such a big occasion?"

"Well, Major, I can only offer an educated conjecture, but, knowing how General Grant feels about General Lee and all, maybe he just wants to add insult to injury. Now that is only conjecture! You will have to take that up with General Grant for the truth."

It was evident to Custis now that it was not of any military value, but more of a personal nature between the two. It was common knowledge how Grant felt toward Lee for resigning his commission in the Union army and going with Virginia's secession. Again, the question confronted him, "What next?"

Chapter Twenty One

On the morning of April 9, 1865, Palm Sunday, other than a couple of small ill fated battles by the rebel forces, control was kept by the Union. It seems that General Lee's nephew, "Fitz" Lee, didn't want to honor the truce that had been given by General Grant and attacked unsuccessfully the Union forces. They came within a half mile of the station, but were driven immediately back to General Gordon's stronghold in a most embarrassing manner. After all, the Union had General Ord's "Army of the James" that made the frontal attack and thousands of the Union infantry that pretty well coined the phrase "coming out of the woods". Fitz Lee had no choice but to run. After this futile attempt and wise advice from General Lee's most valiant officer of the day, General Gordon, General Lee made the decision that there was nothing for him to do but to go to see General Grant.

General Grant had expectations of meeting with General Lee in the Appomattox Courthouse, but when one of his majors, a Major McLean, offered his house for the meeting, his invitation was accepted.

It was a nice brick home in town and had rooms large enough for such. It was actually Grant's secretary, Colonel Charles Marshall, who accepted the invitation for General Grant. General Grant's entourage contained several of his most famous generals followed by lesser ranking officers. It

Verne Foster

was a group that Major Custis was to join. They had ridden hard to meet up with General Grant. Major Custis had left camp at about one o'clock. As he approached the rebel line, he was joined by a Confederate escort. They rode through the area without incident. He did not know that he would cut through the same orchard where General Lee had rested earlier that day before heading for the McLean house. When he arrived at the McLean house, there were armed soldiers in the street and all around the house. No chance was being taken for any problem from either side. He found out that General Lee had already arrived and was inside the house quietly awaiting General Grant. He identified himself to the Captain of the Guard and was informed that General Grant was still enroute. The route they were taking was a muddy one from the recent rain. He realized that the time for the meeting had passed and still no General Grant.

Major Custis then asked permission to enter and talk to General Lee. The Captain reached in his pocket and pulled out his watch. He looked at the time. He said,

"Well, Major, since the General is late and you have been personally selected by him to be in the meeting, I guess it is alright."

Custis thanked him and entered the house. As he entered the ante room, passing two guards, he saw General Lee sitting calmly waiting across from the door. The great General looked at him and politely nodded.

Custis said, "Sir!" and saluted the General.

General Lee, the great gentleman he was, stood and returned the salute. Custis held his salute until General Lee had dropped his arm. There was something that was amazing about this gentleman. His very demeanor demanded respect. Here was a man whose record at West Point remained unchallenged. He was the only cadet ever to go through West Point without a single demerit. Of course, being kin, Custis went through a terrible time as a plebe.

General Lee, still standing, replied, "And to whom am I speaking?"

The Saga of Robert E

The Major defined his relationship to the General. General Lee smiled softly and motioned for him to sit. As both men sat down, Major Custis sat in awe of the General. Even though he was the enemy, Custis found himself automatically treating him like his own superior. There was just something about him that made his very countenance stand out. General Lee was in an immaculate uniform. His clean and spotless gray uniform was perfect. His waist band was a beautiful red sash. He wore a beautiful gold sword at his side. His black boots had apparently been spit shined. They reflected the light. He was a perfect figure of a general officer. "Yes", thought Custis, "It is his countenance that demands your respect." Looking at this epitome of class, Custis became self conscious of his own appearance. However, he wore a clean uniform and his boots were shined as well. "The way he wore his uniform was probably from the genes", he thought.

General Lee spoke first, "What is your status here? Are you an aide to General Grant?"

Custis knew that General Lee had been personal friends with General Grant before the war, but even under these conditions, he spoke of him as "General Grant". "Sir", Custis replied, "I am not an aide to General Grant. I am an aide to General Davis."

General Lee made no sign of recognition. "General Absolom Davis, Sir. He is the commander of our brigade that has just came in from Northeast Georgia."

General Lee winced at that remark. He solemnly said, "This has been the strangest war that has ever been fought. Brother against brother. Here, you and I who are actually in the same family, are on opposite sides and thousands upon thousands have been slaughtered. It is so senseless!"

Custis replied, "But General, they are referring to you as the Confederacy. You are known worldwide. Our causes might be confused, but it can still teach us something."

General Lee looked at him and said, "You know? You come from a long line of patriots. Mary Anne, my wife and your cousin, is the great grand daughter of Martha Washington, who was a brilliant woman in her own right. You speak wisely, but I am afraid the only thing the South has left is pride and pride is nothing but folly."

The General paused for a moment looking at Major Custis. Then, he said, "So, Major, what role do you play in this scene?"

Custis was impressed with the General's analogies. He replied, "Well, sir, I hate to say this, but I really believe I am here at the wishes of General Grant so he can flaunt me before you. To sort of make fun of you. I am not sure because I have not had the opportunity to speak with him as yet. I was ordered here solely for that purpose, I'm afraid."

The Major looked down at the floor and then back at the General, saying, "Well, they have put me in for the Army's Medal of Honor. Seems it was accepted for enlisted ranks only, but General Davis wants to change that and has recommended me for it. I guess I am sort of a guinea pig."

General Lee looked puzzled and asked, "Just what kind of medal is that? I'm afraid you have me there. I know of no such thing."

"Well", said Custis, "it is a medal created originally by George Washington, but went into a sort of hibernation until this war. It was created again for this war and President Lincoln okayed it, but the Army did not accept it until about a year or so after the Navy. It is the only medal I know of for valor we have. You have to risk your life beyond the call of duty>"

General Lee returned, "And I can easily understand that you did this."

"Yessir. I was wounded and lost my memory for awhile; but anyway, the President is supposed to give it to you, so it is quite a big thing, I suppose."

General Lee smiled and said, "You come from good stock, Major. Don't worry about the reasoning of your General Grant to have you here. I am glad to meet a relative."

The Saga of Robert E

About that time, a soldier stuck his head in the door and hollered, "General Grant is here!" General Lee smiled, shook Custis's hand and said, "We'll certainly have to talk some more. What is your full name?"

The Major replied, "George Fitzhugh Custis, sir."

The General almost laughed as he nodded and said, "Oh yes. There is a lot of Fitzhugh's in my family."

At that moment, Grant and his group entered the room. A sloppier bunch of men Custis had never seen. It was such a contrast to General Robert E. Lee. There Grant, Sherman, Ord, Custer, oh, so many of them came into the room with muddy boots and uniforms. They looked terrible. There was General Lee, the surrenderer, in his immaculate and very military appearance and Grant and the others looked like a bunch of street bums. Coats were unbuttoned, not a sword amongst all of them. Custis was truly embarrassed for them. He turned to General Lee with a look of chagrin, but General Lee just smiled as if to say, "It's all right."

General Grant already knew General Lee and made his greeting. Then, he looked at Major Custis and asked, "Who are you, Major?"

Before Custis could reply, General Sheridan, who was the neatest looking one of the whole lot, stepped up and said, "General, this is Major Custis, the one you wanted here with you."

Grant stepped back and cocked his head a little, sizing him up, then over to General Lee. He than said, "Yep. I can see quite a family resemblance there." He looked at General Lee and continued, "Well, Robert, I presume you have met your kin here. I understand that he is a Union hero and is up for our highest medal for fighting you Rebs." General Lee just nodded as Grant took out a cigar and bit the end of it off, spitting the tip on the floor. "I thought it would be a nice contrast to have him here when you came to talk about surrender...his having had a lot of influence towards that end and all."

Verne Foster

Grant was literally smirking now. No one made a sound. You could tell that General Grant was enjoying this, but, Custis knew something General Grant didn't. It was of no importance to General Lee. General Grant stretched out his hand motioning for Lee to precede him into the next room and said, "Well now. Let's go into the parlor and talk business."

All the Generals followed quietly. None had spoken a word since they had entered. Custis stayed in the ante room with the other lesser ranked officers.

Chapter Twenty Two

There was no talking by anyone but General Grant and General Lee. Custis picked up some of their word exchange. At first, it was sort of chit chat as best he could make out, but then, they got down to brass tacks, so to speak. They were discussing the conditions of surrender. General Lee was an amazing person. He did not give the appearance of just a general, but rather, a humanitarian voicing concerns for the whole Confederacy as a whole. He had quite a concern for his men to keep their animals, horses and mules and the like, as well as their weapons. General Grant seemed to understand that this was a request for hunting and farming and not another rebellion. Having been in the midst of a southern area hit hard by the war, Custis thought of the total lack of horses and guns there. His thoughts went back to how he and the girls had gotten a couple of horses and guns and what a big help that made for them. As his thoughts swept through his short lived experience there with those people, his reverie was interrupted by something that the Generals were discussing. Seems General Lee had come to the subject of his Union prisoners. He was explaining that he had a hard time feeding his own men and animals, but that he was expecting a supply train from Lexington that would allow him to feed both the prisoners and his men.

"That must have been the train we saw that General Sheridan had captured." Custis thought. Apparently General

Lee did not know it had been captured. Custis could hear some whispers coming from the entourage of generals as General Grant spoke, "Well, sir, that won't be a problem if you'll release all your prisoners. I promise you we will feed all of your troops and the prisoners."

Custis peeked around the corner of the door as General Grant spoke of this and saw him give a mean look at his Generals. There was sudden quietness immediately among them. Custis remembered well from the day before how the Union troops were elated at having captured this train and quite obviously, General Lee was not aware of the event and was still expecting it to arrive. He could only get a few words here and there from the conversation, but enough to tell him that a quite reasonable agreement had been made between the two warriors. General Lee asked General Grant to write down the agreements, which he had done, and General Lee signed the surrender with those last conditions added to the list. Then, General Lee stood as did General Grant. They shook hands and General Lee nodded to the others and came walking into the ante room. He stopped at Major Custis who had snapped to a salute. He returned it and immediately put out his hand for Custis' hand.

As he shook the Major's hand, he smiled and said, "Son, heroism and integrity go together and if a man has those qualities, it matters not what side he is on. I am proud to have met you."

Tears swelled in the young Major's eyes as the General left him. An odd thing happened as he left. All the officers on the porch and steps snapped to a salute when he exited. Custis thought, "Now that's the kind of man I want to become."

General Grant interrupted his thoughts as he said, "Major." Custis snapped to and saluted with his answer, "Sir!"

General Grant said, "At ease, son. I have approved the request for your medal and I have given orders for you to go to Washington. I will meet you there and we will go to the President together. However, there is something I would like to discuss with you. I am having you assigned to my staff so

The Saga of Robert E

you will report to my headquarters as soon as you can get your things gathered."

The first thing Custis thought about was Pug. He blurted out, "Sir, what about 'Pug', er, I mean Lieutenant MacHenry?"

General Grant replied, "And just who is this 'Pug'?"

Custis replied, "Sir, he has been through this whole campaign with me and we were assigned together for this mission. He is the one who found me and brought me to General Davis."

General Grant thought for a minute, then, he said, "Let him stay where he is for now. He will remain an aide to General Davis. You and I have other things to take care of for right now. How much time will you need to report to my group?"

"Sir, I am traveling light. I can go with you now."

General Grant took a draw off his cigar as he looked at Custis and said, "Son, I think you'll do just fine for what I have in mind." He turned to Colonel Babcock, who had been standing along side the General and said, "Orville, take care of this matter." He smiled as he twisted his cigar in his mouth, then continued, "This Lieutenant 'Pug'. I like that. Orville, wire orders for him to remain where he is with General Davis and transfer Major Custis to my staff, effective immediately."

Colonel Babcock said, "As you wish, General." He motioned for his orderly to come over to him.

General Grant was a great one to talk using his cigar for emphasis. He told Custis to walk with him. He asked, "Well, since you are ready to leave now, where is your horse?"

"He's just next door toward downtown." was the Major's reply.

A soldier came up to General Grant guiding a horse, saluted the General and handed him the reins. The General said, "Well, get your horse and ride back with me. We'll save the talk for later. I'm real interested in where you were while you were missing in action." With that, he mounted his horse and said, "Well, get mounted, Major! You're riding with me."

The Major hurried to his horse, mounted, and as he rode back toward General Grant, he could see the "not so kindly expressions" of the other Generals as they sat mounted on their horses and found themselves waiting for a mere Major. Major Custis shyly rode up along side General Grant. All waited until General Grant moved out, then, forming an informal column, his entourage followed. Even though they rode together, Custis realized why the General chose to wait to talk. It was a noisy enough experience with the snorting of the horses and their hoof sounds against the ground. Even the squeak of the leather saddles as you rode would be sounds that you would end up yelling over. As they rode, a million questions flooded the Major's mind. "What was Grant wondering about? Did he think I might have deserted, then came back?" So many things ran through his head, but as they did, he started thinking of the girls, the farm, the beautiful country side, the girl's laughter, how hard they worked. Even how good they looked dressed like men instead of the very ladylike long dresses. Then, his mind went back to the first day. The way they were dressed in their long dresses. He tried to think of a reason they might have been in dresses instead of their normal attire. Then, he remembered something one of them had said in a random conversation. "Sunday belongs to the Lord. We always dress up for Sunday even though we don't have a church to go to." He then remembered seeing three dresses on the line drying. He thought of how hard it must be to wash those big skirts on a rub board. Random thoughts meandered through his brain as he thought of it as almost unfair for women to have to wear such tedious dresses all the time and them so hard to keep maintained. Not like a shirt and breeches.

It helped him to reminisce so he could refresh his mind of what had been something he experienced as another person, so to speak. His memory had all returned, but there were a lot of things he would suddenly think of as if it were a

The Saga of Robert E

first time experience..."What did they name him? Oh, yes.... Robert E. after their leader. Why those mischievous little devils." The thought suddenly occurred to him, "Oh, how close to right they were and didn't know it, and yet, he was the enemy."

He tried to remember if the "town" they referred to had a name. They had never mentioned it, just something about "town" at times. He didn't even know exactly where it was. There were things he still could not bring to mind. For example, how he got to the place where Pug had found him.

After cleaning up, he reported to General Grant's quarters where a fine supper was laid out. There were only two others present, Lt.

Colonel Babcock and General Sheridan, not counting a couple of orderlies. Major Custis was to sit opposite General Grant with General Sheridan on his left and Colonel Babcock on his right. There was nothing religious about General Grant. The meal started with a remark from Grant, "Dig in, men. I know you're hungry!" As the table was cleared, they walked outside as General Grant lit a cigar. As the four men stood together, General Grant said, "Major, how much do you remember about the time you were missing?"

Custis replied, "Sir, I've been trying to think about it and I can pretty well remember most things. Why"

Grant looked at Babcock and Sherman and said, "Well, how about the people? I understand you were taken in by a family. How much can you trust them?"

"Oh, what I remember about them, the three ladies saved my life and therefore, I can say for sure I can trust them. I only met one other person. He was their neighbor and the local parson."

General Grant went on, "Well, as General Sheridan will verify, it sounds like you were in the very area where we have lost several shipments of guns and ammunition. Do you remember anyone else?"

131

Verne Foster

Suddenly, the two Union soldiers came to mind. He said, "Well, as a matter of fact, I do. When we went to meet the parson, there were two Union soldiers at his place. A lieutenant and a topkick. The Sergeant was top rank and had several service stripes on his sleeves."

General Sherman looked at Grant, then, Grant asked, "Do you remember their names?"

"No, sir, General. It seemed we interrupted them and they left rather abruptly."

General Sheridan then asked, "Do you remember where this place was? A town, or the nearest town?"

Custis shook his head now and replied, "But I think I could find it if I rode south from where my men found me. I can remember saying to myself to just ride north. The next thing I knew, Pug, I mean Lieutenant MacHenry, was talking to me."

General Grant then told Custis it was late and to go get a good night's sleep. They would be leaving for Washington early the next day. He had a wire from President Lincoln to meet with him at the earliest possible time. He added, "And Major. You will accompany me at that meeting. I want him to give you that medal. It is very important that you are given it. I think it is important for all commissioned officers."

He then told Custis that after the appointment, he might just have an assignment for him. An assignment that possibly only he could accomplish.

Chapter Twenty Three

The next morning, General Grant met with General Lee for the finalization of the official surrender. It was mid-afternoon before Custis was able to see General Grant. He was called for by the General to come immediately. They were to board a special train that the General had waiting.

As he joined General Grant on the train, General Grant explained, "We should be able to make Richmond tonight and be in Washington by late tomorrow. I am giving you the responsibility to keep this briefcase in safekeeping. It has all the surrender documents in it that I will be presenting to President Lincoln. We have an appointment with him Wednesday, the 12th. I know you think a lot of General Lee, but here is a man you'll never forget once you have met him. Not just because he is the President, but because of he himself. In many ways, Lee and Lincoln are a lot alike. I'll give him that!"

As the train pulled out of the Appomattox Depot, many thoughts were rushing through Custis' mind. The last few days were almost a blur. So much had happened so fast. The General had a special car of his own. It was quiet and comfortable. The breeze through the open windows kept the coach cool as they sped down the track toward Richmond. General Grant came over and sat beside Custis, cigar in mouth as he usually had. He would smoke about half of it and chew the rest. It wasn't lit and a big wad of it was in the

Verne Foster

General's mouth. He said nothing for awhile as he looked out at the country going by.

Then, without changing his stare, he said, "Sherman was right."

Custis looked at him as he asked, "Sir?"

Grant turned to Custis and said, "Sherman was right. War IS hell!"

Custis softly answered, "I can attest to that, but even so, I have never had to make the terrible decisions you have, General."

Grant looked him in the eye and he appeared to be hundreds of years old as he said, "No, son, and you had better be thankful that you haven't. If you lined up the bodies of the men I've sent into battle and were killed, I suppose they would reach from here to California and back. I guess that's why I drink so much. When I'm awake, I think about it and when I'm asleep, I dream about it. I hear the screams from dying men! Some of them die cursing the enemy. Some of them die cursing me. Some of them die calling for their mothers."

The only words Custis could think of were, "But, it was your job, Sir! You were the bravest just to do it!"

As if he were fighting pity, his look suddenly hardened and he changed the subject, "Well, we have done what we had to do. I told the President that I would deliver him the Confederacy and now, I am on my way to do that!"

This war worn General than turned to Custis and asked, "What about you, Major?" How do you feel about all this?

Custis replied, "Well, Sir, if this is the end of all the bloodshed and woe, I am happy it's over."

The General said, "No. I mean the way we fought the war. So many men dying in a single battle…over and over again. Could we have done better?"

Custis looked him straight in the eye and asked, "Sir. Are you asking me for the truth or just a kind answer?"

Grant looked at him curiously as he threw his cigar out the window. He said, "Major, I've never liked sycophants!

The Saga of Robert E

You have shown courage and integrity. I want your true opinion! Sometimes, a General can get an education from even a private."

As Custis nervously tugged at his collar, the General said, "Let's take off our coats. We have no audience here. Get comfortable."

With that, he removed his coat and even pulled off his boots. He propped his feet up on the next seat and continued, "Now.! Let me have it as you see it. You're a graduate from 'The Point' as Lee and I are. You have done a lot of front line fighting. You have been in almost all the battles of the war and yet, you have survived. So talk to me!"

Custis slowly turned up his shirt sleeves a couple of turns as he started, "Well, General, there was more than one kind of fighting in this war. I know that 'The Point' teaches 'frontal combat'...the Napoleonic method...but I highly disagree with it."

The General cocked his head back at this remark, but remained silent.

Custis a little braver now, continued, "You've obviously seen my record since you seem to know all about me. I am sure General Davis has it entered there. My company had the lowest casualty list in the Battalion. Certainly, I remembered the type of attack we were taught, but I often asked why we had not learned anything from the first Revolutionary War and how the British made such grand targets as they marched in line toward you. I also took into consideration that the Napoleonic system was based on the reloading time for muskets, etc., but it never made any sense to me to just make yourself a target of any kind. My men either dug in, crawled, or fired from trees or anything else they could find to protect themselves. We tried to attack from a forest or from behind some kind of barrier. I believe in killing the enemy without letting yourselves be killed."

The General was concentrating heavily on what Custis said. He held up his hand and motioned for an orderly to bring him a drink. The orderly started to pour him one, but

Verne Foster

he held up his hand to his cocked head and the orderly got the message and brought him the bottle.

He took a slug and said, "Aaaaah! O.K, Major, continue."

Custis referred to General Stuart's success from the Shenandoah Valley with his quick cavalry assaults and just as quick withdrawels. Then Custis remarked, "Well, Sir, I believe we would not be riding this train today if the Rebs had all fought like that. That kind of fighting is hard to control."

Grant had been looking out the window as he listened to Custis. Then, he gave Custis a surprising answer, "Major! You are absolutely right! Lee and I were both sold on the frontal attack we were taught at West Point, but as the battles went on, I slowly changed my opinion. If I had this war to fight over again, I definitely would do it differently."

He took another drink from the bottle and looked at Custis, continuing, "Son, we are going down in history from this. I hope to see you there. You are on your way to becoming the first Union commissioned officer to receive the Congressional Medal of Honor. It's the only medal we have to reward men of your courage who willingly risked and/or gave their lives for their country in combat. I originally had a selfish reason to have you with me at Appomattox. I wanted to flaunt you in front of Lee. You see, we were friends before this war. However, he hurt me deeply when he resigned his commission as a Colonel in the United States Army and went with Virginia when it seceded. Oh, I know he had his reasons, but, I guess I was as interested in hurting him as much as I was interested in defeating the Confederacy."

The General gazed out the other side of the train and said, "I heard the remark he made to you as he left and I can't get it out of my mind."

Custis asked, "Which one was that, Sir?"

"Well, he said something about it didn't matter which side a true hero was on as long as he had integrity. That got me to thinking. You know, as I sat there across from

The Saga of Robert E

him talking about the surrender, I knew the Confederacy was defeated, but I also realized then that I would never defeat him."

Custis smiled understandingly.

Grant continued, "The reason I have you still with me is because I have learned something there. I saw the calmness and peace Lee had in his face when he talked to you. I saw the deep emotion you had for him. My reasoning changed right then. I was face to face with true integrity. Now, the reason you are with me is purely for good. I really want you to have that medal. Not just to change a policy, but for you personally. I think you deserve it."

The change in Grant's outlook astounded Custis. It also created a deeper respect for the man. Even with his irreverent life and weaknesses, he could look at him as a great man now.

General Grant was quietly solemn for a few minutes. He just sat looking out the opposite side windows. Then, he explained to Custis,

"I am holding off talking about the assignment I have in mind for you until I confer with General Sheridan. He has had an investigation going on for a while. Most of the guns and ammo that were stolen were repeater rifles and bullets for them. We are missing better than 2000 of our latest new weapons. They were shipped, but never reached their destination. For example, your outfit should have been issued these weapons. Think what you could do with rifles that can fire as fast as you cal pull a lever down and back."

Custis asked, "How do you know where they might have gone? I mean, can you pinpoint their last location?"

Grant replied, "Well, I will want you to get with Sheridan after we meet with the President. He is presently completing our plans for the surrender and making sure they are carried out. He will utilize that supply train of Lee's and also furnish supplies for whatever is needed to make sure everyone's truly taken care of. It will take some time, but the preliminaries will only take a couple of days. He will then join us in Washington later."

The train started slowing down as we were pulling into Richmond, or what was left of it. The whole southern end of it was a shambles. The capital building was still standing and most of the city north of it,. Yes, war was certainly hell!

General Grant said, "We'll rest here tonight. Tomorrow, we will continue on to Washington. We will have to go to the Quartermaster for appropriate uniforms and clean up before we see the President... or at least, before he sees us." He chuckled as he said that.

Custis thought to himself, "A far cry from how you looked at the surrender."

They slept in beds that night and Custis had his first good night's sleep in a while as he thought about all that had happened and the possibility of seeing the girls again. "Hmm", he thought as he dozed, "Why does that mean so much to me when I am going to actually be meeting the President of the United States in a couple of days?"

Chapter Twenty Four

Tuesday was an uneventful day. Several officers had joined them and Grant spent most of the day discussing events and answering questions. Custis sat back by himself most of the time. He was not that interested in the rhetoric that was going on. At one time, General Grant called him over to ask him some questions. One of them was whether he knew if an army post was near where he was kept.

He answered, "No Sir, just those two soldiers I told you about."

That question, however, did raise some thoughts to him. "Why were they even interested in an old man who called himself a preacher? Where did they come from? Where were they now? And worst of all, were they leaving the girls alone?" That thought seemed to make him uncomfortable. He wasn't sure why he seemed so touchy at the thought of the girls. He had really never been close to anyone before. He had left home when he was fourteen and lived with an uncle and aunt for a couple of years. They had a nice farm and he had learned a lot from them about working the land and putting in different crops. He made a vow to himself, "If I ever have a farm, I will be smart enough to rotate my crops and stay up on what is most in demand on the market."

The train whistle interrupted his thoughts. It was about 4:00 p.m. They had made a speedy trip today. Washington was a big place. There were plenty of soldiers present

Verne Foster

everywhere. Apparently they were still on full alert. "Well", he thought, "the news we bring will certainly put an end to that."

General Grant hollered to him, "Major Custis! We are here and you and I have a mission to complete. Bring yourself and your briefcase with you. We're heading to the Quartermaster."

The other officers cleared the way in the aisle as Custis walked past them and stood by the General. The train came to a stop and they dismounted ahead of the other six officers. General Grant seemed to know where he was going. They walked over to the depot to where a carriage was waiting. There was a sergeant standing by the door holding it open. As the two officers walked up, he very stiffly saluted. They returned the salute and climbed aboard the carriage.

The Sergeant told them, "Sirs, you have an escort that will ride ahead and behind you all the way."

General Grant remarked at the lack of necessity in it, but the Sergeant said, "President's orders, Sir." With that the Sergeant told the driver to move out. That seemed to take the argument out of it.

They were taken to a hotel instead of the Quartermaster. When the General questioned the driver, he was told that uniforms would be brought to them. Seems that the President was concerned about their quarters and a little relaxation. The General shrugged his shoulders in acceptance and dismounted. They were ushered to adjoining rooms that were very stately. Custis had never even been in a hotel this nice. They were told that the President expected them the next morning at nine o'clock.

Shortly after they had taken a bath and the hotel personnel had removed the tubs and water, a lieutenant reported with four corporals carrying uniforms. He knocked on the door of Major Custis' room. When Custis answered, his smile disappeared as he said, "Oh, I was expecting to meet General Grant."

The Saga of Robert E

Custis laughed as he invited him in and led him through to the next room to meet the General. The Lieutenant was obvious in his attempt to be pleasing. Both officers were outfitted with not one, but three new uniforms including boots and even hats. These had all been carried in on a wheeled rack and platform. Custis looked at himself in the mirror in his new Major's uniform and felt the pride as he admired the well made outfit.

Well! Now they were prepared to meet anybody. But first, it was suppertime and they were hungry. When they mentioned this casually, the Quartermaster Lieutenant said, "Oh, I will take care of that. I will send the hotel clerk up to take your orders right away."

The General signed the issue slips and as Custis ushered the little group out, he saw two guards at each of their doors. He asked them why they were there and they replied, "Sir, there is quite a lot of unrest here and we have orders to take no chances. The President wants to make sure you are safe."

Custis reported this to Grant who merely shrugged his shoulders again and replied, "When you're in Washington, you can expect anything."

The hotel Chef knocked on the door and had a menu with him. He was allowed to enter and took their orders. General Grant was more interested in a bottle of fine scotch than he was the menu. As the chef turned to leave, the General said, "cigars and scotch. Remember that."

The chef smiled and left. In very short time, the table was set up in the General's room and it was a feast. Both the men looked at each other as they sat down and one agreed with the other, "It doesn't seem fair that we are sitting down to this when there are so many men out there with nothing."

It was Custis who lightened the moment saying, "Well, General, by now, all those supplies have been distributed and all of them are eating well too." With that, the General

Verne Foster

poured himself a glass of scotch and raised it as he said, "I'll drink to that!"

While enroute to the site of the ceremony the next morning, General Grant said to Custis, "Major, I've not heard any reply to my request for this medal of yours, but with all the recommendations it bears for you, I well imagine that no news is good news."

Major Custis spoke, "General, it doesn't matter to me. What does matter is what you and the other Generals are trying to accomplish."

General Grant answered, "Well, son, that is a great attitude. One I would expect from you. You know...Lee was right. You do come from great stock!"

"Sir, I consider that a great compliment. Thank You." Custis said in admiration.

Now, they were approaching the site. Their carriage was led and trailed by two cavalrymen. As they neared the Whitehouse lawn, the four horsemen were joined by another dozen cavalrymen. As they pulled up to the platform that had been built on the lawn, the front horsemen peeled off and faced the carriage with their swords at "Present Arms". The carriage stopped just in front of the stand and the two rear horsemen joined the file with the others. The carriage door was opened and as they prepared to dismount, General Grant said, "Well, Major, apparently, you are going to get that medal we all want you to have!"

They were ushered up to the platform amid salutes and pomp and circumstance. The President had just preceded them from the other side. They stopped at the opening as the President stepped to the platform first and invited them to proceed. At his signal, they stepped forward.

Abraham Lincoln shook hands with General Grant and said, "Well, General, I've heard you have something for me."

General Grant replied with a loud and proud voice and a smug look of pride on his face, "Mr. President! I promised you the Confederacy and I now present it to you!" With

The Saga of Robert E

this, he stepped forward and presented Mr. Lincoln with the document.

Mr. Lincoln opened it and looked at the signatures. He shook his head and said very seriously, "General Grant, this is a very hallowed document written in the blood of too many Americans, both Northern and Southern. In this war, there are victors and losers, but no winners! Hopefully, the occasion this represents is as sacred to our people as it is to me. I thank you, Sir." With that, he held it up for the hundreds of people to see. The band struck up "Yankee Doodle" and cheers went up for over five minutes.

Just as Major Custis was feeling completely out of place and was preparing himself for a quiet exit (for he felt that a thing like his medal was so minor compared to all this and was probably not even on the agenda anyway) he heard the President ask loudly, "General Grant! Is this our Major Custis?" The fact that the President of the United States even knew his name utterly shocked him as he immediately snapped to. He was frozen with rigidity as he stood stiffly at attention.

It all seemed like he was watching it all happen from inside a box or something. General Grant smiled proudly and said, "Mr. President, may I present Major George Fitzhugh Custis, a most genuine hero in my sight!"

Mr. Lincoln smiled as he looked the soldier straight in the eyes. Custis looked into his sharp dark eyes that sparkled like they were reflecting the sun. Though they were grinning, they could not hide the deep sorrow he felt. Mr. Lincoln looked the Major up and down as if inspecting him. Custis was immaculate in his dress as if he were trying to emulate his cousin General Lee. The Major gave a very stiff salute and as the President returned it, Custis held his salute in true military style of honor until Mr. Lincoln had dropped his hand. It was now extended toward the Major in a friendly gesture for a handshake.

Mr. Lincoln said, "Major Custis, you are here for a most divine purpose. Not only have you proven your bravery by

Verne Foster

risking your life above and beyond the call of duty in combat protecting your country, but you are a representation of all the brave heroes of our Army. Your course is a new course for this medal. A course which I and Congress gladly follow. You are hereby clearing the way for this medal to be awarded to all heroes who have risked their lives, or lost them, in the protection of our now even greater country. This is the first of many that will be awarded from this great battle that has now finally brought us under one flag again. I am privileged not only to meet you, but to make this award official by pinning the Congressional Medal Of Honor on your tunic myself."

General Grant was holding the medal in its box. He took it out and handed it to the President. Mr. Lincoln then pinned it on Major Custis and to the Major's surprise, he immediately snapped a salute to the Major before Custis could even move. Custis returned the salute, but this time, Mr. Lincoln held his until Custis dropped his hand. A cheer went up from the crowd again. Custis just stood in awe as Mr. Lincoln took his hand in his and lifted it up in the air with his great long arm and they faced the crowd and stood listening to the cheering voices.

The ride back to the hotel seemed like a dream. General Grant remained with the President. Shock had set in and he found himself in as much awe of the President as he was of General Lee. As he rode, the thought came to him, "Now, there are two men of great integrity. Both with broken hearts over the bloodshed of the war. General Lee was right. Pride is all that is left and it is oft referred to as folly!"

Chapter Twenty Five

The combination of being in Washington on a pretty day, time on his hands, and the availability of a nice carriage made it an easy decision of what to do for Major Custis. He had never been in Washington before and there was no time like the present for him to tour the city. He did so.

He even had a fine lunch at a very nice restaurant. It was mid-afternoon when he returned to the hotel.

As he neared the desk, the clerk recognized him and motioned for him to come there. By the time Custis approached, the clerk had an envelope in his hand and said, "Major Custis. A messenger delivered this note for you before lunch and said it was very important that I get it to you."

The desk clerk then handed him a sealed envelope addressed to him and marked "Urgent". It read, "Major Custis, General Sheridan will not be joining us here in Washington. I must remain here in Washington with the President. There are multiple problems at Appomattox. General Sheridan has advised me that you are the perfect man for a very important and confidential mission. He has requested you be assigned to him personally at the first opportunity. The President is cognizant of this and we both concur with General Sheridan. Consequently, you are hereby ordered to report to General Sheridan immediately for further instructions. These are your temporary orders and General Sheridan is expecting you without delay. He will inform you of your further orders

Verne Foster

when you arrive. God speed." the note was signed with that famous signature, "US Grant".

Custis was amazed that these high level leaders would consider him as the perfect man for the job. "What could the task be?" he wondered. "It had to be important for the second in command of the U.S. Army to be giving the orders directly. Well, whatever it was, it meant NOW!" So, he quickly collected his belongings and was taken to the railway station where he headed back to Appomattox.

The train came into Appomattox from the east after crossing the Appomattox River. It was early daylight and a slight fog was settled in the trees. The breeze coming in the windows was cool and almost damp.

As they passed near downtown, he could see the red brick house where he had seen and talked with General Lee. He wondered what the General was doing now. The last he saw of him, he was riding his famous horse Traveler west out of town. It seemed so long ago and yet, it had only been a couple of days. So many things had happened in so short a period of time.

The train passed by the downtown area and on out to the depot. There were soldiers everywhere. Even the depot was well guarded. As he alit from the train, the Corporal of the Guard met him, saluted, and asked, "Sir, are you Major Custis?"

The Major nodded and returned the salute. The Corporal went on, "Sir, you are to go directly to General Sheridan."

The Major looked confused. The Corporal continued, "Sir, you are to be escorted to the General. Your escort is bringing your horse up now."

Custis looked up and sure enough, here came a cavalryman leading two horses. One was his. He took the reins from the man and petted his horse's neck as he made his hellos. It was a fine reunion between horse and owner. The Major looked around at the soldier and before he could ask, the soldier smiled and handed him a sugar bar. Custis could tell what a great horseman he was by his attitude. After their

The Saga of Robert E

reunion, Custis mounted his horse. He had a name, but Custis, not one for being superstitious, decided to change the horse's name right then and there. He told his horse, "From now on, you will be called "Traveler" after a great general's horse." He then mounted "Traveler" and the two men rode off for town together.

Arriving at the courthouse, he was immediately led to General Sheridan's office. As the door opened into the huge room, General Sheridan, who was looking at a map spread out on a large table, turned and said, "Oh! Major Custis. Come in. Come in."

Custis removed his hat and no salutes were exchanged. The General seemed very occupied with the map. He said, "Come take a look at this map."

The Major was quite curious at all this. He wondered what role the map would play in his assignment. He then remembered what a great strategist Sheridan was. As he approached the table, the General reached out his hand and as he grasped the Major's hand, he said,

"Major, you can't know how glad I am to see you! I believe you have the key to unlock a major mystery for me. As you know, I have been the Commander of the Western Army for some time now. I also have close ties with the states and happenings going on in the True West."

Custis noticed how intrigued this little man seemed to be with this project. Apparently, the man had been up for hours going over it. Apparently, it concerned the True West. Custis had not noticed before, but since he was over six feet tall himself, he now noticed how short General Sheridan was. He was a little on the plump side, slight of hair in the front, but kept neatly cropped. He had heard that because of his dynamic concerns for getting the task at hand accomplished, he could break bad on you at any time...if he were pushed toward failure by someone. This side of the man Custis did not want to see.

Custis looked at the map. The largest part was of Georgia. There was a circle drawn in a specific area. He looked at it and asked, "What is the circle for?"

"I thought you'd never ask! Do you recognize any of the territory in it?"

Custis looked again and said, "Not really, General."

"Sit down here, Major. I have some questions that I believe you can shed some light on. Let me explain." As Custis sat down, the General remained standing and continued, "Do you remember anything about where you were when your men found you?"

Custis thought and then replied, "Pretty much. It was near where we had been fighting and I must have lost my memory."

"Good! Then we're on the right track!" Sheridan said joyfully.

He then sat down in a chair next to Custis and continued his questions. "Major, you told us you had ridden north during the night. Tell me as much as you can remember. Now think hard, for this is most important!"

Custis sat back and reviewed in his mind that night and started telling the events as they would come to him. The General suddenly broke in, "Major, you said it was after midnight when you left. So how did you know which way was north?"

"Well, I'm not really sure, but for some reason, I knew which direction the moon was traveling and by the time I had my horse saddled and all, it had moved toward me. That made me figure where north was and I headed out keeping the moon to my left."

"Good! Good! Now give me every detail you can remember from then on."

Custis frowned in concentration. "I can remember riding hard for awhile, then, since no one was chasing me, I slowed to a trot. I just kept riding with the moon moving to my left. How far, I have no idea."

The Saga of Robert E

"O.K., Then let's try and figure out just how far you rode. Can you remember deviating your route at anytime?"

"Oh, no sir! I kept as straight as I could. All open country for miles."

"Well, then, let's see. The last thing you remember before your men found you. Was it daylight or still dark?"

Custis could now see what the General was doing. He thought hard and as he realized it, he suddenly said, "It was daylight. The sun was rising over the trees to my right. Yes! I can remember the dawn!"

"Great! Now we're getting somewhere. You said you figured it was after midnight because the moon was already past you moving to the west. That is a good idea, but not a sure thing."

"Oh, yes it was! Somehow, I knew where the moon was at midnight. I remember it all quiet well, now. At first, I was quite confused, but it's all coming back to me now! Both sides of my malady!

Yes! I slept in a barn and was not a prisoner. The three ladies that took care of me called me Robert E for a joke, since I was a Yankee to them."

His relationship to the girls was making sense now.

General Sheridan cocked his head and said, "You're an interesting case. Fortunate for the return of your complete memory. Some men get shocked out of theirs and never get it back. Well, let's go on. So, you left sometime after midnight and rode hard for a short while, then to a trotting gait. Let's figure it was about five to six hours until daylight. So, give or take, you know you rode that long non-stop."

"Yes Sir. I'm sure."

"Well, at that pace, you probably made a speed of somewhere around seven to eight miles an hour, wouldn't you say?"

Custis thought deeply and then agreed.

"So, let's use a wider margin just for an approximate. You rode somewhere between six to eight hours. Let's take outside figures realizing they are approximates. Multiplying seven hours times about seven miles an hour gives us, let's say, fifty miles. So, you were due south from the point where your men found you. Look at the map again."

Sheridan and Custis stood up and moved over to the map. Sheridan put his finger on where Custis was found. He brought his finger down for what he figured was the approximate mileage. It landed right in the circle. He then asked, "See how the Little Chigger River meanders through there? There is a road running north and south right along near it. It sort of doglegs through a little hamlet and then on up into the foothills. We found that the Rebs used that road a lot, so we put a light cavalry unit of thirty six highly trained cavalrymen on the east side of the village. It is a highly strategic point for covering that area and our cavalry unit was a deterrent. There is a Captain Cordell Morgan there as Commander. Can you remember seeing anything like that?"

"No Sir."

"Well, that circle shows where wagonload after wagonload of arms and ammunition just disappeared. Several even after that unit was stationed there. The latest was in the last couple of weeks or so. I am most anxious to find out what happened to them. How they could just disappear without a trace within a few miles of a veteran Light Cavalry

Unit. I am angry about not only the missing arms and ammo, but I an insulted that I was unable to arm that unit with our latest repeating rifles."

Custis gazed at the map, then said, "I can remember the girls, er,

I mean ladies, mentioning something about going into town, but they never did as long as I was there...well, as far as I know, anyway. When you put this all together, I can almost visualize the farm where I was. That road that their farm is on runs east and west as far as best I can remember."

General Sheridan reminded him, "But remember, it makes a dogleg through the town."

"Well, that farm must be on that dogleg just west of town then."

General Sheridan leaned on the table and looked him in the eye and said, "Well, Major, now you see why you are not only the best, but in all probability, the only man that can get to the bottom of this! I want you to solve this mystery for me and I also want anyone... I mean anyone connected with and/or responsible for the theft of those guns. I want 'em bad! I don't know how many of our troops might still be living if only they'd had those new rifles. Also, I consider it an insult for them to disappear right under our noses! I have a strong suspicion that maybe someone in that unit might be connected to it. Your job is to find out and then, I want them brought here for due justice!"

Major Custis was beginning to see that mean streak show through General Sheridan that he had heard about. He offered, "Well, General, just tell me when and what you want and I will make it happen."

Sheridan bounced back immediately with, "Now that's what I expected to hear from you! I am putting you in complete charge of the mission. You will replace Captain Morgan immediately and he will report to me for further assignment. You will report directly to me. I am assigning you a troop of twenty six light cavalry to accompany you to your new assignment. This will make a total composite of fifty men. You will keep your eyes open for any possible traitors. Now there is a sergeant there and he will remain, however, your troop will also have a First Sergeant and you can also take your favorite Lieutenant, Pug, I believe you call him. He has been chomping at the bit to get back into some kind of action. Reorganize this troop and bring it up to maximum.

You can handpick your men to take with you. Don't ask for volunteers because I already know the whole bunch will want to go with you."

"And if I need supplies or equipment, how am I supposed to get them?"

Sheridan smiled as he said, "Custis, you name it and you claim it!

Verne Foster

Whatever you deem necessary, wire me and it will be provided immediately! Top priority! I mean whatever you need! I want this solved at any cost! You have Carte blanc!"

"Well, there is one thing I would like for starters, Sir."

"Anything!"

"I would like our own colors. Red waist sashes, and permission to turn our hat brims up on one side with a silver U.S. shield holding it up for enlisted men and a gold one for officers."

The General looked puzzled expecting an explanation.

"Sir, it's my first step in raising the morale level of the troops. It will be an Elite Corps."

General Sheridan broke into a smile and shook his head as he said,

"I knew it! I knew it! I heard about what General Lee wore to the surrender! Nice! Nice! Good start. I like it. What ever it takes, Major. You are top priority now."

They were standing facing each other. Custis with his over six foot frame and General Sheridan almost a head shorter, but a very commanding picture of an ardent leader. Custis asked, "When do I leave, Sir?"

General Sheridan looked up at him smiling and said wryly, "You should have already been there! Your orders are being prepared as we speak. So, pick your men while your uniform adjuncts are being procured. I will give the order for it to be done immediately. They will work without stopping until you are ready to leave. Good luck and keep me posted."

As Custis started for the door, the General spoke loudly across the room after him, "Major! Your idea is a good one. Your privates are going to look like generals." He laughed and said, "Do me a good job and I will add that to my uniform."

Custis saluted as he said, "I'll have them make you a set too, sir."

Chapter Twenty Six

Major Custis addressed his old unit. There were over fifty men, very capable and top notch veterans of the war, who all wanted to follow him. At first, they thought he had returned as their commander. Many were to become highly disappointed to find their unit was being dissolved and only part of them would be going with Custis. It was a most difficult task to handpick the men for the job. He, of course, kept the Sergeant that was the NCO under Pug, promoting him to "topkick". The senior corporal was moverd up to the rank the Sergeant left. Major Custis now further exercised his "carte blanche" and, instead of picking twenty-six men, he ended up with thirty-six. Of course, Lieutenant Pug MacHenry was his adjutant and all were overjoyed at the opportunity. The disappointed ones were left behind reluctantly. However, many of them were replacements that had not actually ridden with Custis. That made it a little easier.

Custis called on the Quartermaster for new uniforms and the additions thereto. The Quartermaster was an officer of integrity and was proud to be given the task of creation. He handed Major Custis a polished brass insignia he had created and forged. It was a beautifully artistic design with a U.S. inside a pair of lightning bolts coming out of a star at the top. It was two inches in diameter and a beautiful piece of handiwork. Major Custis had Pug with him and they

Verne Foster

both were beside themselves with admiration. It fit the idea perfectly. This is the pin that would hold up one side of their hat brims. Custis asked how many they had. The Quartermaster proudly said, "Four of the brass ones for the two officers and they were working on fifty pewter ones. Pug looked at Custis quizzically.

Custis then stated, "Well, there have been some changes and we will more than originally planned.. I have added ten more men to this half of my unit and, counting the men we will be joining to form this group, we will need another thirty-six. That makes a total of sixty men.

The brass ones are fine. They look just like gold. Make one pewter one for each of the men immediately and then store a number of them for possible replacements. Take your time on the spare ones. Now, how about the sashes?"

The Quartermaster proudly produced a sample for approval. It was a beautiful specimen. Much like the one General Lee had. The Quartermaster offered, "Now Major, if you like this, I suggest you allow us to put a gold edging on it."

Custis held it up looking at its construction. Quite ingenious actually. It was made like a belt with a catch in the front, but allowed a tail to hang as if it were wrapped in itself. He tried it on. It was adjustable in size and he took it up a little and looked in the mirror. It was similar to a cummerbund. It set the uniform off with a very colorful look. An attention getting look. It was just what he wanted. He thought to himself whimsically, "Shades of George Custer."

He handed it back to the Quartermaster and told him to only put the gold edging on the ones for the officers and to also keep some replacements in stock as well. Then, he asked, "Now. How soon can we get these? By noon tomorrow?"

The Quartermaster accepted the challenge and said, "We will have to work around the clock to do it, but they will be ready for you."

"Can I count on that Lieutenant?"

The Saga of Robert E

"Done, Major! I am proud to be a part of a brand new unit. I am labeling it 'The Custis Elite Corps Project'." The Lieutenant looked quite proud.

Custis cocked his head a little in thought and then said in a rewarding tone, "Have your people initial each piece, Lieutenant. That will be a reminder to us of your and their help in this. Oh, by the way, I want you to make a special gold one. I have plans to give it to General Sheridan later. Your cooperation will be duly noted in my report to him." Custis and Pug then left to finish other business. The Lieutenant was visibly very pleased.

It was afternoon the next day that the two officers stood and watched, with pride, their troops boarding a specially ordered train. One that would provide a comfortable trip for both man and beast. His men were now outfitted with the new look and were a most proud group. All had prideful smiles as they boarded. Pug looked at Custis and winked as he said, "I believe they're ready to ride into hell with you, Major."

"They might very well be, Pug. They might just very well be."

Then the two officers boarded the train and the conductor signaled the engineer and the train started the trip to the "Little Chigger" location. It would not be able to take them all the way, but the men would be well ready to ride horseback for awhile after their long trip. A good two days later, they were mounted in rank and file with the Corporal riding guidon holding their new unit banner. It was a red triangular banner with gold edging and their new insignia the same as their hat badges. The two Sergeants rode side by side ahead of the guidon and directly behind the officers. It was a marvelous looking sight. A sense of pride was felt all through the ranks. Every man was hand picked and was well qualified. There was not an actual road to follow. They traveled more "as the crow flies" to reach the hamlet from where they had left the train. They had a marked map that showed a trail leading into the hamlet where they could turn and go on out to the camp. This pleased Custis since he wanted their appearance to be noticed by everyone. By the time they reached town, it was a tremendous parade. Apparently, people had gotten the news they were coming and were lined up along the sides of the town thoroughfare. The column proceeded through town and on out to camp. The troops at camp had been alerted by wire and were expecting them.

When Captain Morgan saw them, his jaw dropped open and he remarked, "Oh, my God!"

There had been no formality at the camp since it was an outpost. Military courtesy and regimen was lax. This was about to change drastically. The sight of this crack and well dressed group set everyone who saw it aback. The people in the town were amazed. They had never seen such a thing. The troops at the camp, well trained, but having been lax for such a long period of time, felt not only a sense of pride as they watched the new troops approach, but suddenly felt ashamed of their own appearance. Some began buttoning up their tunics and others went scurrying for their hats. The morale rating there started rising immediately. Custis' idea was working on first sight. He noticed this and thought, "It won't be long before they find out that their uniform will not be the only changes made here."

Major Custis raised his gauntlet covered hand and Lieutenant Pug immediately gave the command, "Column.... Halt!"

The company halted in a very orderly manner. Then, Major Custis dismounted in a very matter of fact fashion. He walked over to Captain Morgan. They exchanged salutes and then shook hands. No formal introduction was necessary. The Captain had already read his orders sent by wire and knew exactly to whom he spoke. However, he could not help but to think of how he had underestimated this man. The troops remained mounted and silent. A very impressive scene to say the least.

The Saga of Robert E

The Captain spoke, "Major, this is quite a display of military might. I am deeply impressed. I was well aware of the fact that you would be reorganizing this unit completely, but I had no idea it would be this large."

Major Custis smiled and said, "Sir, we have a mission and this is just the start of it. My men have ridden quite a while and I would like for them to bivouac immediately. Can your men be of service to that end?"

The Captain turned to his Sergeant and told him to get things started for the new arrivals. Lieutenant Pug had already dismounted by this time and had joined the other two officers. Custis nodded to Pug who immediately turned and gave the order to dismount. The First Sergeant echoed the command and the troops dismounted and stood by their horses. Custis introduced Pug to Captain Morgan as his adjutant and he will handle all the problems of setting up our quarters with your men's help. The Captain was quick to agree. Lieutenant MacHenry and the Sergeant left together. Then, the Captain asked, "Major, tell me the truth. Is this a sort of punishment here or what? I am a little confused."

Custis assured him it was not. It was a maneuver to set up a new unit with a special mission. Not knowing just how big a situation they might encounter, there was deemed a need for more troops and that this was a simple transfer of command. He was to report to General Sheridan for debriefing and reassignment."

As they arrived at the Captain's tent, he ushered Custis in. They entered and sat down. Morgan took his pipe and stuffed it with tobacco. He lit it, drawing a few puffs from it and blew a couple of smoke rings as he turned and looked at Custis and said, "Well, I had to ask about this complete change of status, you know. I mean, after the death of President Lincoln and all, I was wondering if there would be any other changes."

The news hit Custis like he had been thrown off a horse. His mouth dropped open and he gasped as he replied, "What was that about the President?"

The Captain suddenly realized Custis had not heard about the assassination and said, "Oh, I am so sorry. I assumed you had heard about it. He went to the theater Friday night last and some maniac actor shot him in the head. He died the next morning about 7:15 a.m. Johnson has already been sworn in as president."

Custis could not believe it. He tried to shake off the shock of it, but it was too overwhelming. He felt a gnawing in the pit of his stomach. As tears swelled in his eyes, he reached into his tunic pocket and took out the medal Mr. Lincoln had given him just days before. He looked away from Captain Morgan in an attempt to hide his tears, but the Captain had already became cognizant of Custis' pain. He offered, "I am so sorry. It has taken us all aback. Even the locals here are saddened. He was a much respected man. I just didn't think."

Custis looked up and said, "We've been traveling hard and fast. We left the train some time ago. Apparently we missed being informed. Wow! I was just with him last Wednesday. Shook his hand and he took it and held it up in his in a show of pride for me and this medal. It was unbelievably awesome. And now, he's dead!"

Morgan asked in amazement, "You were with him? I had not heard about that! I knew my replacement was being sent by the highest authority, but I didn't know it was that high!"

"Aw, it was a medal he gave me and it was at a ceremony. It's a long story. Look here...getting back to matters at hand. Is there anything you can tell me about the missing weapons and ammunition?"

"Well, we are aware that there have been several incidents of hi-jacking, but, no clues have been found as to how and why. There have never been any witnesses left to tell the story. That's about it."

Custis thanked him for his information and said, "We will make this as simple as possible. No ceremonies or

The Saga of Robert E

such. Here are your orders to report to General Sheridan immediately."

The Captain was quite polite and understanding. He offered mess for the troops and the Major. Custis agreed that would be a great idea. Captain Morgan told him that fresh venison was the entrée for the day.

He then said, "I will see to it while you get yourself and your troops settled in."

Custis thanked him and left the tent. As he looked over the camp, there was a great hubbub of getting tents up and wagons unloaded. One wagon contained the new additions to the uniforms as well as some supplies. The camp soldiers and his troops were already working well together and he could hear some of the conversations, mostly about the new look of the uniforms. All the men's spirits seemed to be up. He then headed for a special tent he had brought which was intended to be their headquarters. The job of change already had begun.

Chapter Twenty Seven

It didn't take long for the change of command and integration of the troops to take place. Major Custis called for a mass meeting of the troops with a question and answer agenda. After a tour of the camp, his special training as an engineer took over and he decided to start improving the living conditions there even though it might be a temporary camp. No one knew the future of the many camps scattered around the south. There were so many problem areas that it would take a well organized rehabilitation program to be planned and carried out. The Major made a quick decision. Strike while the iron's hot. While he had carte blanche status, he decided to exercise it a little boldly. He told Pug to make plans for the construction of wooden floors and walls for the tents and other miscellaneous improvements that a little planning would come up with. He put Pug in charge of that project and knew he had left it in good hands. He has studied the position of the camp and had decided it was a very strategic position guarding a main road and also a navigable river. It was a junction that was perfect for a territorial control point. He would use this as a justification for improvements and his only instruction to Pug was "ASAP".

It took most of two days to get the transfer and integration of troops taken care of. Now that he had that settled, he wanted to check into just where he was from the girl's

Verne Foster

place. It was kind of fuzzy in his mind, but he knew it was close. On the third day, he rode out by himself toward town. One thing he noticed was there were people coming and going into the town. As he rode into the main part, he noticed a new building coming up. The studs were already in place and the men were preparing to put a roof on it. It looked like it was not going to be a residence, but another store or business building. As he rode into town, the people stopped what they were doing and all looked at him. He was quite a sight in his immaculate blue uniform with his red sash around his waist, his highly polished black boots, his hat with the left brim turned up and that beautiful badge of identification on it.

Was he going to be accepted or not? He decided to test it and with a smile. He nodded to them and waved. To his surprise, they returned the gesture. One man came out in the street to him and said, "Hey Major, are you the new commander we've heard about?"

Custis nodded smiling and answered, "Yessir, I am."

At this, he dismounted in front of the construction site and asked the man what they were building. No sooner than he had done this, the people that were present in the street started coming over to him. The man said, "This is going to be a church. Our town is starting to grow already."

Custis wryly asked, "By any chance is the preacher going to be a man named Reverend James?"

This surprised the listeners as the man replied, "Why yes. Do you know him?"

Custis thought a minute and then replied with a tongue in cheek attitude, "Let's just say I've heard of him."

The people laughed as they all agreed, "Sounds like you know him. Fine fellow. Has his faults, but a fine preacher."

Custis could not help but remember the white lightning incident as he chuckled. By this time, Custis was almost surrounded by curious onlookers. As he looked around at them, they all had a pleasant look, though hardened by the

The Saga of Robert E

times. Even the women weren't the soft and pale skinned ladies of the north. These ladies were all tanned with skin that seemed as tough as leather. Their hands showed hard work. All had been through hell here. He took this opportunity to put out the news. He began, "Ladies and gentlemen, I am the new commander of the camp. As you probably already know, I brought more troops in with me. We are here on a mission. I want to assure you, though, that we are also here to make sure no one does any harm to you or your property."

One of the men spoke up, "Yep. We saw ya'll come in the other day and there were a lot more troops than we have ever had here before. Is there something special going to happen or what?"

Custis realized he suddenly had a town meeting on his hands as more people came up. Some of them came riding in on their wagons and saw the little assembly and stopped to join it. Within a couple of minutes, he had a crowd. They must have come out of the woodwork or something. He seized the moment, though, and continued, "Oh yes! There is something very special going on here. I want you to know General Sheridan is very concerned for you and has assigned me personally to carry out this mission, part of which is to make sure you and yours are safe from any harm. I was at the surrender and it is the wish of all concerned that General Lee's requests be carried out to the utmost. I am here to make sure your men return without incident and that you can begin to live again without concern for your safety."

The people seemed to be quite pleased with this and all wanted to shake his hand and welcome him. There were many compliments on his appearance and of his men as they had ridden through. They seemed to all take the attitude that these might be Yankees, but they had brought pride with them.

Well, at least his strategy for increased morale seemed to be working both with his troops and the people. After he had spent a little time answering questions, shaking many hands, and exchanging assurances in return for compliments, he asked one of the people, "I am looking for the 'Lee's' place. Can anyone tell me how to get there?"

More than one person immediately started telling him just how to get there. He thanked them and remounted his horse. He smiled and saluted the small crowd and rode off in the direction of the girls' farm.

As he rode for a little while, he began to sense familiarity with the area. Sure enough, he soon recognized Reverend James' place. He then knew he was on the right track. It would be only a few minutes ride to the girls' place.

Sure enough. It was not long before he saw their gate ahead. He had been in familiar territory for quite a while now. The gate was open and he rode on in toward the house. He could feel his heart beat a little faster in anticipation. He drew within a few yards of the front porch and stopped his horse. He turned his horse a little so he could look at it from his side. He patted his horse's neck as he looked and felt it all coming back to him. That first day when he woke up on the porch and the girls were around him and their conversation about who he was and all. About that time, he heard Rose scream, "Oh my God!"

He looked over to the left of the house and there she was. She had apparently heard him come up and came around to see who it was. Hettie heard Rose and came running up. He dismounted and they came running up to him and, at first, were a little cautious, looking for his reaction to them. He smiled and held out his arms and they ran up to him and hugged him immediately, tearfully crying, "Robert E! Oh, Robert E!"

Hettie noticed him looking around and hollered loudly, "Mercy! Come out front quick!"

About that time Mercy came running around the corner of the big porch. When she saw the three and who it was, she stopped short. She looked wide eyed as if in shock. Her mouth dropped open. Then, she seemed to suddenly become intimidated as she slowly walked toward them. Her

The Saga of Robert E

head a little bowed. Rose said enthusiastically, "It's Robert E, Mercy! It's Robert E.! Don't you recognize him? Ain't he beautiful?"

That was just the trouble. She recognized him from the very first look. All she could think about was what a handsome picture of a man he was. Even though it was a Yankee uniform, he was absolutely beautiful. But, she was now scared to show her real feelings that suddenly came flooding over her that she had not even admitted to herself. However, she now, at this moment, realized just how much in love with him she was. Tears swelled in her eyes. She shook her head slowly, afraid to show her real anxiety to just touch him. She was perplexed by the thought of how he might feel toward her and she just could not face rejection at this time.

Hettie and Rose had long realized how she really felt even though their sister could not accept it herself. Hettie and Rose stepped back away from Robert E. All his attention was on Mercy now anyway. It seemed an eternity that they stood there just looking at each other. He drinking in the beauty of her slender little body with her long shiny black hair in the sunlight made her a picture of beauty and she, wondering what he was thinking of her standing there in all his glorious splendor. A half-breed Indian girl with just a country upbringing. What kind of chance would she have for her dreams to come true?

It was Hettie who finally spoke, "For God's sake, girl! Come over here and hug him!."

Robert E held out his arms and Mercy ran to him. He leaned over as she neared him and jumped into his waiting arms hugging him around the neck like a little child. They embraced each other so tightly that you would think they were trying to crush each other. All three girls were now crying and snubbing. They all knew how much this meant, but it was now up to their Robert E. Would he feel the same love this little half-breed sister of theirs had for him? They knew the social graces that had to be embraced plus they

Verne Foster

did not really know this man that was now here. How much of Robert E was he and just how much Union Major was he. Could he be both? They didn't even know his real name. He soon answered all their questions. He let Mercy back down and she started to back away from him afraid she had bared too much of her feelings prematurely, but he took her hand and pulled her close to him. He ran his hand through her long black hair and just shook his head as he looked at her. Rose and Hettie looked at each other as they held back their giggles of delight.

Custis asked Mercy about her fiancee. Before she could answer, Rose piped up, "We got word he's dead."

The Major looked at them and frowned as he said, "I'm sorry. What about your husband, Hettie?"

"Oh, we just got word yesterday that they were in a prison the whole time. Jeremiah died there, but Jefferson Lee is coming home."

Rose, the more romantically aggressive of the girls piped up, "Now, that should make a lot of difference for Mercy. I mean, well, she IS eligible now."

The more reserved Hettie scolded her for being so brazen. Custis just smiled and hugged Mercy again. He looked down into her eyes, but addressed Hettie as he said, "Hettie, I'm presuming that you are more or less the head of this family, so I will ask you something.

Hettie nodded and replied, "Go on!"

Still looking into Mercy's eyes, he said, "I would like your permission to court your sister here."

Both Hettie and Rose laughed and said in chorus, "We just knew you would! Yes! Yes!" With this, they all were hugging each other.

Hettie said, "Well, this is the quietest we've ever seen Mercy. But, then again, we can surely see why." Mercy was holding on to her "Robert E's" arm tightly and could only smile as the tears streamed down her face.

Rose said, "Oh, for goodness sakes, Mercy. Here, let me wipe those eyes." She took her kerchief from around her neck and dabbed the tears away. Mercy was still silent. It was as if she had lost all speech.

Hettie said, "Well, this calls for a toast."

Mercy's eyes widened and the Major said, shaking his head, "Oh no! No more of that!"

Hettie came back and said, "Don't be silly! Let's have a big glass of tea." Seeing the Major would not be able to tie his horse to the whipple tree because of Mercy's hold on him, Hettie took the reins and wrapped them around the crossbar. As they walked around the house to the kitchen, Hettie said, "We have a lot of catching up to do. I do hope you have some time here."

Custis looked down at Mercy and smiled as he said, "All the time we need."

Chapter Twenty Eight

It was a grand time of questions and answers. The girls wanted to know all about this Major. There were many questions like, "Do you remember this? Do you remember that?". After awhile, all was caught up. The Major had explained how he had apparently lost his memory, wandered away from the battle, and ended up in their care. It had taken him awhile but all of it had come back to him. He told them about waking up unaware of his time spent with them, but only thinking he was a prisoner and had to escape. He was Captain Custis and was obviously missing in action. Though confused, he had direction enough to know to head north and so he did. Over an hour had passed in a steady flow of conversation when he randomly asked, "And how about that old man preacher that snockered me with his booze? How's he doing?"

The girls looked around at each other and then Hettie said, "It's a wonder that old fool is still alive. At least, I think he's still alive."

Custis asked, "What in the world? Did something happen to him?"

Rose almost hollered, "Did something happen to him! He almost got himself killed and of all we know, it ain't over yet!"

Hettie said calmingly, "Now Rose, we don't know that much about it. It has been a while now."

Now this bothered the Major and he insisted they tell him what was going on. Hettie started explaining what had happened and as she told him about the rifles, his heart almost skipped a beat. He told them to get one of the rifles for him and was so excited, he had to pace. The girls were completely lost at his actions. Mercy came in with one of the rifles and a handful of bullets. Custis took it and inspected it, looking for its serial number and all. He cocked the lever several times to make sure it was empty. Mercy assured him she would never hand him a loaded gun to look at. He went to the edge of the porch where they were sitting around the table and held the gun up aiming at a tree. He squeezed the trigger and heard the click of the firing pin as it slammed forward on the empty breech. He turned to the girls and with delighted excitement showing all over him, he said, "Girls, sit down. I have something to tell you and I want you to pay special attention to what I say. It's very important for me to get all the information I can about this little gem. Start from the beginning and tell me everything you can remember."

Hettie asked as she sat down, "Just why is this so raving important to you? You look like you just found out that Santa Claus was real!"

With this, Custis told them about the primary reason he was there. He told them all about General Sheridan thinking it was important enough to solve the mystery. Custis emphasized, "It is not only a personal matter to General Sheridan, but it is also a personal matter to me!"

"Well", said Hettie, "Welcome to our side. It couldn't get more personal than it is to us. Those crooks might be stalking us right now!"

Custis urged them to tell him everything they could and leave nothing out. So, the girls told him all that had happened and how they nursed old Reverend James back to health. Hettie also told him about going out to the camp and talking to a couple of soldiers there and how she was curious as to whether the Captain was involved or not. Custis told

The Saga of Robert E

the girls that this was the best information he could have gotten. It gave him a direction for the tracking of these men. He said, "Actually, I'm more interested in finding the men responsible for all this than I am the weapons. They are responsible for the deaths of a lot of our men. I can see I need to go talk to Reverend James now."

Mercy insisted, "We're coming with you."

He looked at the girls and they all nodded as Hettie said, "You'll get a lot more out of Reverend James with us there than not!"

He nodded and said, "Then, let's go."

They saddled their horses and as Hettie mounted the third horse, she saw the slightly puzzled look on the Major's face and said, "Borrowed her from Reverend James. He doesn't need her right now.

He still ain't up to bouncing 'round in a saddle."

The Major smiled and said, "Lead on, girls. Time's awastin'."

The four of them headed off back toward town to Reverend James' place. They reigned up at the side porch and Hettie hollered, "Reverend James! It's Hettie! We're comin' in."

They dismounted and as they started up the steps, the door eased open slightly. They stopped for a minute and then Reverend James called out, "O.K. Come on in."

The Major had been standing aside from the girls a little and the Reverend had not noticed him until he stepped up to the door. He was walking back to his chair and when he turned around, he was startled at the Major's presence. The Major took off his hat. It was then that his scarred up face crinkled with a grin and he cocked his head and asked, "Hey, you're Robert E, aren't you?"

They all smiled and sat down with him. Hettie started the conversation, "It's a long story, Reverend, but that can come later. Right now, you need to tell the Major here everything you know about them guns and the guys you were dealin' with. I mean everything!"

Verne Foster

Reverend James paled as he stared at this Union Major in his fancy uniform. His first words were, "Uh, I need a drink. I need a snort bad!"

He picked up his jug and took a slug letting out a long breath afterwards. He looked over at Hettie questioningly. She assured him it was alright. He then related to them how he had gotten lured into the business by these men and emphasized how dangerous they were. Once they had helped him make a little money by smuggling out a couple of slaves, they told him he was then a partner in their enterprise and had to do what they told him. He wasn't sure of all the names of several of the guys, but the Lieutenant went by Jordan and the Topkick Sergeant was a man named Wilson. Jebediah Wilson. "I'll never forget that one because one day, when I was a little lit, I laughingly called him Jebediah and he told me if I ever did it again, he would kill me. Man, they're dangerous men. Killers!"

Hettie said, "Tell him about the guy named Sam. Fancy dressed and riding an appaloosa." The Reverend's face showed his fear as he told how the man would shoot people down for nothing.

The group talked about an hour and finally, the Major said, "Well, I've got to get back to camp. There's a lot I have to do."

The Reverend asked, "Major, whatcha goin' to do to me?"

Custis stood up and put on his hat. "Well, it all depends on how accurate this information is and how it turns out, and ladies, I am going to assign a patrol to keep watch on both your places. I don't want anything to happen to you. I'll be back as soon as I can."

Mercy said, "Let me walk you out."

Custis ushered her toward the door and said, "Maam, it will be a pleasure." He looked at Hettie and Rose and winked as he trailed behind Mercy. Once outside by his horse, he said, "You are one heck of a beautiful woman and you are as strong willed as you are pretty. Don't do anything to

The Saga of Robert E

get yourself hurt before I can get back out here. If I can't be back tonight, it will be tomorrow. I've got some heavy business to take care of."

Mercy looked up at him smiling as if she were so proud she could burst. She asked, "Major Custis...would you think it forward of me if I were to tell you just how glad and honored I am to be the girl you want to court?"

He just smiled his big grin and stroked her cold black hair back off her forehead and, with a soft voice, he replied, "I can't imagine myself thinking anything like that about the girl I would like to marry."

Her face lit up and she looked into his eyes and almost stuttered, "Marry me?" He nodded assuringly. She grinned excitedly and hugged him and said, "Well, then, I don't mind telling you. I've loved you from the very first time I saw you. Well, at least since after we dragged you out of that water and all." She kissed his cheek and backed away. He climbed up in the saddle and as he reined his horse around to leave, he pursed his lips to her and rode off.

On arriving at the camp, he rode up to the command tent in a hurry. Pug came out and could see the excitement on his face. Pug said, "Major, what in the world have you been up to? I ain't seen that look on your face since the last battle we were in."

Custis told him of his findings and said, "I want you to get a wire off to General Sheridan's office immediately. I want to know the serial numbers of the last two or three shipments of arms and ammo. Also, I want to know if there is any record of a Lieutenant Jordan...might even be cavalry. And also a Sergeant Wilson..Jebediah Wilson...probably a first sergeant. Oh, and also..."

Pug broke in, "Hey, slow down, Major! I can't write all that fast. How do you spell Jebediah?"

Custis told him and continued excitedly, "Also, I want all the information I can get on an Indian Agent named Sam something."

Verne Foster

With this, Pug just shook his head and kept writing as he mumbled, "Sure...Sam something! Right!"

"Well, this might narrow it down a little. He dresses real fancy eastern style, is quick with a gun, and rides an appaloosa. There can't be that many agents like that."

Pug finished writing the information and gave it to the telegrapher. He told the clerk to give it top classification and priority. He turned back to Custis and asked, "How about us putting out an all points call to all the camps and forts near here or near any Indian reservation?"

"Great idea, Pug! I want that information as soon as I can get it."

The adrenalin was pumping in Custis and forcing him to pace back and forth. He decided to take a walk. As he walked through the camp, he could sense a good feeling about it. He noticed the men were neat and clean and wearing their appropriate uniforms. The ones on work details were allowed to wear their shirts without the tunic. They all had their new hats and waist sashes now for their Class A attire. Military discipline had settled in already and he said to himself, "Damn, I'm proud of these guys!"

Chapter Twenty Nine

It was the next morning, Friday, April 21, 1865, when the telegraph started clicking out its da dits for the telegrapher to identify himself and receive a message. The camp had been up and busy since before dawn. A typical military atmosphere was present in the early morning dew dampened reservation. Major Custis and his aide-de- camp, Lt. Patrick McHenry, better known as Lt. Pug to his men, were having another round of boiled coffee after their breakfast when the telegrapher came running into the mess tent with a message for Major Custis. Custis had been anxiously awaiting some kind of reply since the afternoon before. He was quite battle seasoned, though, and had long ago learned to cope with waiting. He had expected a mere reply acknowledging receipt of his priority request. His responsibility of being directly under the personal command of General Sheridan made all requests top priority. Sheridan was known to have a side of him that no one wanted to encounter. He had proven that on more than one occasion. Consequently, when he gave an order that was top priority, you stopped what you were doing and responded immediately. This apparently explained the lack of recognition of his wire being received. Since he had received no receipt acknowledgement, he had wondered what might have been going on with the General's office. Well, he now was going to find out. The clerk saluted as he reported to the Major. He said, "Sir, I apologize for the

Verne Foster

delay this morning, but it is quite a lengthy message and it took time to copy it all for you."

The Major took it and started reading it. Not only was there a list of serial numbers for the arms, but there was also a verification on the identity of this "Sam". It seems there was an Indian Agent that fit that very description to a "T". His name is actually N. Samson Bright. He was appointed as Indian Agent at large for the district of southeastern Oklahoma. His appointment was contested from the beginning due to his questionable activity in business; however, being very well liked by certain powerful congressmen, he was given the job early in the year of 1864. There had been several complaints lodged against him during that time, but they all were discredited and labeled as just so much Indian hullabaloo.

Custis handed the message to Pug and as he finished reading it, he looked up at Custis and said, "In other words, this man is just another political pet that gets away with anything."

Custis was sitting with his elbows on the table looking in deep thought. He replied, "Until now, old buddy. Until now!" He then thanked the clerk who saluted and departed. Custis was in that deep thought. A grin came across his face as he said to Pug, "Pug, get our horses. You and I have a visit to make and I want you to meet some friends of mine."

Pug took a last sip of his coffee as he got up from the table. As he stood up, he asked, "Where we goin' Major?"

"You'll see. As a matter of fact, there is someone I'd like for you to meet. It's a long story, but you know part of it already. I'll tell you on the way."

He then left the mess tent and Pug went for their horses. Pug came up to the stable crew and ordered their two horses and then went to the officers' tent to pick up his sash and weapon. As the two men rode toward town, Custis brought Pug up to date. Pug was awestruck. The fact that the Major was seriously involved with a girl, especially a southerner, was completely unexpected. Custis said, "Well, I didn't realize it myself until I saw her again yesterday. It's funny, but we both knew it in our hearts."

As the two came up to the gate and turned in, Custis said to Pug, "Here is the house where I spent those days of unknown identity...and with three of the finest women in the country."

They reined up at the porch and dismounted. They could hear someone around back and walked around the house. It was Mercy and Rose in the yard chopping some wood at the back porch. They were busy and did not hear the men ride up. As the two men approached the porch area, Hettie came out of the kitchen, When she saw them, she said loudly, "Land sakes, look who's here, girls!"

The girls stopped and turned to the men. When Mercy saw them, her face lit up as if it were reflecting the sun. Both the girls immediately started fidgeting with their hair and brushing it back off their foreheads. Rose just stood there with the axe over her shoulder. She was looking at Pug curiously, but with a smile of approval. Pug wasn't as tall as Custis nor was he as thinly built. He was of good frame and quite muscular. His bronzed face showed many days in the sun and weather.

Custis finally jokingly spoke first, "Well, Rose, are you fixing to use that axe on us?"

It was only then that she realized she was still holding it. It was obvious to Custis that she had taken an immediate interest in Pug. An interest that he had hoped for. Pug was a career soldier and had always been married to the Army with no serious love affairs. He looked at Pug to see his reaction. Pug seemed just as interested in Rose as she was in him. It was as if they were all alone with no one else around. Custis took the moment to introduce everyone.

Hettie said, "Ya'll come on up to the table and have a cup of fresh coffee. Let's sit down where we can talk."

Custis really wanted to conduct business and had a high interest in getting on with discussing it with the girls, but looking at Mercy made him forget all about that and also Pug and Rose were all but holding hands by now. He shrugged his shoulders and said, "Good idea."

Mercy came and took his hand shyly smiling and they walked in pairs up the steps to the table. They sat down together and Hettie asked, "You two want some grits and red eye gravy?"

They declined, saying they had just had breakfast. Custis spoke, "Uh, Pug, I believe Rose has a Rebel boyfriend."

Rose immediately denied it and said, "Ugh, that was a long time ago. Lt. Pug, sir, Robert E never mentioned you before. I would like to hear about how you and he got together."

Pug, with a puzzled look on his face, replied, "Who is Robert E?"

Custis laughed and said, "Oh, I guess I neglected to tell you that is what the girls named me. I am still Robert E to them." Pug just grunted as he continued his pre-occupation with Rose.

Hettie giggled, "Now, darn it, ya'll can get all this lollycoddlin' done later. I think we have some important business to discuss!"

This remark brought the four out of their rapture and back to reality. Hettie asked Custis, "Well, what kind of information did you get from Washington?"

Custis told them of the message and went over everything with them again. He wanted to know every detail. Hettie told him everything she could remember about the men at the barn and then, the girls discussed their day at the ravine. Custis determined they should go take a look at the ravine to see if there were any clues they might gather. The girls agreed and started to go saddle up. Pug quickly volunteered to help. Custis also took the opportunity to be with Mercy and they all went to the barn to get ready. Mercy seemed to be unusually quiet around Custis. She just hugged his arm while they walked. As they walked, Custis remarked, "You're sure quiet lately. Is anything wrong?"

The Saga of Robert E

Mercy looked u p at him and replied, "Oh, I still can't believe this has happened. If I am sleeping, I don't want to wake up."

Custis stopped and held her chin up in his hand and bent down and kissed her lightly on the lips. She closed her eyes and sighed. Custis felt the warmth flow from her body filling him with emotion. He looked into her face and as she slowly opened her eyes, he looked deep into those two black pools and would have been engulfed had it not been for Hettie shouting, "O.k., you two! Let's get mounted!"

The five of them were soon on the road to the ravine. As they rode, they discussed all the possibilities of such a situation. Questions were addressed like where would the gun runners be now? What route would they have taken? Where to start, etc? The information from the girls combined with the wire from Washington was clearing up a lot of questions that had them baffled before. If they were lucky, they might determine which way the culprits went and then, by estimating the miles per day they would probably make, multiplied by the number of days it had been since the girls had seen them, would give them a great insight as to where to head.

By the time the group got to the ravine, all were seriously involved in the mystery. Romantic thoughts had been put aside for later and all were now interested in any possible clues that might be there. The nearer Mercy got to the site, the more her natural instincts took over and she found herself noticing things that were overlooked before. For example, she spied a cartridge casing near the site of one of the shootings. She drew up and dismounted. She walked over to the casing and picked it up. She then walked over to where the shallow graves had been. She found the tip of a kerchief sticking out of the dirt. She pulled it up and it looked like the one the Westerner had been wearing. Custis and Pug were following her every move. She handed the items to them and said, "Maybe we ought to dig around in here and see if there might be anything else."

Verne Foster

About that time, she spotted something several yards up the river and partially in the water. The water would lap over it and ebb back out. She quickly went over to it, but her alert eye had caught it even from a distance. Custis was witnessing all this and thought to himself what a wonderful tracker she would made. He would later consider that very thought seriously.

She dug around it enough to get a grip on it and pulled at it. It took some more digging to free it, but she finally pulled it up. It was a U.S. Army saddlebag and was full of something. Now how did it get there? Was it that Lieutenant's or the Sergeant's? Why was it left and why was it buried? And, more importantly, what did it contain? Custis undid the buckle and opened one of the pouches. He reached in and pulled out what looked like a log book. They opened it and looked at each other amazed at what they saw.

Chapter Thirty

There were several items in the saddle bags, but the most interesting was a thick book with writings in it. All the items were soaked from being in the water. The book was apparently the Lieutenant's log. It was in poor shape from being so wet, but most of the writing was legible. Most of it had been written or drawn in pencil. Custis carefully peeled the last few pages apart looking for any dates to show how recent these writings were. They dated back a couple of years, but the final one had the date printed on the top of the page. It was apparently his last day to be alive. The day when all this happened here in the ravine. They could barely make out the printing, but it gave them some valuable information. It mentioned the gathering of the guns and ammo and schedule to meet Sam and his party from the West that day. The Lieutenant's last words were that he would be rich before the day was done and then he would be on his own. The most interesting of the all was a crude map drawn in apparently India ink because it had not been blurred by the water and was clear. It showed a route for the wagon train. Well, here was the most important information they had.

Custis asked Mercy if she recognized anyplace on it. She looked at it blankly as if nothing were familiar. Then, her face brightened. She turned the book around so she could face the map from a different direction. There it was! A small "x" was on the eastern end of the trail. She held the map up to Custis and pointed to the "x" and said, "That's us right there!"

Custis frowned in his confusion. She pointed to the markings on the map and showed him it was the ravine. He looked at it and saw the trail leading north, then splitting and heading west-north-west. He asked the girls, "What does this road do at the other end of the ravine?"

They almost said in chorus, "It splits and continues north or heads west. Why?"

Mercy was ahead of him. She said, "They followed this trail west. We've never been very far down it to the west, but you can go around this foothill to the north and come back in on the main road we live on."

Custis asked if they knew anything about where it ended up to the West. Hettie offered, "Well, it's supposed to just keep going west. I understand there is a ferry for it at the Chattahoochee River. It heads sorta' north and follows a railway west. I think it runs about a mile south of that railroad."

They suddenly looked at each other as the reality of where the hijackers went sunk in. Mercy added, "They've headed west with the goods and I thought they might have circled around to come back at us since Reverend James' escapade."

Custis shook his head, "Well, I don't think they were even interested in you all. This must have been their final haul and they were clearing out."

The girls agreed as Custis rubbed his brow and said, "I wonder how that saddlebag got there?"

"Fate!" answered Hettie.

"Exactly", Mercy added, "That Lieutenant was killed and left here before they came back and cleared everything out. They probably threw him across a horse to take him wherever and it fell off into the water."

Custis reasoned, "Well, that could explain how it got to where we found it in the edge of the river."

The Saga of Robert E

Rose offered, "They were probably in a real big hurry to get out of here and didn't see it or didn't bother with it."

Pug had remained silent all this time, but now queried, "I've got one question. Why did they bother to clean up the mess and what did they do with the bodies? Surely, they had no intention of taking them all the way with them."

Hettie said, "I've asked myself that question too. When that trail splits north of here, it goes on up into the mountains. The trail west follows a ridge and there is a steep drop on one side of it."

The other two girls were nodding in agreement and seemed to know what she was going to say. Rose piped up, "That's it! They dumped the bodies and stuff they didn't want down that mountain where nobody would ever find them!"

Custis was studying the map and finished going through the saddlebags. Nothing else of interest to them was there. He looked around making a last look of inspection when Hettie said, "Well, we've done about all we can do here. Let's go back to the house where we can dry that book out and see if we can determine where we can go from here."

Her opinion was well accepted and the group headed back to the farm. It was still just a little crisp and the air smelled clean. The little clan gathered in the kitchen and Hettie stoked the fire in the big iron stove where the big coffee pot sat on the warming burner. Rose got out the coffee mugs. They were an admixture of kinds. Most of their nice "china" had either been taken or broken over the last couple of years. A mug was better for coffee anyway. She quickly set the mugs down in front of the three at the table. She smiled as she set a mug before Pug and then one next to him for herself. She cooed, "Mind if I join you for coffee, Sir?"

Pug, pleased with her flirting, quickly stood up and moved the chair out for her as he answered, " T'would be my deepest pleasure, maam."

Verne Foster

Further around the table, Custis and Mercy had their heads together looking at the map. Custis noticed the closeness and, as they slowly looked at each other, he said, "Mmmm. You smell just like Lavender, little lady."

She smiled sheepishly and replied, "Why, thank you, kind sir."

After looking at each other for a minute as if they both were wishing they were somewhere else in a different time, they returned to the map as Mercy asked, "Do you think it would be a good idea to draw a copy of that map just in case?"

He replied, "Well now, that's a good idea. Then, we can try and dry out the whole book. No telling what we'll find written in there."

Hettie came up with the coffee pot and filled their mugs. She stopped for a moment, looking at the map, and said, "You know, he must have made that map himself. It only goes up into the mountainside. Besides, I've never seen a map of that trail before."

Custis nodded and replied, "Well, it's not unusual for someone to do that of a territory they're trying to remember."

Hettie continued as she gave the pot over to Mercy to do the pouring, "That's not exactly what I was talking about. Look at where it ends. I just noticed. That is where they dumped all the junk and the bodies. The trail is pretty high there and there is a steep drop off right about where this map quits."

Custis looked again at the map and Mercy came back to join them. The girls agreed in wonder why he stopped the map in that particular spot. Custis said, "Well, maybe it just coincidence."

Hettie answered, "And maybe it's not. It probably wouldn't be a bad idea to have a look-see."

Custis came back, "Well, just how deep is that drop off there?"

Mercy looked at Hettie as they pondered an answer. As Hettie replied, Mercy nodded in agreement, "Right in that area, it drops off out of sight in the woods. It's real steep and goes down probably over a couple hundred feet or so." She thought for a minute as Custis looked curiously at her. She defended, "Look, I ain't very good at stuff like that. It just keeps going out of sight into the trees below. You could climb down it, but it's steep."

Custis, with a thoughtful look, said, "Well, maybe you're right."

"You mean how steep it is?"

Grinning, he said, "No, no. I mean it's probably a good idea to go have a look-see."

They chuckled at this as the humor took over the seriousness. Custis looked over at Pug and then explained, "Only thing is, I don't believe it's a good idea for you girls to go climbing down there. Furthermore, we don't have any idea what all we'll find. If they did dump the bodies there, it won't be a thing I want you girls to be getting into."

The girls all started to disagree at once, but he stopped them and said, "Look here! This is a job for the Army and I will have a detail carry it out. I don't want you girls out there, you hear me?"

They looked at each other and acquiesced at this sudden official tone.

Custis told Pug, "Well, we need to get on this right away. Let's get back to camp and get it started. You pick a detail of men for the job and I'm going to wire the General for a possible map of that trail they're on."

Pug and Custis made their goodbye's to their respective girls. Custis tipped his hat to Hettie as he climbed into the saddle and said, "Thanks for the help. This might just be our breakthrough."

She raised two fingers to her eyebrow as if to salute him. The two men rode off as the girls watched from the yard. As

Verne Foster

they rode in a slow gallop toward town, Custis told Pug, "You know, Pug, I want these guys. I want 'em bad!"

Pug nodded and replied, "I know, Major! I know! Me too!"

Chapter Thirty One

When the two officers came to the camp, the sentry saluted them as they rode in. Both headed toward the command tent. Pug called to the First Sergeant as Custis dismounted and went in. He heard Pug start telling the Sergeant what he wanted.

As the Major came into the tent, the telegrapher jumped up and reported with a salute, saying, "Sir, I have some information for you."

Custis returned his salute and sat down at his desk. As the clerk came over to him, Custis told him to sit down. Then, he said, "Well, Corporal Johnson, I have some work for you to do also."

"Sir, this is very important information and I think you will find it most interesting."

With his curiosity aroused, Custis told him to continue.

"Well, Sir, I have many contacts on the wire. It has been a boring job until you came and I, sort of, well, Sir, set up a communications news line with many of the other telegraphers."

Custis stopped him and asked, "Are you telling me what I think you're telling me?"

The Corporal looked worried and asked, "Er, what is that, Sir?"

"Are you telling me you have been keeping in contact with some of the Forts and all?"

Verne Foster

As the uncomfortable Corporal tugged at his collar, he asked, "Uh, would the Major be upset with that...Sir?"

Custis smiled as he realized he just might have a treasure of information in this Corporal. He assured the Corporal, "Quite the contrary. If you're going to tell me what I think you are, I might just promote you to Sergeant!"

Corporal Johnson beamed as he explained how he had set up a news network with all the forts and even many of the railroad telegraphers. He even knew them by name. They were always exchanging information about what was going on at their location and keeping all alert to changes and so forth.

Custis sat back with his elbow on the arm of his chair and his finger to his chin. Suddenly, his grin changed to a serious look as he said, "Corporal, I've got some terribly important questions that need immediate answers. You said railroad telegraphers. Do you know anything about a trail heading west out of town they call 'The old wagon trail'? I understand it follows a railroad out west."

The Corporal was up to the challenge. Corporal Johnson smiled as he nodded his head, "Sir, I am quite familiar with that trail and know about the railroad. I have talked to many of the clerks along it and also, there are several forts near it along the way."

Custis felt as if he had just struck gold. He listened intently as Corporal Johnson told him of the trail, how it crossed the Chattahoochee and meandered on westward past several towns and forts.

"Can you get hold of a map of it for me?"

"Sir, as a matter of fact, I can do better than that. Since I've been communicating with these guys and they have told me about their areas, I have drawn up my own map of how I think it looks. How far west do you want to go?"

"Well, it depends on you, my friend."

Corporal Johnson was truly impressed. He stuttered as he answered, "On me? How so, Sir?"

The Saga of Robert E

"Well, I need you to find out if any of them have seen or heard of a wagon train traveling that trail lately."

The Major described the outfit to the Corporal and gave him the peculiarities of the men and the wagons. When he mentioned three men on Appaloosas, the Corporal raised his eyebrows and sighed, "Wow! I can't believe this!

"Can't believe what?"

"The important information I had for you was that if you ever wanted some information right away, I might just be able to supply it since I have so many connections on the wire."

Custis leaned forward with both elbows on the desk as he looked into the Corporal's eyes, "Corporal, I need that information yesterday! Can you help me?"

Corporal Johnson answered with a big grin, "Sir, if I can't, no one can! I'll have it for you as soon as I can send the messages. Give me an hour at the most!"

Custis was elated. He thought how things are suddenly falling in place. . As he got up and went to exit the tent, he considered just how much of an asset this Corporal was. He exited the tent and saw Pug coming his way. Pug came up to him and said, "Well, Major, the search detail is forming as we speak. You want them to go out there immediately?"

"Yes. They've had lunch, haven't they?

"Yessir, and they have been briefed just as I thought you'd want them to be."

"Pug, sometimes I think you can read my mind."

Pug grinned and replied, "Well, we make a good pair, Sir."

Custis agreed, "That we do. That we do."

Pug seemed concerned and said, "Sir, since I have an idea where we're going and what we're looking for, I'd like to lead the detail."

Custis thought for a moment, then agreed, "Good idea, but I suggest you stop and take one of the girls with you. She might possibly be of a great help to you. But...don't let her off her horse. Keep her away from whatever you find out there."

Pug smiled broadly saying, "I fully agree with the Major. Any orders as to which one, Sir?"

A mischievous grin came on his face as he replied, "I leave that up to you. Oh, and also, take the First Sergeant with you. Fill him in on the way to the girls' place. I want him to be aware of what we're getting into here."

Pug nodded he understood. Then, Custis told him to stay back himself with the girl and let the Sergeant and his men do the job. Pug gave an understanding nod just as the troops rode up. The First Sergeant was with them. Custis watched as Pug told the First Sergeant to join him. Pug mounted his horse and told the Sergeant to ride next to him. He held his hand up and yelled out, "Trooop! Forward!" The Major smiled proudly as he heard the Sergeant echo, "Trooop! Forward!"

Custis watched them as they rode out in file. He thought to himself, "Man! I love the way these men have come along!"

Custis knew there would be no problem no matter how gory what they find might be. There is nothing they haven't been through. The ones on the detail were all from his original outfit and very seasoned veterans of the world's worst war. Anyone who can stomach 50,000 men being killed and blown apart can take anything. He then realized he was hungry and headed for the mess tent where he knew that at least, there was coffee waiting.

As the long file of twelve men moved toward town, Pug filled the First Sergeant in and why he had been picked to be the enlisted officer to lead this detail. Pug also told him of the three girls who knew the countryside, and that they were going to take one of them with them on this detail. He said, "And Sergeant, even though I just met them today, I think I might just be marrying one of them someday."

The Saga of Robert E

    The Sergeant almost fell off his horse. He asked, in surprise, "You? Pug MacHenry? Now what girl is going to fall for a tough old Irishman like you?"

    They both laughed at the friendly humor of two old buddies as Pug said, "Wait'l you meet her. She's the youngest of the three. Cute as a pin and just as sharp....and, don't go getting any ideas about the other two. They're all pretty, but tough as nails. They've had an awful hard time and have weathered all kinds of bad treatment from both our troops and renegade rebels. My girl's name is Rose. Then, there's Mercy. She now officially belongs to the Major. The oldest, Hettie, well, her husband's due back any time. He's been in one of our prison camps for about two years. What ever you do, don't make no mistakes. The Major's girl is part Indian and she is a natural tracker. We're going to take Rose with us to help us find what we're looking for."

    "Well, Lieutenant, if this Mercy is part Indian and a good tracker, why are we taking Rose?"

    Pug just smiled and said, "'Cause the Major left it up to me and she's my choice." The Sergeant shook his head in utter amazement and said no more.

    As the column approached the girls' place, Pug called a halt. He told the Sergeant to explain to the men what they were going to do while he went in. He then rode into the gate and up to the house. Mercy and Hettie came around the corner from the back. Rose came out of the front door onto the porch. She beamed when she saw Pug. He dismounted and doffed his hat as he greeted the girls. He couldn't help notice the girls looking inquiringly at the troop still mounted outside the gate. He explained that this was the detail Custis had mentioned and that they were on their way to search out the trail.

    Pug then asked, "Mz. Hettie, we need one of you girls to help us find the place we talked about." Hettie started to say something when Pug cut her off, "I would like Rose to go with us. I assure you, no harm will come to her."

He grinned as he continued, "I'll guard her with my life. I may be Irish, but first, I am an officer and a gentleman."

Hettie pondered, then replied, "Well, I was going to suggest we all three go, but I can see why you'd pick one. Just remember that if anything happens to Rose, you will answer to us."

He nodded as he said, "Understood maam."

Rose gleefully said, "It'll only take a minute for me to get my horse."

The Sergeant came up about that time and Pug said, "Ladies, I want you to meet our First Sergeant, an old war buddy of mine. He likes to be called Sergeant because, well??? He turned to the Sergeant and coyly asked, "You want to tell'em your name?"

"Not particularly, but since you are ladies, I guess it's O.K. My name is Bartholomew. Bartholomew Grimsley, maam."

The two girls smiled and as Hettie cocked her head wryly, she said, "Now that's a fine name. I think we'll just call you Bart. Now how's that?"

Sergeant Grimsley smiled as he thought about it. He asked proudly, "Now why didn't I think of that years ago?"

They all laughed as Hettie continued, "And since you like to be called Sergeant, we'll always call you Sergeant Bart."

The Sergeant seemed quite pleased with this and he turned to Pug and said, "Dern, Lieutenant, you're right. These girls are very smart...verrry smart!"

Rose came around the corner of the house leading her horse and said, "Well, I'm ready to go."

Pug then asked the Sergeant, "Are the men updated on our guide?"

"Yessir. That's what I came to tell you. Seems the girl is as ready as we are."

He introduced Rose to the Sergeant as they mounted their horses and Hettie yelled after them, "Rose...we call him Sergeant Bart."

The Sergeant just raised his hand and kept on riding. Once out of the gate, the Sergeant took his place in front of

The Saga of Robert E

the column as Lieutenant Pug and Rose took their place side by side in the lead. Lieutenant Pug ordered loudly, "Trooop! Forward, Ho!"

The Sergeant echoed the order and they all moved out very orderly. Hettie and Mercy stood and watched them ride on down the road out of sight. Mercy quipped, "Hmmm, Rose seems to fit right in beside him, huh?"

Hettie thoughtfully smiled, "She sure does." Then, she mumbled, "Almost as much as you fit in with Robert E, I mean, the Major." They smiled as they walked back from the gate toward the house.

Chapter Thirty Two

It was jut over an hour when they entered the ravine. Pug and Rose rode side by side followed by the Sergeant. The "Guidon" followed directly behind the Sergeant. The "Guidon's" banner rippled in the breeze as they moved slowly along. You could see the look of curiosity on the soldier's faces as they looked up at the top of the ravine with forestry growing on the top and a tree or two extending out over the edge. It promoted an habitual alertness in these battle experienced veterans as they scanned all possibilities of an ambush. All was quiet, though, in the ravine except for the sound of the river as it ran its course.

Once in the ravine, Pug raised his hand for halt. The column obeyed. He looked around to see if there were any change since he'd been there last. He then asked Rose, "Are you sure you're up to this, Missy?"

Rose nodded in affirmation and said, "I'm as ready as I'll ever be. Let's get on with it."

"How far have you girls been up the trail?"

"We've gone all the way around the foothill and back home on the main road several times."

"How about the trail west?"

"Well, we've been up a pretty good ways, but not more than a mile or so. It keeps rising into the foothills and all looks the same."

"Then you know it pretty well?"

Verne Foster

"Oh, sure. Well enough for what we need today."

Pug then raised his arm and motioned forward. The column moved out. As they traveled, Pug noticed a narrow trail going off to their left. He pointed to it and Rose advised, "Oh, that's just an animal trail. The fork is up ahead a ways."

After about fifteen minutes, they came to where the trail split. The trail they were on continued on a more even level and led off to the right. The trail to the left started an immediate rise. They started up it and soon came to a gap on their right. Rose reigned to a stop and Pug quickly raised his arm for a halt. She pointed to the slope that was formed as the trail made a turn to the right up ahead. She said, "This is the place we talked about."

Pug dismounted and walked ahead for a few yards up toward the curve. He inspected the slope scanning closely the mulch covered terrain. It was dotted with trees. Once spotting a good sized rock resting at the edge of the trail, he tried to push it over the edge. It was heavier than he thought. Sergeant Bart quickly dismounted and came to his side. They pushed the heavy stone easily together. It began rolling slowly at first, then picked up speed as it tumbled down the grade. It rolled about seventy five yards before crashing into a tree. The Sergeant looked at Pug and asked, "Testing the momentum of the grade, Sir?"

"Exactly. You reckon a dead body would roll down that easily?

"I think it would, Sir. Dead or alive."

Pug gave the order to dismount and make ready for the descent. The "Guidon" jammed his flag pole into the soft orange clay and it remained erect. He then quickly dismounted and went to assist Rose. The other soldiers moved on by. Two of them carried coils of rope on their shoulder. These had been fastened over their saddlebags. The Sergeant told them to spread out. He then said, "You're aware of why we're here. Let's see what's down there."

The Saga of Robert E

The men started the descent as the "Guidon" brought Rose to the Lieutenant. Pug walked her over to the opposite side of the trail. He explained, "I don't want to see you go sliding down that slope. You stay back here and wait."

She nodded, but looked with interest at all that was going on. She asked Pug, "Why are the men carrying ropes?"

"That's in case we need to repel or maybe bring something up. Best to be prepared for all circumstances."

Rose nodded with understanding and watched the organized way the troops very quickly descended the slope as if they had planned it ahead of time. Watching a well trained and experienced group of soldiers move into a detail fascinated her. There was no idle chatter between the men. They only spoke when it seemed necessary. They worked quietly and with quick accomplishment. She was amazed. As they waited for any word from below, the Sergeant asked Pug, "Just what made you pick this area instead of going on up a little further?"

"Two reasons. First was my instincts. I stick with my gut feeling. This is where I'd have done it. Secondly, the stone told me this was the place."

The Sergeant said coyly, "Oh. I thought it might be because this was the place Miss Rose pointed out to you."

Both men grinned at this and with a chuckle, Pug said, "Well, that too."

It wasn't long before one of the lead men yelled from down the hill,

"Hey Sarge! Found something! Looks like that Lieutenant you spoke of."

The Sergeant immediately started down to him. Sure enough. As soon as he neared the sight, he smelled the odor. There lay what was left of a person. As the two looked at it and smelled the stench, the Sergeant said, "Well, we've certainly been here before, haven't we?

The soldier nodded and continued, "Not much left after nature and the animals got through with him, huh?"

The coat was definitely a Union Lieutenant's blouse though torn to shreds. The boots had been torn off the feet and lower legs. They were definitely military. The Sergeant yelled back to the Lieutenant, "We seem to have the Lieutenant, Sir."

Before Pug could reply, another soldier further over yelled, "Hey! Got another one here. Looks like a cowboy."

The Sergeant went over to him and viewed the chaps and high heeled boots. About that time, a third body was found. The Sergeant moved toward the site. The soldier said, "Looks like he was a 'topkick'. Not much left of his jacket, but the sleeve is full of gold stripes."

Sergeant Bart hollered to Pug, "You get that, Lieutenant?"

"Yes! Just leave them there and call it quits. We have what we need to know. Come on back up."

The soldiers obeyed immediately. The Sergeant came up to Pug and asked, "Sir, since they're one of us, do you want a burial detail?"

Pug almost hissed as he answered. His eyes were slits as he replied, "First, they are not one of us! They are nothing but murdering thieves! They are responsible for the hijacking of our new rifles and killing our troops just for their own greed! We're not even sure they're real soldiers! Secondly, either way, they are a disgrace to our uniform and to us! Leave them there! That's what men like that really deserve!"

It was quite evident how emotionally affected the Lieutenant was. The Sergeant nodded and said, "I understand and fully agree, Sir. The truth was never more evident."

"Then go and explain it to the men for me...and tell them they've done a fine job here."

Rose quietly watched and heard. She was seeing the soldier side of this man Pug. His face was as if it were cut out of stone. She could not help but see the sorrow in his eyes as well as the contempt on his face. She quickly realized he was the Lieutenant and it was his responsibility to accomplish the mission. This was to be quite an education

The Saga of Robert E

for her today. She considered herself fortunate to see the business side of this Irish born soldier,. Gentle as a lamb, but hard as a rock when the need arises. She stood in admiration of him. Knowing Robert E and seeing him as the Major, told her where Pug got his metal.

The Sergeant responded to Pug's order, "Quite right, Sir." He then moved over to where the men were forming on the trail. Pug gave the command to fall in and remount. He and Rose led their horses past the other ones. When all the troop was mounted, Pug got on his horse and faced the men. He told them, "Men! Do not think of them as soldiers or even humans. They murdered our soldiers and stole our weapons. They intended to sell them out west. I am proud of the way you have conducted yourselves here. Good job." With that, he then gave the command to move out.

It was late in the afternoon as they neared the girls' farm. Pug raised his arm for a halt. He and Rose moved out of ranks and he said to the Sergeant, "Continue to the camp and make an immediate report of what we found to the Major. I'll be along shortly."

The Sergeant nodded, saluted, and yelled, "Forward ho!"

The column moved out. Pug stood his position and saluted them as they passed. It was a show of respect. They all returned it as they passed. Rose was on her horse at the gate and watched all this. She marveled at what she'd learned this day. She witnessed a whole different way of life. A very regimented way of life. They rode to the house and Pug dismounted and came around and helped Rose off her mount. He took her hands in his and said very softly, "Missy, I am so sorry for what you had to see today. I hope I have not seemed the demon to you. It is what I had to do."

She shook her head as she cooed, "Oh no! No! Don't even think such.! You were perfectly right in what you did. I would have done the same thing if I were in your place."

The tenseness left his face as it softened. She put her hand to his cheek and reached up and kissed him. He looked

Verne Foster

deep into her big blue eyes for a moment and then said, "You are one fine lady, Missy! I would consider it an honor if you would let me see you again."

Rose smiled sheepishly and replied, "The honor would be mine, Lieutenant Sir."

He took his two fingers and put them to his lips, then, touched them to hers. He then said, "I must go, but I will be back."

With that, he swung up into his saddle, tipped his hat, and rode for the gate. As he reached the gate, he turned back and held up those two fingers he had touched to her lips. She smiled and waved as he rode off toward camp.

Once back at camp, he reined up in front of the command tent. As he entered, the Sergeant was still there with Custis. When the Sergeant saw who it was, he said, "Oh, here he is now, Major."

Custis told Pug to have a seat. Pug pushed his hat back and sat down. Custis said, "Well, Pug, looks like we have the information we need. You have anything to add?"

Pug asked, "Do you want us to take a burial detail out there?

"Not on your life! The Sergeant and I agree with your decision completely! They lived and died in their own obscurity. Let them lie in it forever!"

This eased Pug's mind a little. Riding back, he had thought it over and was concerned if he had let his feelings guide him wrong. He gave a deep sigh and said, "Major, I just want to say I'm damned proud of our men. And you, Sergeant, are to be commended for your leadership!"

Custis said, in a humorous tone, attempting to lift the soberness of the moment, "Hey, now, don't make his head grow any bigger. I just told him that myself." The three laughed.

After a much needed laugh, Pug inquired, "Well, Major, what now?"

"I'm glad you asked." With that, he called out, "Corporal Johnson, come join us."

Corporal Johnson answered with a "Yessir" and immediately came over. Custis then said, "Drag up a chair and tell Lieutenant MacLean and the Sergeant here what you've found for us."

Custis then leaned forward with his elbows on the desk and said,

"Men, you're just not going to believe this!"

Chapter Thirty Three

The Corporal began proudly, "Well, to start with, I have built up sort of a web of contacts that I keep up with almost daily and we exchange information as we need it. I am in contact with over two dozen military posts or forts and thirty or more railroad stations. Consequently, when the Major asked me to put a trace on your perpetrators, not only did I find someone that had seen them, but possibly, we can come close to pinpointing where they are."

He leaned back as if expecting applause. Custis said, "Corporal, just cut to the chase."

The Corporal lost his smile and took on a more serious expression as he continued, "Uh, yes sir! Well, it seems that the people we are after are sorta different enough so as to be remembered if they're ever seen. The railroad clerk at Opal Junction, which is just southwest of Anniston, Alabama, uh...his name is Johnson, same as mine...Hank Johnson. He's been with the railroad right there for ten years and.."

Custis interrupted, "Corporal, get on with it."

The Corporal gulped and smiled meekly as he continued, "Yessir, Major, I'm sorry. I just sorta chase rabbits sometimes. Anyway, it just so happens that a couple of Indians that looked like Apaches and a well dressed easterner wearing a brightly colored vest, came riding in on, of all things, Appaloosas. Those are horses that people notice since they are rarely seen around there. There was another Indian driving a

Verne Foster

wagon with water barrels on it. They were looking to refill them. When Hank asked them where they were headed, the fancy Dan told him it was none of his business. A real mean character. Oh, and another thing. He wore his gun real low. Looked like a gunslinger."

Pug looked up at the Major and then at the Corporal, then asked, "When was this?"

Corporal Johnson said, "Late yesterday. I asked Hank which way did they come from and he said they came and went from the direction of the old wagon train trail."

Major Custus looked at Pug and the Sergeant as he remarked, "And here is the kicker, gentlemen." \

Refusing to steal Corporal Johnson's thunder, Custis told him to tell them. The Corporal just beamed at this and replied, "Thank you, Sir. Hank said he felt real uncomfortable about them. They got their water from the refilling tower and while they were there, he noticed they all three were carrying new lever action repeating rifles. He walked out to where their horses were to get a closer look, but got scared when they saw him and started to come over to him. He walked back inside and closed the door. They let him alone and went about their business."

There were a few moments of silence, then Pug spoke, "Major, I think this Hank guy got the same kind of feeling about these guys as we got out there on the trail." Pug looked at the Sergeant, who was nodding his head, and said, "You get that feeling too, Sarge?"

"Man, I sure did. It's like it's pure evil all around you."

Custis said, "Well, men, that is just why we are here. To find that evil and wipe it out. Corporal, give us that last report you got."

Corporal Johnson cleared his throat and started, "Well, I got to thinking about that particular place and went to our land chart and figured that since yesterday, they must have covered about twenty or so miles."

He quickly got up and went over to his desk, He brought back a big printed map of the Eastern United States. He

The Saga of Robert E

spread it out on the desk and pointed to a dot he had put a circle around and said, "Now, this wasn't on the regular map before I put it there. There's a railhead further west. A little better than thirty miles that is now an official town. It even has a name. They call it Eberton. So I rung it up. A guy named Jimmy works that station and you know, he has seven kids and.."

Custis gave him the look and he gulped, "Sorry, Sir. Well, anyway, that trail is less than a mile south of him so he sent a couple of guys out to see if there was any action on it."

He stopped for a minute, as if he wanted them to ask him what they saw. The Major drummed his fingers on the desk and said, "Corporal Johnson, give us the news!"

Corporal Johnson knew that when the Major called him by his rank and in that tone, that he had better get on with it, so he continued,

"Well, Sir, they came back and told Jimmy that they didn't see anything. Since there wasn't any sign of tracks or anything, they just rode east for about fifteen minutes and saw nothing."

Pug asked, "Now when was this?"

Custis spoke up, "That was this afternoon about an hour ago. He just got the wire then."

Pug and the Sergeant looked at each other. They were all three thinking. Then, Pug asked, "Major, looks like we know where they are. How do you want to handle it?"

The Major then told them that the Corporal had already wired an order for a special train that can handle forty mounted horsemen and a supply wagon. He then said, "I'm waiting for a reply as to when it will be here."

He looked over at the Corporal and said, "Corporal, you have done a superb job. If this allows us to catch this bunch, I'm promoting you to Sergeant."

Pug and Bart said in unison, "We support that!"

Corporal Johnson's face was filled with a smile of pride. You could tell he was about to float.

Custis gave instructions, "Pug, I want you to pick the men for this job and Sergeant, I want you to start getting everything set up to move out first thing in the morning."

Pug interrupted, "Uh, Major, we need to go ahead and get started now. We still got a couple of hours of daylight and you know yourself, we have a lot of ground to cover."

Custis shrugged his shoulders as the Sergeant agreed. About that time, the telegraph at the other end of the large tent started clocking out its code. Johnson was on it before it even quit. They listened to the da dits as the Corporal wrote down the message. Sure enough, it was from Sheridan's headquarters. It confirmed the approval for the train and gave an estimated time of arrival of about six hours or so. It depended on how much time it took to get the cattle cars and all together. Otherwise, it would be at their siding a little before midnight. Pug was exuding pure adrenalin as he said, "Yes! That will be fine! That will give us enough time to get set and make the trip up to the railroad."

Corporal Johnson injected, "Uh, Major, I also requested a telegraph set up as well so that whenever you stop, you'll be able to send and receive."

Custis smiled and said, "Good boy! And how about a telegrapher? You want to go with us?"

Johnson gave a loud "Yessiree!"

Custis nodded to Pug and Pug said, "Done! We've got to get to work right away."

Custis stopped him and said, "Hey, guys. Get something to eat first. We've got time."

"Good idea, Sir", the Sergeant agreed, "I was wondering what that empty feeling was in my gut."

It was early the next morning and the girls were finishing their daily chores. There were over a dozen chickens now and as many biddies. There was always wood to chop and get ready for the stove. Emptying out the ashes wasn't the favorite job for any of the three. They were sitting down to a restful cup of coffee when a lone rider came riding into the yard. It was a soldier from the camp. He dismounted

The Saga of Robert E

and led his horse around to the back yard. By this time, the girls had heard him and were coming out of the kitchen to the porch. They looked at each other questioning in their mind as to what had happened. The soldier removed his hat as he looked at Hettie and asked, "Maam, are you Mrs. Hettie Lee?"

She nodded her head as the girls looked at each other. He then continued, "Well, maam, the Major and Lieutenant send their regrets that they will not be able to see you all anytime soon. They had to move out on an urgent mission last night."

Mercy and Rose were wide eyed as they listened to the young soldier. He continued, "The Major said you all would know where they were going and what they had to do."

The girls nodded together and Mercy asked, "When did they leave?"

"Well, maam, they had to be up at the railroad to catch the train when it arrived, It was due at midnight and it's about an hour's ride. They moved out early, though, just in case. Of course, they were quite anxious, you know."

Hettie quickly did the math and said, "Well, if it were me, I'd have left about ten thirty or so. Is that about right?"

Nodding, he replied, "They apparently mean business and are going to be gone awhile, judging from the supplies and armament they took with them. Two thirds of the camp went."

The soldier stopped for a minute and then continued, "Oh, yes. Lieutenant MacHenry said to tell Miss Rose..." He stopped and looked questioningly, as Rose identified herself. "Right, maam. The Lieutenant said to tell you he would tell you about the other end of the trail when he gets back...er, does that make sense to you?"

Rose and her sisters nodded as they laughingly answered, "Yes."

Hettie suddenly stopped and said, "Land o'goshen, girls. Where's our manners?" She turned to the soldier and said, "We were just having a fresh pot of coffee when you rode

Verne Foster

up. Taking a rest from our chores. Please, won't you stay a minute and have a cup with us? We have so many questions to ask you."

The young man replied, "Well, as a matter of fact, I missed breakfast awhile ago. A cup of coffee sounds good."

Rose seized the moment to extend her southern politeness and said,

"Do you eat grits, Soldier?"

The man smiled and said, "Yes maam. I've been down here long enough to know you don't put sugar on 'em."

Hettie smiled as she said, "Well, now. There's one more Yankee that's been converted. How do you take your eggs?"

He told her he liked them over light since he had learned how to mix them up in his grits. The girls asked him several questions about the mission, but he had limited information. As he finished his breakfast, he sort of summed it up with, "Ladies, that was a great meal and I really appreciate your hospitality. I wish I could tell you more, but everything happened so fast, none of us that are left know much about just what all is going on. We just know that the Major and both Lieutenant Mac Henry as well as our Topkick were real excited and anxious to get gone.

And...that's just what they did. Quite frankly, I've never seen so many things happen in such a short time as since the Major came. Man, we never had much of anything to do. Now, every day brings something new. It's like he brought a storm with him when he came."

This delighted the girls and they felt proud of their Robert E. After making his farewells, the soldier got in the saddle, nodded as he tipped his hat to the girls and rode off. Mercy, Rose, and Hettie looked at each other for a few minutes without saying anything, but they all three had a feeling of anxiety in their stomachs.

Chapter Thirty Four

It was well past midnight when the troops were all settled in their temporary home for possibly the next few days. The special cars that had been sent made good quarters for both man and beast. When all was loaded, the engineer pushed the throttle forward and the huge locomotive wheels quickly answered the force of the steam pressure and spun until they gained traction with steel against steel. You could feel the jerk of each car as it was suddenly pulled from its resting place. In minutes, the train was moving full throttle down the track headed west. Nothing had been left out. A private car had been included to be used as a command car (compliments of General Sheridan). It belonged to a railroad executive. Custis did not question it. It would be well used. There were sleeping quarters as well as a large room to be used for the office. Custis considered Pug and the First Sergeant as his immediate staff. When he included Corporal Johnson, the young man was so excited that he couldn't sleep and spent most of the rest of the trip tinkering with his equipment and getting it ready to send or receive. He had a nice table he used for laying out the map and started drawing his own for the journey.

Certainly there was enough adrenalin to go around for everyone. The troops had been completely filled in while they were waiting for the train to arrive. They knew the full account of their mission and this was the topic of interest

Verne Foster

that replaced sleep for them. They were all battle hardened and found themselves anxious to get into battle again. Custis had laid out the plan of attack well. As the train moved down the tracks, the lulling movement of the cars and the clack clack of the wheels against the rail sections soon had its affect and overcame the adrenalin, as all were soon asleep getting much needed rest after their long day of events. Custis had given orders to the train crew as full speed ahead. It was a long distance to overcome and they needed every minute of make up time they could get. The engineer obliged and opened the throttle.

As the sun came up, it was enough to awaken most of the men. Custis was up at first light and delighted in the onboard facilities that the railroad had provided. This truly was a special train. The men were served in the mess coach while Custis and his staff were served in their car. By now, Johnson had put together a new map of the area where they were headed. He had a special talent for such. Custis studied the new map carefully familiarizing himself with the stations and even the nearby forts. These were important for possible assistance if needed. That, he hoped, would never be a necessity. He had learned by experience several things. One was to choose your time and place of battle, if possible.

Two was to plan to have superior numbers to start with.

Three was to have the element of surprise on your side. He had fought against the man and though he was a Confederate, he mustered not only respect, but admiration for General Forrest. Custis stopped for a moment and relived that night in Memphis in August of 1864 when General Nathan Bedford Forrest rode in suddenly with 2000 cavalry in an audacious raid. Had it not been for Custis' ability to learn from the enemy and use knowledge gained in battle to his own advantage, Forrest would have taken two Union generals captive. Custis was reminiscing how his men were able to move the generals just in time and his cavalry was affective in turning the tide. He thought of how he suddenly rode up

The Saga of Robert E

face to face with General Nathan Bedford Forrest himself in the heat of the battle. They looked at each other for what seemed to Custis as forever. He remembered the General's face not five feet from him. He wore a heavy goatee. Sweat was pouring down his face as he suddenly reined up and could have easily killed Custis and visa versa. However, over all the noise of the battle going on around them, he merely said, "I remember you from when I hit Sherman at Brice's Cross Roads back in June. You got a good head on your shoulders and one helluva fighter, so remember what I always say, "The fustest with the mostest." With that, he turned and rode off. He thought of how easily they could have killed each other, but that tremendous respect for each other as warriors kept them alive. Custis had practiced that every since. Even in this case, though he figured about a dozen adversaries, he would take no chance and, like General Forrest, gave no quarter.

They had spent thirty six long hours on their train, but now, they were pulling into Opal Junction. It was really nothing but a couple of buildings as far as he could see, but when he thought about it, it was about like the little hamlet where camp was. He pondered to himself, "Hmmm, our little town should have a name."

The troops took a break from the train and exercised their horses around the area. Custis studied the lay of the land and compared it to the new map Corporal Johnson had drawn up. He looked at the map and there was a rail stop and a fort a few miles further down the track. He noticed that the wagon trail came quite close to it. Just as he was about to call Corporal Johnson to get him to contact them, Johnson came out from the car and reported, "Sir, I've just got through talking to my buddy at Fort Mercer. It's a little over twenty miles from here. I thought you'd like to see if they had any sign of a wagon train lately."

Custis just shook his head as he muttered, "You are starting to read my mind, Corporal." The Corporal just stood there

Verne Foster

for a minute as he took that for a great compliment. Custis broke his reverie as he asked, "Well, what did he say?"

"Well, Sir, they have no sign of anything like that. The Army has a daily patrol of the area and they usually check out the trail in case someone happens along and breaks down or something."

"When was the last patrol?"

"Just this morning. They usually do it a couple of times a day."

"Well, I wonder if they've gotten this far yet?"

"Well, what if we sent out a patrol to check it out for ourselves?"

Custis thought about this, then said, "These guys are probably well acquainted with that trail and know it comes close to an Army post. They might have taken a detour." He then told Pug to have a couple of men take a quick ride to the trail and see if they could check out any tracks. He added, "Have them keep out of sight. Make no contact. If they see the wagon train passing, just come on back as fast as they can and report."

Custis and Johnson went to the station and talked with Hank. Hank expressed his pleasure in meeting his "on wire" buddy in person. He was impressed with the apparent importance of the matter with the special train and all the troops. Custis was coming out of the station office when their patrol returned. They reported to him as soon as they rode in. The senior man saluted and spoke, "Sir, we saw tracks on the trail. Several wagons and horses. No attempt to hide them seemed to be made. We tracked them west for about a mile. Apparently, they're somewhere near here on the trail, because the tracks are fresh. Some of the ruts are deep, too. They're carrying a heavy load."

The Major thanked them and called for Pug. Apparently, the culprits were between here and the Fort Mercer cut off. This seemed evident. Pug came over to him and Custis gave his orders, "Lieutenant, you take half the men and hit the trail from this end. Send point men ahead. If they locate

The Saga of Robert E

them, try not to let them know they're being followed. Meanwhile, I'll take the rest of the troop and continue on to Fort Mercer. Hopefully, we'll be able to double back and cut them off. However, if they do see you and make a run for it, chase them toward me and we'll be waiting for them ahead. Don't hesitate to attack. According to the information we've gathered, the land is rather flat with some big rocks on either side of the trail. So, remember now, I want to box them in. When our scouts spot them, we'll form a flank and wait for 'em. By then, you should be close enough to see what is happening. Then, if they make a brake, we'll make a full charge from all sides.

He stopped for a moment to let that sink in, then, he added, "Remember, we don't want any of them to get away. Stop 'em dead or alive. It doesn't matter an iota which."

He looked away for a minute toward the men, then said, "Now if I can get this Sam what's his name alive, it would be nice, but definitely is not necessary. You understand? This is no different from any of our battles."

Pug grinned and replied, "We've never lost one yet, huh Major?" He hesitated a second, then added, "Me and you, that is!"

The two officers shook hands and parted. Pug called for the Sergeant. They would separate the men for the mission. The Sergeant pulled half the troop out of the way of the train. He would be going with Pug. Pug did a quick job of outlining their battle plan. He then gave the order for the remainder to board the train. The preparation went smoothly and quickly. Within thirty minutes, the troops had their horses back on the train and ready to ride. Some of the men preferred to stay with their mounts while the others took to the cars. Custis was already aboard by now and was instructing Corporal Johnson as to what he expected of him. He was to remain with the train when they moved out. There would be a rear guard with him. He was to be in charge. His main responsibility was to keep the train ready

Verne Foster

for anything that might come up and for communication with the Fort just in case.

Corporal Johnson was very pleased with this assignment. He loved the chance to be of actual field service. He was a capable soldier who knew his job well. He also was a thinker. As a result of their conversation, he quickly followed the Major's instructions and got off a wire to Fort Mercer. It explained the situation and requested a rear guard unit to protect the train during the maneuver. He privately, on his own, sent a wire to General Sheridan's office. He thought to himself, "Might as well cover all areas." This type of personal action was proving his high capability in serving his Major. He had already gained a high regard for Custis and was a dedicated fan as were all the other men in the unit. Custis seemed to have that charisma that made you want to join him in his efforts. The Corporal thought, "I'll bet he was a leader even when he was a kid."

He got the reply from the Fort just as the train was ready to pull out. He disconnected his wire from the line that ran along side the track. As the train moved forward, he informed the Major, "Sir! The Fort acknowledges receipt of your wire."

Custis asked him was that all. He replied, "Yessir, but I am sure you will get their full and ready cooperation."

Custis nodded as he settled down at his desk. Johnson smiled as he thought to himself of his wire to General Sheridan's office, "Yes, I am sure you will get COMPLETE cooperation."

Chapter Thirty Five

By the time the train reached Fort Mercer station, which was about a half mile south of the Fort, the rear guard detail from the Fort he had requested was waiting for him. There was a corporal in charge of the eight man squad. All cavalry. The Corporal reported to Major Custis as the men were getting off the train and forming their company. He said, "Major, our Commander offers any assistance you might need. He received a wire directly from General Sheridan to do so."

Custis looked at Johnson and Corporal Johnson just smiled and shrugged his shoulders. Custis wanted this to be his battle though, so he told the squad leader he appreciated the offer, but he would need nothing else for right now. He went on to explain to the Corporal, "Acting Sergeant Johnson here will be in charge of this scene."

The Corporal nodded and quickly said, "I understand, Sir. We'll take our orders from him." He then saluted the Major.

As the Major returned the salute, he looked around at Corporal Johnson, who was now basking in glory, and through squinted eyes, quietly said, "It sure looks like I'm going to have to watch you." Then, he grinned letting Johnson know it was in jest.

Corporal Johnson beamed as he said, "You can count on me, Major! Uh, Sir, when you said that about acting sergeant..."

Custis cut him off and said, "I meant it, soldier. You're earning it!" Custis looked at him for a second and thought to himself, "I hope I don't have to tie him down to keep him from floating off." The thought made him chuckle out loud as he walked toward his horse.

The troops were lined up in two columns on their horses when he swung into his saddle. He said, "Men, let me have your attention. You already know why we're here. You've been briefed. Are there any questions?" No one had any, so he went on, "Well, troops, we've certainly been in this position many times before, so let's get on with it."

With that, he reined up in front of the column. He called out, "Guidon! Post!" The trooper moved into position behind him and in front of the right file. He watched as the unit's banner fluttered in the breeze. The trooper yelled, "Guidon posted, Sir!"

Major Custis raised his right hand and yelled, "At a gallop, Forward Ho!" The troop moved rapidly over the short distance to the trail. As they approached the intersection, the Major raised his hand for a halt. He could see a good way up the trail from where he was at the crossing. He inspected the dirt and saw no recent tracks. It had apparently rained recently and made for a clean slate as far as tracks were concerned. Off in the distance, there were some big mounds on either side of the trail. He noticed the trail seemed to work its way through this hilly section of land. Trees were on both sides, but none grew really close to the trail. His heart raced as he could see they were apparently ahead of the wagon train.

He called out two of the front men and assigned them the point position. They rode off back toward the east. He had no idea just where the wagon train was, but he was sure it was between him and Pug. His plan was to form a rank as soon as he was within sight of them. Then, if they had not seen Pug's troop and turned around to run, he would pursue. If they saw they were being followed and ran toward him, then Pug's troop would pursue and they would wait. Either

The Saga of Robert E

way, one would chase them into the other. He expected also a report from the scouts as to the lay of the land for battle purposes. It would dictate whether nature would keep them on the trail or whether the soldiers would have to surround them. They moved toward Pug's group at a slow pace waiting for the scouts to report back.

It was close to a half hour when the scouts returned. Custis' unit had traveled almost two miles. The scouts reported they had found the group. They were stopped and it looked as if they were taking a food break. They had built a fire and were cooking something. Apparently, they saw no need for lookouts. They were camped by a small creek that ran a short distance by the trail and disappeared into the next hill as quickly as it came out of the other one. Custis thought about it. This was too good to be true. Maybe the souls of all the men they'd killed were having an influence on fate to set it up like this. Surely, Pug's group will see this as well; however, he might not be anywhere near there yet. He thought again, "Knowing Pug, he probably had moved at a gallop all the way." Pug was not one to hesitate to get into battle. Custis knew though that he could count on him to follow the plan and not deviate for the sake of self satisfaction.

This latest development changed the plan a little. On one hand, it gave him the advantage of a surprise attack, but on the other, unless Pug was in place, some of them might get away. This was not an option to Custis. He really didn't care about any particular one except this guy Sam. He was the whole cheese as far as the Major was concerned.

The lead scout inquired, "Well, Major, I know this changes the plan. What now?"

Custis replied, "If I only knew where Pug's troop was."

"Well, Sir, it looks like our prey had just stopped shortly before we located them. They'll probably be there for awhile. As a matter of fact, they were starting to unfasten their teams to take them over to the stream to water them. Now that'll take awhile."

He hesitated and the Major sensed he had more to say, so he asked him what he had on his mind. "Well, Sir, I was thinking maybe we could skirt around them and make contact with Lieutenant Pug. A man on horse could skirt those hills in just a little while. The Lieutenant can't be too very far away and, if I know him, he probably has his scouts in tandem. While one is reporting, another one is forward."

The Major marveled at the common sense this made. He had long ago learned to listen to his men anytime they had an idea. This is what made him as successful as he was. He called the two men together and told them of the plan. He asked, "How far are we from them? "

"Only a little over a mile, a mile and a half at most, Major."

Custis said, "Then, let's do it. You two want the job?" They both jumped at the chance. They had already become familiar with a little of the area, so they were the choice anyway. The Major told them to contact Pug and tell him to close in from the East. He would move his column up until he was as close as he could be without being seen. They would stay out of sight in case the culprits decided to send out a scout ahead. He then told the scouts to tell the Lieutenant to move into position and wait for the signal.

The soldier asked what it would be. Custis said, "Tell him to listen for the gunfire. Since we will be coming in from the West, they will probably try and head back east. That's when Pug can cut them off and stop them."

The scout asked, "Sir, the lay of the land is so that they could head either north or south, too. What about then?"

"We'll anticipate that and handle that as it happens. I believe they will go for the wagons for protection if we come in shooting."

The soldier saluted and left. Major Custis watched the pair ride off in the distance. The men had heard this discussion and knew what they had to do. Custis spelled it out for them. They would wait for the return of one of the scouts. This would tell them Pug was in place. They would

The Saga of Robert E

then attack. He also told them that these were ruthless cutthroats that would not hesitate to kill. He emphasized to be on the lookout for the men on the Appaloosas. He then instructed them to be careful and not shoot the Appaloosas. He wanted them for a prize.

After waiting for only about a half hour, the scouts returned. They reported that Lieutenant Pug was almost even with them on the other side by the time they got around the crooks. They further told Custis that the Lieutenant said he would be in position and would attack on the signal.

The men were already mounted and ready for the charge. The Major's heart raced with anticipation as he climbed into the saddle. He remembered well the last time he made a charge into the enemy with only one gun. This time, he had the second one tucked into his sash on the left side with its butt facing his front. When they were within earshot of the hijackers, Custis yelled, "Charge!" He was in the lead when one of the hijackers turned from his chore and grabbed for his rifle. Custis' aim was true and deadly. He was a white man and not an Indian. He never got a shot off. He lurched backwards and hit the ground with a thud. Custis looked specifically for this Sam. He figured he would be a fighter. As his eyes searched the bedlam of men running and shooting, dodging behind wagons and yelling, his eyes caught a glimpse of something he had not expected. Something he had hoped would not happen!

Chapter Thirty Six

Pug's forces quickly moved in from the opposite side and the battle was short lived. However, in the middle of the bedlam, the one man Custis wanted the most apparently wasn't there. The troops literally ran over the camp and when the body count was in, eight of the raiders were dead and the other six were begging for their lives. All of the Indians were dead. There were only two Appaloosas accounted for. Where was the leader? This Sam was really more important to Custis than the rest of them. He had hoped to catch him in battle and thereby put an end to him. He knew, with his connections, he stood a chance of getting off. Custis also knew General Sheridan would not like that any more than he did.

The attack was so overwhelming and fast, it left the raiders who were still alive literally in shock. They had never been exposed to such and yet, this was the hallmark of their leader. Custis was beside himself. He just couldn't let Sam get away. Where was he?

The remaining six raiders were all tied together in a special roping technique the Sergeant offered. They were tied to one of the wagons. This wagon had several kegs of black powder on it. Custis heard Pug give the order, "If they so much as try to get away, don't bother to shoot'em! Just shoot into the powder and we won't even have to bury'em."

The fugitives looked at each other in fear and one of them hollered to the Major, "You can't do that! It's inhuman!"

Custis just laughed as he got off his horse and walked over to them. He got face to face with the man and sneered, "Just give us a reason! Give us a reason! You've tangled with the wrong men here!

We've survived most of the battles in the war and we're still alive because we know when and how to kill."

One of the six tested the Major with, "You won't do anything to us. It's against the law and you know it."

Custis queried, "And just who do you think is the law way out here in the lonesome? We are!" He looked at the other men and said, "You know you probably won't make it back east, don't you?" The men looked at each other and the fear could clearly be seen in their faces. Seeing this, Custis seized the opportunity and continued, "Of course, we could be sure nothing will happen to you if you decide to cooperate with me."

One of the men quickly said, "Major, whatever it takes. Please have mercy on us. We know what we've been a part of and we know we're going to die for it."

Custis cut him off, saying, "If you ever told the truth in your life, you just did!"

The first prisoner that had called to him said, "I know you apparently hate us, but if there's any bargaining to be done, we're ready to do anything you say." He turned to the rest of them and nodded his head as he said, "Ain't that right, fellers?"

Pug had silently witnessed all this and knew well what his Major was after. He drew his revolver out and placed it to the man's crotch. He looked him straight in the eyes as he said, "Major, I think he's lying."

Custis picked up on Pug's lead and said, "Me too. Show'em what we do to liars!"

Pug pulled the hammer back with his thumb. All six men screamed as Pug squeezed the trigger. The man just flooded his trousers as the hammer slammed against the empty chamber. That loud Colt click was drowned out by their screams. Pug was nose to nose with him as he took him by the collar and hissed, "Oops. Guess I forgot to reload." The man went limp and slid down to the ground pulling the others with him to a sitting position.

The Major was standing with his feet apart and hands curled into fists. He softly and distinctly said, "I will only ask you once. If I do not hear what I want to hear, I will turn you over to the Lieutenant here who is very anxious to work out his frustrations on you. We've seen what you did with the bodies of your fake Lieutenant and Sergeant. This Lieutenant and Sergeant here take it very grimly and personal. Did you know we didn't even bury'em? Well, we classify you guys the same garbage as them."

The six were silent. No one spoke. They waited intently leaning on every word he might say. As Custis spoke, Pug was very noticeably reloading his revolver and smiling and would steal a deliberate glance at them each time he loaded a chamber. The original spokesman for the six was a limp soggy mess now and couldn't even speak. Finally, one of the men almost screamed, "What do you want!!! For God's sake, man, just tell us what you want! We'll do anything! We'll tell you anything you want to know!"

The Sergeant stepped over to him and looked down at him in a steely glare and said softly, "The truth. Just tell the Major what he wants to know and no lying!"

They all nodded their heads except the first man. He just sat there staring at the ground. The man next to him asked pleadingly, "Uh, would it be possible for you to let him clean up? He's making me sick."

Custis was now convinced that he would get honest answers. He stepped over to them. He looked down at the first man and then said to the one next to him, "You're right. He stinks." He then moved away a little and said, "I am looking for Sam. He is not here. Tell me where he is and I won't give you to these guys."

Verne Foster

He raised his index finger to emphasize his question as he continued, "Now think before you answer. You have only one chance. If even one of you lies, your bodies will not be recognizable if someone finds them."

The men did not have to even hesitate. They all started at once. "He went and hid in them woods back there when it all started! He was watering his horse. He was right over there next to those trees." The man talking motioned with his head in the direction he spoke of.

Custis asked again, "Where does that stream come from and where would you look for him now?"

"It comes out of some rocks about a half mile up stream from here. I'd look for him to come out about half way from here to the railroad. He'll probably head west."

Custis looked at Pug for a second, then bolted for his horse. He reined the animal around and headed upstream. There was a lot of area to cover and he did not want to waste another minute. He heard Pug shout, "Major! Wait!" With that, he disappeared into the woods.

That scene brought back to Pug's mind when the Major had disappeared from him in battle before and did not come back. This gave him an anxiety to quickly follow. He called the troops together and quickly gave the orders to secure the wagons. There were five wagons of arms and ammunition. Then, there was a water wagon and a supply wagon.

The Sergeant yelled out, "Give me drivers for these wagons and a guard for each one. Remove those barrels of water and use that wagon for these guys and their dead buddies."

Pug stepped up and said, "I want you to take them to the train. When you get there, have Corporal Johnson send the prisoners and the dead to the Fort. The detail from the Fort can do this. Your orders are to not let the guns and ammo out of your sight. No one messes with them until the Major returns. We will inventory it all when we get back. Corporal Johnson will be in charge."

The Saga of Robert E

There was no hesitation or lack of volunteers out of these men. Immediately, the men started pushing the barrels out of the wagon. As they hit the ground, the wooden barrels burst as the weight of the water overcame the staves and their straps. By this time, they had taken the one prisoner loose from the others and bared him from the waist down. They let him clean himself and his clothes from the one barrel of water remaining. In jig time, the wagons had drivers and outriders. These men all were used to taking orders quickly and quietly. As they were preparing for the trip back to the train, Pug told the Sergeant, "You take the rest of the men and cover every inch from here to the road that goes over to the Fort. I'm going after the Major! I lost him once, but never again!"

Before the Sergeant could say anything, Pug was riding off in the direction the Major had gone. The Sergeant shrugged his shoulders and walked over to the wagons which were now prepared to move. The troops had let the loosed man retrieve another pair of trousers and had him trussed again. He was a lot more alert now, but still heavily shaken. The Sergeant couldn't help but grin as he thought about the man. It would definitely be worse than a fatal blow for someone to shoot off your testicles. The Sergeant wondered if the Lieutenant really thought his revolver was loaded or knew it wasn't and did that just to put a scare into the guy. He knew fully well that Custis or Pug was fully capable of doing either. That is what made it so weird. The Sergeant said to himself, "I've got to know the answer to that one." That thought brought him back to the subject at hand.

The wagons were pulling out just as ordered. The soldiers driving them had fastened their mounts to the rear of the wagons and the soldiers riding "shotgun" were riding along side their assigned wagon with rifles in hand. They had the butt of the rifle against their thigh and held it upright with their trigger finger placed outside the trigger guard. He called the rest of the troops together and told them how he wanted them deployed. With rifles drawn and in place, they

Verne Foster

would travel into the wooded area about thirty feet apart. At no time were they to ever be out of earshot from the next man. They then moved out in the direction they had come from. He had told the troops with the wagons to also scrutinize the woods and trail as they traveled back to the railroad.

So they began their search together in a line. They were close enough to see each other and slowly guided their horses around trees and boulders. The ground was covered with millions of leaves which made a thick carpet to walk on. This helped muffle the sound. It was an eerie picture of stealth and search as they moved ever so deliberately and silently through the trees. If there were anyone in their path, they would be found.

Chapter Thirty Seven

Pug headed upstream and found an easy trail to follow. Custis had made a clear trail as to where he went. One could tell he was in a tremendous hurry. Pug thought, "I sure hope the Major don't get in too much of a hurry and get himself shot."

He suddenly came upon a clear trail leaving the stream and heading, as best Pug could tell, south to southwest. The forest was not nearly as thick as it was near the stream and one could see quite a distance around oneself. Pug had a lot of tracking experience and soon could tell he was following two men on horses. He thought, "Well, that certainly makes sense."

He continued patiently for close to twenty minutes. By now, though, he had dismounted and was leading his horse behind him as he searched more closely for clues. It was then that he hard a loud voice. It was near enough to understand what was said and recognize the voice. It was the Major. He heard Custis say loudly, "It's over, Sam!"

Pug then headed toward the sound of the voice. As he hurried along through the trees, he could see a sort of a clearing up ahead. As he approached it, his heart beat triple time. There was Custis facing the man he easily recognized from his description. It was the fast gun Sam that the girls had talked about. He came out of the woods into the clearing slightly behind Custis. He saw the low slung holster and all.

Sam saw him walk up and Custis heard him behind him. The two men were about forty feet apart. Custis never changed his look. He shouted over his shoulder to Pug, "Stay out of this, Pug! You're looking at a piece of garbage that is an insult to all that is good! I'll deal with this!"

Pug knew this was not a request and backed off a bit, but Sam told him to "stay put!" Pug was ready to assist at any time, but wanted to wait for his Major's play. Anyway, he had his orders and obeyed. He watched as Sam tried to con Custis into a duel with him. Pug did not like this, but he remained still.

There was this eerie calm about Custis that he had not witnessed before. Custis told the man, "I'm taking you back to hang."

Sam laughed and said, "Never, soldier. I can take both of you anytime I want." He looked at Custis curiously and asked, "Just who are you, Major? And why are you so concerned that you will even face me gunning you down? You're nothing but a tin soldier that knows from nothing!"

"Oh, you are right about that. I am a soldier that has the duty to bring you back. Now, slowly undo your gunbelt and let it fall free!"

Pug's hand had been on his revolver the whole time. Sam knew it, but it did not seem to bother him. His hand tensed at what would happen next. The man sneered and mockingly said, "Well, looky here now. See the little blue coat acting brave and trying to tell me what to do!"

Custis's eyes were like firebrands. His eyes never left Sam's eyes.

He spoke again in a calm but emphatic manner, "I won't tell you again! Unbuckle your gunbelt and let it fall free!"

Pug was wishing he had a better position. He needed to be farther away to the side of the Major. Even though he was well behind Custis, Sam had the advantage of having them both close enough together not to have to change directions for a second shot. Pug also realized he dare not move. As sweatbeads began to form on his forehead, he wondered

The Saga of Robert E

at the extreme coolness of his Major. Custis was not only relaxed, but he had a cold confidence about him as if he already knew what the outcome would be. He wasn't the only one who noticed this. Sam had apparently noticed it too and could tell his taunts were making no impression on this soldier.

Sam's face went stoic as he changed his stance and was face to face with Custis. It was plain to be seen that Sam's curiosity about this man was not about to get in his way of killing him. It was now time to get down to business. He threw out his challenge, saying, "Well, soldier boy, I can't help but wonder about you, but I don't have the time to play anymore. I guess I'm just going to have to kill you both so I can be on my way."

Custis said nothing. He was like a stone statue. His eyes were searching Sam's eyes intensely. He seemed completely relaxed. Pug had never seen this side of him before.

Sam said sarcastically, "Well, sonny boy, I guess it's time to teach you not to mess with a real man!"

Custis never batted an eye. Then it happened! Sam went for his gun with the speed of light itself. He was as fast as the girls had said. A shot rang out and Pug heard it echo through the woods. Sam lurched and staggered back. His gun hand went limp and his revolver fell from it. He was fast enough to have cocked it as he drew it out of the holster, but that was as far as he got. His face showed extreme shock, as if he couldn't believe what had just happened. He looked at Pug with a quizzical look as if he might have thought the shot came from him. He dropped to his knees as he tried to look at Custis. It was Custis who was holding his six gun in his hand. Sam then fell over on his back on the ground.

Pug had that same look of puzzled shock on his face. He also looked around to see who fired the shot. At first, he thought it might have been one of their men shooting from the trees. Only the three of them were there. He looked at Custis who was putting his second gun back in his sash. He was watching Sam as Sam just lay there. His left leg crossed

Verne Foster

under his outstretched right leg. He had a pained grimace on his face. Blood was flooding his shirt and vest. The ball had not hit the heart, but it was a lethal wound.

Pug just stood there and watched as Custis slowly walked over to the man on the ground. Sam was trying to say something. Pug overcame his amazement now and walked over and stood by Custis looking down at the man. Custis leaned down to hear what Sam had to say. Pug did likewise. His curiosity tearing at him. Sam was having more and more trouble breathing and was trying to speak in great effort as if he had to know something. He said, "I'm dying. Just tell me one thing. How can a mere soldier like you handle a six gun like that? I've got to know!"

Custis grinned as he replied, "Well, Sam, my Uncle Eustice finished raising me from a young teenage boy and he had a close friend that used to come over all the time. That man took a liking to me and through the years, taught me all the tricks of the trade. Now, my Aunt Emma never did take to violence, but Uncle Eustice said it was good for me and might just save my life one day."

Pug could tell Sam didn't have long, but he heard him ask almost pleadingly, "Tell me who he was. I gotta know! What was his name?"

Pug looked at Custis as the Major smiled a mischievous smile. He replied, "Well, I always called him Uncle Bill, but most everybody that knew him called him Wild Bill. Wild Bill Hickock."

Sam grimaced and had trouble speaking now as he slowly said, "Wild Bill Hickock! Of all things. Me and him had trouble out West before I came back to the East. He said he would get me someday. I guess he did after all." With that, Sam let out his last drawn breath. His body went limp.

Custis just stood and looked down at the dead man. Pug stood up and looked at Custis for a minute and then asked, "Major, have you got any other secrets I don't know about? I mean, I just knew he was going to get one of us and more than likely, both of us! The girls saw him draw and they said

The Saga of Robert E

it was so quick, they hardly saw it! You beat him! You out drew a fast gun!"

Custis cautioned, "Pug, don't go telling anybody about what you saw. We were just lucky today. We got the bad guy and that's all anyone has to know. Promise me!" Pug nodded and reluctantly promised.

It wasn't long before one of the soldiers came riding in. He had heard the shot and headed in the direction of it. He reined up. Seeing his two officers were alright, he dismounted and reported with a salute. Pug and Custis told him all was fine and the mission had been accomplished. In a short time, the other soldiers came riding in from the woods. Custis gave instructions for them to put Sam over his horse and to take him back to the Fort. As the men picked up the body, Custis asked the Sergeant, who had just arrived, "Has everything been taken care of?"

With a look of awe, the Sergeant answered, "Well, Sir, it sure looks like it...er...I mean, Yessir." He then gave a full report on what he had done. Pug and Custis both approved.

"You've done well, Sergeant. Now let's get on back to the train and see how our acting Sergeant's doing." Pug and the Sergeant chuckled, but they had the confidence all would be well.

They mounted their horses. It was obvious to them to just head south for the trail to the Fort instead of backtracking all the way to the wagon trail. As they rode, Pug asked Custis, "Why were you so dead set on getting this one man? I mean, it was like you had a vengeance."

Custis rode thoughtfully for a minute or two before he answered and then, he merely said, "I have no idea. I really don't know."

Pug started to say something, but the Major cut him off with, "I know what you're going to say, but, it was just a coincidence. I don't believe in that weird hogwash about him and Wild Bill." Yet, Custis thought to himself, "I wonder. I wonder." Then, he dismissed the thought with "Naaaaaa!"

Chapter Thirty Eight

Soon, they were back at the railhead. Corporal Johnson came running out of the command car and before the Major had even dismounted, he was asking when the Major would like to make his report to General Sheridan. Custis dismounted and simply said, "Not yet."

Custis was more interested in getting the three Appaloosas taken care of than sending a report. As military protocol dictates, Johnson was relieved of his command when the senior officer came upon the scene. Custis didn't have to ask Johnson for a report, Johnson was already updating him as they walked toward the horses. He had been in constant contact with the Fort and they were ready to process the prisoners and the dead. The Major told Johnson he would need to make a full report of the incident, but would do it later. The train had sufficient empty cars. One of Custis' traits was that he always approached a plan in the positive. He anticipated accomplishing what he came to do and was prepared for it. Now, he gave orders for a quick inventory of the arms and ammo. The dead and the prisoners were turned over to the detail from the Fort with a report of what happened and they were shipped off. As for the horses, they would take them with them on the train for later use with the wagons. The riders' horses were considered spoils and would be taken back with them also.

Verne Foster

Once all the details were handled and Custis was back in his command car, he could concentrate on the report to Sheridan. The Troop had been invited to the Fort for a meal before they left. Custis accepted and formed the Troop for the short ride there. He told his men, "We are a proud group and we want to look like it, so be at your best.

Red sashes and all."

Custis and Pug took the lead followed by the First Sergeant. The Guidon in place leading the right file with the Troop riding in pairs behind the Guidon. The guard detail for the train was not left out. They had gone ahead and were fed ahead of the Troop. As the Troop entered the Fort, they caused quite a stir with their elegant dress and perfect formation. Custis was not the only proud one.

Major Custis had planned to move out immediately, but the Fort Commander was so gracious, and his men deserved a much needed break, that the trip back was postponed. Little did Custis know that General Sheridan's office had been in contact with Corporal Johnson constantly during the episode. The General gave orders for the Corporal not to disclose what he was doing. In Custis' communication to the General requesting the special train and what it was for, he had included the reason he was able to zero in on the culprits was directly due to the information the girls had supplied. He had made the remark that he wished they were in the Army so he could give them an award.

The trip back took longer since they were not under "full speed ahead" conditions. They could even enjoy the countryside as the train whistled through the valleys and knolls. It was impressive to cross the big Chattahoochee River heading into Georgia. When the train finally arrived at its railhead, there were a couple of cars already sitting there. Custis wondered whose or what they were there for. He paid them no mind though, since the railroad also used that siding. The train pulled onto the long siding, thus clearing the track for use. There was a rear guard left with it and Custis and the troop rode south toward the camp.

The trip had taken almost two complete days and he knew the men were ready to get back to camp. Their quarters on the train were comfortable, but, it is still nice to get back to where you live. It was still fairly early in the day, so he decided to just take the animals back to camp and deal with the train later.

This time, they did not go through town, but cut across on a hypotenuse and saved about a half hour as well as avoiding taking the horses through the street. As the Major rode up to the guard, he noticed that he seemed almost excited as he snapped to attention and saluted. Custis returned the salute and rode on into camp. It was then that he noticed an unusual stir about the place and an extra guard was at the command tent. The Troop drew to a halt as Custis was dismounting.

Who should come bounding out of the tent but General Sheridan himself. Now this was an astounding surprise to Custis. Custis was now the one who snapped to attention as he saluted the man whose troops referred to as "Little Phil". Sheridan was all smiles as he returned the salute and said, "At ease, Major! At ease!" With that, he put on his hat with its brim turned up on the left side and the medallion holding it in place. It was only then when Custis noticed the red sash as well.

A wooden floor had been constructed for the tent and it extended out in front of the entrance as a stoop. As General Sheridan remained on it facing Custis, he was still not as tall as the Major standing down on the ground. Pug thought to himself, "He might be only five feet tall, but when he is in the field, he is at least ten feet tall." The General said, "Dismiss your men, Major, and come on in."

Custis nodded to Pug and as he stepped up on the deck, the General put his arm around his back as he led him through the entrance. Corporal Johnson was right behind them. As he came through the door, Custis turned to him with a look that caught the General's eye. The General was quick to reply, "This must be the Corporal Johnson I've been in contact with."

He noticed the worried look on Johnson's face and had seen Custis' look. He continued, "The Corporal and I are old friends now. He was acting under my orders to tell no one I planned to be here. Sit down. We have a lot to discuss."

Custis looked around at the Corporal. Johnson had the silliest grin on his face Custis had ever seen. He was holding his chin up and had a smile so big, it closed his eyes. He looked like an editorial cartoon. Custis thought, "Oh, God! That did it! Now, I'll have to give him special permission not to wear a hat! We'll never find one to fit him anymore."

Custis just grinned as he offered the General his chair behind the desk. As the Corporal took their hats, Custis dared not look at him for fear of laughing. He did smile, though, as he sat down across from the General and said, "Well, Sir. Your uniform is certainly becoming to you. It makes me proud that you like it."

The General nodded, but was excited in his demeanor. "I'm aware you brought the missing arms and ammo back with you. Did you leave them at the railhead?" Custis nodded. Sheridan nodded thoughtfully, "Hmmm, that was a good plan. I want to return those rifles and ammo to the Quartermaster. Not letting them out of your sight was just what I would have done."

"Well, General, I left them at the railhead under guard and plan to unload them later."

"I'll save you the trouble, Major. I have enough men with me. Just leave them on the train and we can take them back with us. You have the inventory."

"Yes Sir. It's all in my report."

"Great. The Quartermaster will be delighted." Sheridan then leaned forward and said, "Major, one of the main reasons I came here myself was because something you said in your message. It was about those three ladies."

Custis was curiously puzzled. "What about them, Sir?"

The Saga of Robert E

"Major, it was because of them you were able to solve this mystery and complete your mission as rapidly as you did. An astounding feat! They may be Rebels, but they are also Union heroes, or heroines, whichever."

He stood up, too excited to remain sitting, and continued, as he paced, "I want to take any possibility I can to re-unite the country. You might not realize it, but here are Rebels who think enough of their country to help capture the enemy of both the North and the South! I like it and I have made arrangements to do something about it!"

Custis just sat in awe and listened, wondering what was coming next.

"You probably haven't had the time to get acquainted with Mrs. Bowden, but she and her husband run the local general store here. I had your men here contact her to see if she had any idea the sizes of those three ladies. She did, so I brought three fine dresses with me and have told her to take them out to the girls and make sure they fit. Now, it seems the girls were reluctant, at first, but this woman is, in my opinion, a social climber. Not wanting to lose this chance to be of service, convinced the girls to take them and between the girls and her, the alterations were made."

Now, the General seemed more excited about this social engagement he was planning than the business at hand. He joyously continued, "Major, I am planning a celebration for not only the solving of a terrible crime and ending the career of a traitor, but also the rewarding of those three girls for their contribution to it. It will take place tomorrow here at the camp. All the locals are invited."

As Custis started to say something, Sheridan continued, "Major, you have just gotten the highest award this country has to give. I have contacted General Grant and he is in complete agreement with me to do two things. You will find out those things tomorrow at the ceremony,."

Major Custis and General Sheridan spent the rest of the afternoon in conference while the men finished a raised platform out in the field that faced the road. Custis told

Verne Foster

the General about the Appaloosas. He wished to give them to the girls. He also told him about the riders' horses and how he would like to also give them to the girls to help them get started again. Sheridan thought it was a great plan and he would handle it personally. They made plans to escort the girls out the next morning. Custis and Pug both wanted to ride out to see the girls, but the General had put out the order that no one was to leave the camp except on business. By nightfall, the ceremonial stand was finished and decorated with red, white, and blue cloth. Custis wondered how the Southerners would accept this. He would find out the next day.

Chapter Thirty Nine

It was a beautiful morning and the temperature was perfect. A slight breeze was wafting through the camp as townspeople started coming in. It seems the word had been spread far and wide. Custis and his crew were up and the General complimented the cook on breakfast. He was introduced to a dish he had not savored before. Since he was from the North, well, if you call being raised in Ohio north. However, it was far enough to not be familiar with this southern dish. Grits and eggs. He took note of how Custis and Pug had mixed their "over light" eggs into the grits and how they turned the dish into a light yellow mixture. Being one who believes in the old cliché, "When in Rome", he did likewise and thoroughly enjoyed his meal.

It wasn't long before there was quite a crowd gathered in front of the stand. Apparently, Custis had made quite an impression on them with his speech in the street. They seemed to have no problem with the red, white, and blue decorated stand. The time for the ceremony was set for 9:00a.m. By 8:30 a.m., there were wagons parked randomly on the grounds, families gathering together, and exhibiting anticipation for the event to start.

Out at the Lee place, the girls quickly finished their chores. Then, they got themselves all cleaned up and put on their new dresses. They weren't sure just how these dresses came about to be given to them. All they knew was that they

Verne Foster

had been invited to a ceremony for the Major. They were full of wonder as they awaited the arrival of the escort they had been told would be sent for them. They weren't aware that all the people would be there also. A messenger had come to them the evening before and informed them that the troop had returned and the Major and Lieutenant were both fine. They kept looking in the long mirror at themselves, each trying to improve on what could not be improved on. They were three beautiful ladies in their fine attire right down to their parasols. Hettie had a brief thought of how Mrs. Bowden had acted that day she was in the store in her pants and coat and what a contrast to her attitude when she brought the dresses. She thought, "Well, I guess she ought to be quite happy now. We're all in dresses."

They heard horses outside and they scurried down the stairs to the front door. As they came out on the porch, there were three soldiers in their best attire approaching them. The first was Corporal Johnson. He had been selected to lead their escort. The men quickly dismounted, doffed their hats and held them to their chests. The Corporal said,

"Ladies, we are here to escort you to the Camp."

A fourth soldier driving a carriage pulled up to the whippletree. Corporal Johnson said, "Whenever you ladies are ready, we need to go."

There was a little nip in the air, so the girls reluctantly had to put a coat over their shoulders, hiding their beautiful dresses. The three were so different today from their usual appearance. It seemed that as they wore the dresses, they became the effeminate darlings the dresses called for. They giggled as they daintily came down the steps and the soldiers quickly took their hands and led them to the carriage. It was a fine carriage that even had a top that was folded down in the back. Corporal Johnson knew better than to tell them it was General Sheridan's personal carriage that went with him everywhere. The Corporal took the lead and the other two soldiers fell in behind them. As Hettie stepped up on the carriage step, she noticed her new shoes that Mrs. Bowden had so generously supplied. She wondered again why this lady had been so generous. She would not let them pay her anything. The Corporal had ushered her into the carriage. She took the front seat facing the rear. Mercy and Rose sat in the back seat facing the driver.

Corporal Johnson and the two soldiers then mounted their steeds and as the Corporal moved out in front in the lead, the other two took their positions at the rear of the carriage. They began to get excited as they moved out toward town. Odd, they thought, though, as they rode through town, no one was on the street. The town looked deserted. Actually, it was. Everyone apparently was out at the camp or on their way.

Back at camp, Custis and Pug were busy getting ready for the ceremony. General Sheridan had remained in camp the night before instead of retreating to his railcar. It was a gesture to lift the moral of the troops, so to speak. He was already in the command tent and came out as they walked up. Before they had a chance to salute the General, he rubbed his stomach and said through a big smile on his face, "That meal was extraordinary." They all chuckled at this remark.

They were still standing there when they saw the escort bring the ladies in. The girls were so beautiful that it didn't seem to matter if they had their work coats draped over their shoulders. The three men walked briskly over to the platform. The girls were speechless when they saw all the people there. As the carriage moved through the crowd and toward the platform, they were looking around at all the people in curious amazement. The carriage pulled up to the platform about the same time the three officers arrived. The little General smiled and tipped his hat as he said, "And a very good morning to you ladies. You look absolutely stunning. Never before have I seen such beauty."

Each gown was a different color with white parasols. Mrs. Bowden could not supply the matching colors on that short of notice. The yellow for Hettie with her long auburn hair. The blue for Mercy with her long silky black hair and the pink for Rose with her blonde hair. The General held his hand up in front of his mouth as he told Custis, "I picked those out myself. Good job, huh?" It was a great job, but, it wouldn't have mattered. He was the General and would Custis not agree?

By now, Custis was just along for the ride. He did not know what was going to happen next. This little man had the mind of a giant. He knew also that if this guy planned it, it had better come off without a hitch. Custis opened the door of the carriage. The General stepped up and offered his hand to Hettie as she stepped out, lifting her skirts up high enough that her new shoes were noticed. He escorted her to the stand where chairs awaited them. Custis took Mercy by the hand and was absolutely lost in her beauty. It was as if he'd went deaf. All sound was obliterated. He thought he could hear his heart beat. Likewise, Pug led Rose to the stand with similar problems. The two men were not prepared for the women in all their beauty. It was a grand event for them. The carriage was moved out of sight.

The General's aide stepped to the podium and called for silence while he offered prayer. In it, he asked the Lord to smile down upon a torn nation that was ardently trying to heal itself. At the end, there was a loud and unanimous "Amen" given by all. Custis took note of this as it told him things were looking up for these people. The aide then introduced General Sheridan and he came to the podium. He told the people that he believed they were important enough to be considered a town and recommended they select a name for their settlement. He spoke of how it seemed to be growing daily. He then said, "Well, let's get down to the business at hand. I hope all people will take to their future as you all seem to be doing. Yesterday was spent on sorrow. Today is before us and we need to use it to our best advantage so that our tomorrow will be truly better."

He turned toward the three girls and called them to join him. They left their coats on their chairs as the officers on the platform stood and ushered them forward. General Sheridan then explained how cutthroats had been operating in their area and how they were a detriment to both the North and South. He then went on to say, "But to show how the two sides could willingly come together for the stabilization of their united country, these girls put their concern about their politics aside and were responsible for the downfall of these traitors. So, as I do this, I am representing the United States of America as we wish to show our appreciation for their contribution."

He then took Hettie by the hand and brought her next to him. Then, he continued, "This is the first one of your three little neighbors that I wish to recognize. She has a husband whom she has not seen in over two years. He went off to fight for his beliefs. None of us argue with that. I also have information that he is well and due back home here anytime."

He then reached out for the other two girls and they stepped up to his side. Custis wondered how he had gleaned all this information. He then almost said it out loud, "Johnson! Of Course! But little did he know what was coming next. The General nodded his head as he acknowledged the girls. He turned back to the audience and began, "Now, to show you how great this country can be, I can think of no higher calling than to put aside the past and ignore all the politics and thereby feel free to intermingle the North and South. As I understand it, two of my finest officers are quite interested in these two fine young ladies here. I believe a lot of you have already met him, but my camp commander, Major Custis, has asked permission to court this young lady."

With that, he brought the Major up to stand with Mercy. Those who had met Custis that day had been truly impressed with his honesty. As they started the applause, it quickly spread through the whole crowd. Custis looked down at Mercy and she was looking up at him. He quickly became lost in those big dark eyes. A voice from his inner self softly questioned, "Is this going to happen every time I look at her?"

Then, the General looked at Rose and over at Pug. He motioned for Pug to come over by Rose. He had her hand in his and gave it to Pug As they stood there, the General again turned to the crowd and asked, "And what do you think of the possibility of romance between these two?" Again, the crowd applauded.

The General continued, "The reason I am here is to recognize these young ladies. I have a special award for them and I would like to formally present it now."

With that, his aide brought up three gold medals on three gold chains. Also, he had three framed certificates to go with them. The General placed one around each of the girl's necks and handed the certificates to them. A round of applause went up. Sheridan then said, "Now, I have something that comes from the camp commander here and I call him to make the presentation."

With that, a soldier cleared the way to the platform as three others led the three Appaloosas to the front of the stand. Custis stepped forward, unaware that this was going to happen. He nodded to the General and then to the crowd. He loudly announced, "These three very special horses were taken from the murderers we defeated. It is only fitting that I give each one of these brave ladies one. Some of you may not be familiar with this horse, but it is a fine breed used mostly by the Western Indians. I can think of nothing more fitting as the prize goes to them." The crowd went wild with cheers and applause. Both the General and Custis realized what their reaction meant to the Country. Also, they were in great need for something to cheer about. Custis looked around at the girls and they were crying. He thought, "I guess I'll never understand them."

Just when he thought the ceremony was over, General Sheridan stepped back up to the podium and, in a loud voice, asked, "From your reaction, can I take it that you are accepting this camp and its men?" The response was almost deafening as each one remembered how it had been there for them at different times. He then announced, "Well then, I will help you in deciding whether you should give your town a name or not by the next thing on my agenda. I have had this Camp officially named." With this, his aide gave him a document and he held it up for all to see. He announced proudly, "From this day forward, this will be called, 'Camp Custis'. It has been named after the Camp Commander here who is not only the Army's hero, but yours too. And, if I am correct, has aspirations to be one of you!"

A cheer went up showing their agreement. Sheridan then said, "As you were notified, this would be as big an event as you wished to make it. So, is it over?"

A big "NO!" came from the crowd.

"Then what should we do now?"

The people yelled, "Let's celebrate!"

Custis watched as they went to their wagons and started bringing out tablecloths and putting them on the ground. Food was brought out and set up on them as well as quilts and spreads. The General then turned to Custis and said, "I don't know whether you smelled it or not, but your chef has been roasting and also has prepared venison most of the night. I believe it is time for us to integrate with the South."

Someone brought out a fiddle and another a gut-bucket. Another joined in with a jug and suddenly, music filled the air as did the aroma of roasting meat and the different kinds of food. Mercy was holding on to Custis' hand and when he looked down at her, he just couldn't help himself. He kissed her and mischievously said, "Now you know I have to obey orders, so, I guess we'll have to get married." He had leaned down to kiss her and she threw her arms around his neck. He straightened up and held her tightly as she was softly saying, "Yes! Yes!"

Everything was so wonderful until Custis looked around and saw Hettie standing by herself. Her hands were clasped in front of her as she just stood looking at the crowd. She

Verne Foster

unsuccessfully fought back the tears as she saw him looking at her. She tried her best to smile and said, "I think I'll check out those Appaloosas."

Custis started to move toward her, but General Sheridan stopped him. He nodded to the horses as he said, "Wait, Major. See the man who is now holding the Appaloosas?"

Custis did not recognize him. He wore civilian clothes. He was quite thin and a little pale. Mercy gasped, "Oh, my God!"

General Sheridan quickly said, "Shhh, little lady."

They watched as Hettie walked up to the horses. The man could hold back no longer. He almost shouted as he reached for her, "Hettie, darlin'!"

Hettie almost fainted as she saw her own Jefferson Lee there holding the reins of the horses. He let go and they embraced. As they just held on to each other not saying anything, both crying, everyone began crying. Even the General and Pug were now unashamedly letting the tears roll. General Sheridan looked at Custis as the girls ran down to the couple and said, "Well, Major, I believe that takes care of everything I had on my agenda. How about you?" Custis could only nod.

"Well, Major, General Sherman is taking over the Western Command and has shown interest in you. I would like to keep you in my command, but I will leave that decision up to you."

The General then shook his hand and said, "Well, I must get back to my command. I know I am leaving this one in good hands. Sherman will not move you without my O.K., so let me know your decision when the time comes."

With that, the General and his entourage left to go and prepare to leave. Custis looked around at the people who seemed to be having a joyous time for the first time in a long time. As he looked out over the crowd, Mercy came running up to him and Pug and said, "Robert E! Jeff wants to meet you two. He's still a little weak, but game." She took Custis by the hand and said, "Robert E! I want you to know that this is the most wonderful day of my life!"

With that, she took them both by the hand and led them down the steps to the others.
THE END

Printed in the United States
30234LVS00004B/142-159